THREE RIVERS

A DI Tanner Mystery

- Book Four -

DAVID BLAKE

www.david-blake.com

Proofread by Jay G Arscott.

Special thanks to Lorraine Swoboda, Kath Middleton, John
Kincaid, Anna Burke and Ali Dunn.

Published by Black Oak Publishing Ltd
in Great Britain, 2020

ISBN: 9798618210225

DEDICATION

For Akiko, Akira and Kai.

BOOKS BY DAVID BLAKE

CRIME FICTION
Broadland
St. Benet's
Moorings
Three Rivers

CRIME COMEDY
The Slaughtered Virgin of Zenopolis
The Curious Case of Cut-Throat Cate
The Thrills & Spills of Genocide Jill
The Herbaceous Affair of Cocaine Claire

SPACE CRIME COMEDY
Space Police: Attack of the Mammary Clans
Space Police: The Final Fish Finger
Space Police: The Toaster That Time Forgot
Space Police: Rise of the Retail-Bot
Space Police: Enemy at the Cat Flap
Space Police: The Day The Earth Moved A Bit

SPACE ADVENTURE COMEDY
Galaxy Squad: Danger From Drackonia

ROMANTIC COMEDY
Headline Love & Prime Time Love

SHORT STORY COLLECTION
Fish Fingered

"But go and learn what this means: 'I desire mercy, not sacrifice.' For I have not come to call the righteous, but sinners."
Matthew 9:13

- PROLOGUE -

Friday, 9th June, 2006

THE STRAP FROM an over-stuffed holdall cut deep into James Boyd's shoulder as he staggered his way over the car park. Cradled awkwardly in his arms was a gleaming wooden rudder, its stock empty, the tiller left jutting out of the bag. Directly ahead was a narrow steel gate, hidden from casual view by a tangled mass of ivy whose strands twisted and climbed their way through the gate's rusty wire mesh.

Through dawn's early light, James could easily read the gate's sign, but he doubted he'd be able to make out the numbers stamped on the security keypad. Hoping he wouldn't be forced to dump everything down to dig out a torch, he stooped to squint at the numbers. As he suspected, they were indecipherable, but he reckoned he'd opened the gate enough times to know their position relative to each other.

Recalling the sequence in his head, he pressed C to clear the locking mechanism before punching in what he hoped was 1-8-0-5, a number memorable for being the year local hero Admiral Horatio Nelson led the British Royal Navy to victory during the Battle of Trafalgar, only to lose his life moments later to a French sharpshooter.

Turning the metal handle, he was relieved to feel it twist all the way around, allowing him to push open the gate and forge his way through, stopping briefly to tug at the holdall, the pedestrian access too narrow for the bag to fit without snagging on the gate's frame.

With his shoulder beginning to ache, he kept lugging his way forward, heading for the pontoons where his parents' Wayfarer dinghy was moored, rocking gently to and fro between two larger yachts.

Reaching the edge of the floating platform, he began rattling down its length, leaning forward to watch ripples of water spread out from underneath his feet.

Glancing up, he was just in time to see a shadowy figure step out in front of him, only inches away from his face.

'Jesus Christ!' he exclaimed, jumping back. 'You scared the crap out of me!'

'Sorry. I didn't mean to.'

'What are you doing here, anyway?' James demanded, barging past.

'I've been waiting for you.'

'That's nice,' he said, his voice thick with sarcasm.

Reaching the dinghy, he let the holdall's strap slip off his shoulder, allowing the bag to fall hard onto the pontoon's grey wooden slats. 'You do know who I'm taking, don't you?'

'I heard you'd broken up.'

James took a moment to glance around at the boat, checking to make sure everything was as he'd left it the evening before. 'Oh yes? And who told you that?'

'She did.'

'Well, we got back together again,' he said, with casual indifference.

Confident that everything was as it should be, he laid the varnished wooden rudder down next to the bag. Taking hold of the dinghy's starboard side shroud, he swung himself on board, balancing his body as the boat pitched and rolled under his weight. 'And she'll be here any minute, so you'd better skedaddle.'

'But what about me?'

'What about you?'

'I thought – I thought that because you'd broken up, you might want to take me instead?'

'Whatever gave you that idea?'

'You did!'

'Er…I don't think so.'

'Maybe not in so many words, but…'

'Not in *any* words.'

'OK, so you didn't say it out loud, but I know you like me.'

'Of course I *like* you. I wouldn't let you hang out with us if I didn't *like* you.'

'Then why can't you take me instead of her?'

'You know why.'

'What – because I'm not your type?'

'It's not that.'

'Then what is it?'

'I just don't think of you in that way, that's all.'

'But you could. I know you could. We just need to spend more time together.'

'I think we spend quite enough time together as it is!'

'And what's that supposed to mean?'

'Nothing,' muttered James, instantly regretting having said it.

'It didn't sound like nothing.'

Letting out an exasperated sigh, James leaned forward to grab hold of the bag, dragging it over the pontoon towards the boat. 'Listen, if I'm to be completely honest, you've been getting a little – well – a little *needy* recently; always hanging about.'

'I suppose Jelly told you to say that?'

'Please don't call her that.'

'Call her what?'

'You know – that!'

The conversation lapsed for a moment as James lifted the holdall onto one of the horizontal wooded seats.

'I bet she did.'

'She didn't!' stated James, zipping open the bag to slide out the tiller.

'What do you see in her, anyway?'

James shrugged. 'I don't know. She laughs at my jokes, I suppose.'

'So do I.'

'She's pretty as well, of course.'

'You're saying I'm not?'

Ignoring the question, James gestured at the rudder, still lying on the pontoon. 'Pass me that, will you?'

Watching his precious rudder as it was slowly picked up from off the pontoon's floor, he thought it might be prudent to apologise for his earlier remark. 'Look, I'm sorry about what I said, that you're always hanging around. I *do* like you. I mean that, and we'll only be away for a few days.'

'Everything was all right before *she* came along. She's called Jelly for a reason, you know.'

'What, you're seriously suggesting that she's jealous of *us?*' James was unable to stop himself from snorting out a condescending laugh. 'Anyway, I think the break will do us good,' he continued, holding his hands out for the rudder.

'I'm sorry, but I'm not going to let you leave. Not unless you take me with you.'

Giving in to his growing irritation, James blurted out, 'And just exactly how're you going to do that? Sit on me?'

'I'm not fat!' The comment had clearly touched a nerve.

'Whatever,' James shrugged again. 'Anyway, she'll be here any minute, and I've got to get the boat ready; so if you could hand me the rudder?'

Instead, the rudder was held away, tears spilling down a plain chubby face.

'Just give me the fucking rudder!' James demanded, fast losing his temper.

'Not unless you promise to take me instead of Jelly.'

'Listen, fatso, if you don't give me the rudder right now, I'm going to climb out and beat the shit out of you.'

'I'M NOT FAT!' came the furious reply through sobs of raw, unconstrained emotion.

James felt a primal rage surge through his veins. He launched himself out of the boat, making a grab for the rudder he so desperately needed. But his friend was too quick, lifting it out of his reach before bringing it back down, its edge glancing off the side of his head.

Staggering with shock, the boat rocking violently beneath him, James was just able to take hold of the shroud before toppling over backwards.

'You little bitch!' he exclaimed, his free hand reaching up to where the rudder had struck him.

'I'm sorry, but you shouldn't have been so mean.'

'You stupid fat little bitch,' James growled, staring in horror at his open hand, the palm thick with blood.

As his face contorted with fury, he raised his eyes to meet those of his attacker. 'I'm going to fucking kill you.'

Blubbing uncontrollably, his friend swung the rudder again. The edge hit the top of James's head with a dull hard thud, instantly splitting his skull clean open, like a sharpened axe burying itself deep into a freshly hewn block of wood.

- CHAPTER ONE -

Sunday, 31st May, Present Day

A COLD BRISK breeze buffeted Tanner's face as he followed Jenny along an unkempt concrete hardstanding. Grouped around them were about a dozen sailing dinghies, all perched on tubular steel launching trollies, hoisted sails flapping with violent rage above. Surrounding each was an array of neoprene-clad sailors, some young, some old, most bearing the sagging appearance of being the wrong side of forty. They were all as busy as each other, some frantically feeding coloured lines through a complex network of pulleys and blocks, others making more minor adjustments to system controls and halliard tensions.

Ducking their heads to avoid being hit by the ends of aluminium booms that swayed from side to side with dangerous unpredictability, Tanner and Jenny emerged unscathed to put their shoulders to the wind and fight their way along a concrete incline. Up ahead was their destination: a black two-storey clubhouse with a wide veranda overlooking Barton Broad on their left, a red, white and blue RYA flag flying horizontally out from the roof.

With his hands buried inside the warm deep pockets of a dark grey offshore sailing jacket, a Christmas present from Jenny, Tanner raised his voice above the noise of the thrashing sails behind them. 'Isn't it too windy for all this?'

'It's probably too cold as well, but that's dinghy sailing for you,' commented Jenny.

'I actually meant, isn't it too windy for me to be having a go, seeing that I've never done it before?'

'Don't worry. The worst thing that can happen is that you'll capsize.'

'Right,' Tanner replied, not sounding convinced. 'And what happens then?'

'You'll go for a swim, obviously,' Jenny remarked, before offering him a broad cheeky grin.

'And after that?'

'Everyone will laugh at you.'

'No, seriously.'

'OK, they probably won't. But don't worry: I will!'

'I appreciate that, really I do, but I meant, what do I do *after* I capsize?'

'I think that's up to you.'

'How d'you mean?'

'Well, some people prefer front crawl, whilst others opt for breaststroke.'

Tanner was in no mood for his girlfriend's seemingly endless string of jokes, especially as they were being aimed squarely at him.

Jenny had joined the sailing club a few weeks before. Having been reminded just how much fun dinghy sailing was, she'd encouraged Tanner to have a go, telling him that it would be a good way to develop his sailing skills, whilst having fun at the same time. When they'd had the conversation it had been a perfect summer's day, with nothing more to worry about than a cool gentle breeze. Had he known she'd be dragging him along during what felt like a hurricane, he doubted he'd have been so easily persuaded, and he was feeling increasingly anxious about the whole affair.

'Yes, ha, ha, very funny. And after I've spent half an hour providing you with some top class visual entertainment?'

'Then you'll right the boat and climb back in,' she replied, in a matter-of-fact way.

'And how do I do that?'

'Don't worry. They'll teach you.'

'Before it happens, I hope.'

As a particularly gnarly gust of wind tore into them, stopping them dead in their tracks, Jenny took a moment to gaze about; first at an orange windsock which was flying from the end of a bending pole, then over at the wide stretch of water that made up Barton Broad, the length of which was lined with twisting streaks of dark turbulent water.

Wearing a more serious expression, she said, 'To be honest, I can't see them running a beginners' session today. There's definitely more wind than forecast.'

'Oh dear, what a shame.'

'Anyway, whilst we're here, we may as well get you signed up. Hopefully we'll then be able to watch some of the sailors head out.'

'You mean they're going to go out in *this?*' questioned Tanner, as another heavy gust ripped its way into them.

'As long as they know what they're doing, they'll be fine. As I said, the worst thing that can happen is that they'll go over, and there's always at least one safety boat out, just in case there are any problems.'

'But you just said that the worst that could happen would be that they'd capsize.'

'Well, yes, but there can be complications.'

'Like what?'

'It's possible that someone could get knocked unconscious by a boom, or have a mainsheet caught around their neck, or be trapped underneath a sinking boat.'

Tanner's unease was growing by the minute. 'And at what point were you going to mention any of those?'

'Er...' Jenny hedged, 'probably not until you were about halfway out.'

Seeing the look of bemused horror etched over his face, she punched at his chest. 'I'm just kidding with you. I've never known anyone to actually die whilst sailing a dinghy. Not personally, at least.'

'That's comforting.'

'Anyway, as I said, I doubt they'll be running a training session today, but let's see if there's someone around we can chat to about getting you signed up.'

- CHAPTER TWO -

REACHING THE CLUBHOUSE, Tanner and Jenny climbed the five or so steps that led up to the decked veranda. Huddled at the end was another group of people, these dressed in more conventional clothes than those wearing the wetsuits, all chatting and laughing boisterously amongst themselves.

Stopping where they were, they turned to gaze out at the Broad, which looked as if it was being swept away from them by the wind towards the horizon. To their left was a dinghy park, where over a hundred small boats were lined up in rows, their bows pointing towards the air, a criss-cross of masts rising up through a variety of grimy plastic boat covers. To the side of the dinghy park were the dozen or so boats they'd ducked and weaved their way through earlier, sails still flapping with vehement fury.

Tanner overheard the group around them discussing whether or not they should risk going out. After a while, one particularly large middle-aged man called, 'Well, it looks like we'll be going for a swim then!' – a comment met with a round of laughter, as they all began heaving over-stuffed holdalls onto their shoulders and marching their way inside.

'They seem keen,' mused Tanner, turning his attention back to the Broad.

'No doubt they'll be fine,' Jenny said.

'How about those two?'

Tanner was pointing down at a couple of stick-thin elderly gentlemen wearing faded buoyancy aids over sagging black wetsuits. Together they were attempting to ease an enormous wooden dinghy down a steep concrete slipway into the water below.

'Well, at least they look *old* enough to know what they're doing,' commented Jenny, with a notable lack of confidence.

The moment she said it, one of them slipped on the jetty to fall hard onto his back, leaving the other to be dragged down the slope by the boat he was attempting to control.

'Are you sure about that?' Tanner said.

They continued to watch as some of the younger members of the club rushed down the slope to their aid.

'They'll be all right, once they're out on the water.'

'I'd have thought the opposite would be true!'

'The hardest part of sailing a dinghy can be launching, especially when the breeze is up. But once you're off, everything seems to flow into a more natural rhythm.'

'What – even in this?' Tanner queried, as yet another savage gust tore over their heads to plunge down into the boats below with such ferocity that some of the smaller ones lifted off their trolleys and tipped over while their owners scrambled to hold them down.

'I must admit, in these conditions, you could be right. But as I said before, they'll have safety boats out. Anyway,' Jenny turned her attention back to the clubhouse, 'let's see if we can find someone to talk to about membership, shall we?'

Stepping over to the entrance, she tugged at the door, just as someone else pushed at it from the inside. Jumping back, she found herself staring into the sparkling blue eyes of a handsome young man with boyish good looks, a high-collared sailing jacket zipped up to his chin.

'Sorry about that,' came the man's surprised response.

'My fault,' Jenny responded, eyelashes flickering.

'Can I be of any help?' he asked, stepping to one side.

'We're looking for someone to talk to about membership.'

'You can try me if you like, although you've certainly picked quite a day for it.'

'It is blowing a bit,' agreed Jenny, moving away from the entrance to allow some more people through.

'Can either of you sail?' enquired the man, studying their faces.

'Don't look at me!' stated Tanner.

'I'm already a member,' Jenny said, 'but I was hoping to get John here signed up.'

'I assume that means you can sail?'

'Well, I'm only just getting back into it after a rather long absence. I used to be a member of Horning Sailing Club, where I had a rather misspent youth mucking about in Oppies and Toppers.'

Hearing that, the man stopped to stare at her. 'Forgive me, but – you wouldn't happen to be Jenny Evans, by any chance?'

Blushing slightly, Jenny stuttered, 'I-I am, yes.'

'You don't remember me, do you?'

'Um...' Jenny hesitated, taking the chance to study his face.

Unzipping the top part of his jacket, the man offered Jenny a near perfect smile. 'It's Rob! Robert Ellison?'

'Christ! Rob! I'm sorry, I didn't recognise you!'

'Well, it has been a while. How've you been?'

'Good, thanks, yes. And you?'

'I'm still living in Norfolk. I'm not sure if that's good or bad.'

Remembering Tanner, Jenny turned to introduce him. 'Robert, this is John, who's in desperate need of learning how to sail, especially as he lives on board a boat.'

'A boat!' Ellison repeated, observing Tanner more closely.

'I know,' Tanner replied, waiting for the usual response of, 'That's very adventurous of you,' or something similar. But their conversation was interrupted by the sound of shouting, drifting up from the launching area through the still howling gale.

Turning to find the source of the commotion, they spied a group of people gathered at the end of a pontoon, all watching the wooden dinghy they'd seen trying to launch earlier taking off downwind, one of the crew with a rope caught around his ankle, the other leaning over the back of the boat, trying to do something with the rudder.

As they watched, a teenage boy came sprinting up the veranda steps to charge over towards the entrance.

'Hey! Kai!' Ellison called. 'What's going on?'

'Fred and Jim have gone out, but there's still nobody to cover the safety boats.'

'Why didn't they wait?'

'They weren't tied on to the pontoon properly. They hadn't even got the rudder in when the wind caught them.'

'Shit! OK. I can take a safety boat out. Can you crew for me?'

'Well, I can, but I haven't done a course yet.'

'You'll have to do. Find the keys for boat number three. That should be working.'

Nodding, the boy threw himself towards the club's entrance, Ellison calling after him, 'And grab a couple of radios: a lifejacket as well.'

The three of them turned back to the Broad to see how the escaped dinghy was faring in the unrelenting wind.

'At least they're still upright,' remarked Jenny.

'They're good sailors,' Ellison replied. 'I can't say I'd have been too worried if they hadn't set off without a rudder.'

'If you need a crew, I'd be happy to go out,' Jenny offered. 'I've got my safety boat licence, and I did a first aid refresher course last month.'

'You wouldn't mind?'

'Not at all.'

Seeing the teenager come bursting back out through the doors, keys in one hand, radios in the other, and an old lifejacket slung over his shoulder, Ellison brought him to a halt. 'Change of plan, Kai. You stay here and monitor the radio.'

'But who's going to crew for you?' the young man asked, handing over the items he carried.

Ellison nodded over at his old friend. 'Jenny here's volunteered.'

'Oh!' the boy said, his eyes shifting to rest on the attractive young woman.

Jenny raised the corners of her mouth at him as he glanced away.

Remembering the buoyancy aid over his shoulder, the teenager slid it off to hold out for her. 'You'll need this,' he announced, with a stern, serious expression.

'We'd better go,' Ellison said, spinning away to run down to a nearby pontoon, where a handful of small orange motorboats could be seen, each with an outboard engine attached to the back.

Jenny reached out to touch Tanner's shoulder. 'You don't mind, do you?' she asked, catching his eye.

'Of course not,' Tanner smiled. 'You go and do your thing.'

But his accommodating demeanour hid a layer of jealousy which he found himself struggling to shake off. The man she was about to head out on a rescue mission with was younger, thinner, and far better-looking than he was. Not only that, but they clearly had a shared history, along with a mutual interest in all things sailing.

Returning the smile, Jenny skipped into a run to catch up to Ellison, leaving Tanner standing beside the teenager.

Watching as they made their way down to the line of safety boats, as casually as he knew how, Tanner asked, 'So, what's this Ellison chap like?'

'Who, Rob? Oh, he's great!' the lad replied, glancing up at Tanner. Mistaking the anxious look he saw etched upon his face for concern over his female friend's safety, he added, 'Don't worry. She's in good hands.'

Turning to stare out over the Broad at the troubled dinghy as it continued tearing its way downwind, Tanner muttered to himself, 'That's what I'm worried about.'

- CHAPTER THREE -

WITH HER BUOYANCY aid on and the safety boat's engine started, Jenny untied the rope leading out from the bow to shove the nose out with her foot.

Within less than a minute they were planing down Barton Broad at full speed, the boat skipping over the turbulent surface as Jenny's hair whipped around her head.

Spying the stricken dinghy in the distance, she pointed towards it, turning to glance at Ellison as she did.

Seeing him nod to alter course accordingly, Jenny couldn't help but think how handsome he'd become – nothing like she remembered. The way he stood behind the steering console, one hand on the wheel, the other resting on the throttle as the boat jolted and thumped its way over the water, he looked every bit the hero of her more passionate dreams.

She was about to start mentally undressing him when she remembered Tanner, waiting for her back at the clubhouse. A wave of guilt crashed over her, and she scolded herself for having entertained such thoughts, even if they'd only been for a second. Shaking her head clear, she brought her focus back to the here and now. Looking forward again, she called out, 'At least they're still upright.'

'Not for long,' Ellison replied, his sparkling blue eyes squinting ahead.

Following his gaze, Jenny watched as the boat they were fast approaching pitched one way, then the other, its mast swaying like a giant pendulum as its sails filled to near bursting point.

As the occupants fought to regain control, the boat came over again, but this time it didn't stop. As the entire dinghy plunged onto its side, the bow buried itself into the water, forcing the aft end high into the air before crashing back down, the whole thing turning over as it did.

Unable to see anything but the sight of an upturned hull, wallowing in the wake of its own capsize, Ellison called out, 'Can you see two heads?'

Craning her neck, Jenny desperately searched the water around the overturned boat for any sign of the sailors.

'They must be trapped underneath,' she called back.

'Shit! We need to get it upright again, and fast!'

Nodding her understanding, as Ellison pulled the safety boat up alongside, Jenny leapt out onto the upturned hull. Accepting the fact that she was going to get wet, she took a firm hold of the dinghy's centreboard, sticking out from the base like the fin of a shark, and allowed her feet to slide down the hull into the water below. When they met the hull's narrow lip, she began heaving back on the centre board with all her might, attempting to force the dinghy to come over. But with the sheer strength of the wind blowing over its surface, and her lack of weight and strength, the dinghy remained stubbornly where it was.

Feeling it sinking beneath her feet, its two elderly occupants trapped underneath, she shouted back to Ellison, 'It's no use! I can't right it!'

'Let me have a go,' he replied, tugging out the engine's kill cord to swap places with her.

Once in position, he began forcing his weight down onto the lip, heaving back on the centreboard as Jenny had done. But it still wouldn't budge.

'The mast must be stuck on the bottom,' he called. 'Can you try bringing the bow around, into the wind? That may help twist it out.'

Following his instructions, Jenny reversed the safety boat away before expertly easing its nose in towards the stricken dinghy's bow. The moment she was close enough, she wrenched out the kill cord to leap forward. Plunging her hands under the water, she frantically searched for the painter, tied to the dinghy's bow. Finding it, she yanked it out to loop twice around the cleat bolted to the front of the safety boat. Bounding back to the steering wheel, she re-attached the kill cord and began reversing, dragging the dinghy steadily backwards into the unrelenting wind.

The moment its bow came round, she shouted, 'Try it now!'

Ellison once again began forcing his weight down onto the hull's now fully submerged lip, heaving back against the centreboard, and the upturned dinghy finally began coming over.

As the opposite side of the dinghy cleared the water's surface, Jenny leaned out to peer into the gloom underneath.

Seeing the two old men, their arms hooked around the toe straps above their heads, she asked, 'Are you OK?'

Gasping and spluttering, they nodded back.

'Are they all right?' called Ellison, unable to see.

'They're both good,' Jenny replied, reaching forward to begin dragging them out from under the dinghy before helping to hoist them into the safety boat.

The moment Ellison saw that they were both safely on board, he re-commenced his efforts to bring the boat up. Feeling it coming over, fearing the possibility of it capsizing again, this time directly on top of his head, Ellison instructed Jenny to motor around to the back to grab hold of the mast as it came up.

Once in position, Jenny signalled for him to continue as she stared down into the blackness below, hands outstretched, waiting to grab the top of the mast the moment it came into view.

Ellison continued his efforts, and the dinghy began to right again, leaving Jenny to watch as a dense black shadow began creeping up from the broad's murky depths towards her.

'I think there's something caught on the end,' she called up, trying to make out what it was.

'Whatever it is,' said Ellison, breathing hard, 'it's certainly heavy enough.'

A moment later, the water's surface was broken by what appeared to be a large waterproof holdall, oozing thick grey slimy mud.

'What is it?' asked Ellison, gazing down from his lofty position.

'It's just a bag, I think,' Jenny replied, reaching

to take a firm hold of what she assumed would be the top section of the mast underneath. Whatever was hidden under the bag didn't feel anything like the hard touch of aluminium she'd been expecting. What she felt was firm but soft, and moved under her fingers like heavily kneaded dough.

Noting a small tear in the bag, she prised her fingers inside to force it apart. As the material ripped, from inside rose the stinking putrefying head of a man, its skin the colour of slime, its lips like purple sludge.

Jenny screamed, the sound piercing the still howling gale.

Shoving herself away, she let go of the bag, together with the mast caught underneath.

With Ellison still kneeling on the centreboard, his weight launched the mast into the air, leaving him to scramble up and over the side.

As Jenny, Ellison and the two rescued old men stared up, the unrelenting wind caught the bag and ripped it away, revealing the body of a man, fully clothed, the mast impaled through his chest.

As the dinghy's sails flapped around it with demonic fury, they witnessed an apocalyptic vision: a fallen angel, rising up from the darkest, most terrifying corners of Hell.

- CHAPTER FOUR -

JUST OVER AN hour later, Jenny emerged from the clubhouse, one hand clutching at a foil blanket wrapped around her shoulders, the other cradling a mug of steaming hot soup.

Since the rescue of the dinghy sailors, and the subsequent discovery of the body hidden at the bottom of Barton Broad, the scene at the sailing club had been transformed. In place of eager neoprene-clad sailors were police forensics officers dressed head to toe in white, and where there had been an assortment of dinghies lined up on the hardstanding, waiting to launch, was now a fleet of emergency vehicles, including squad cars, two ambulances and a forensic services van. Over by a grass verge, near to where a dry-standing training dingy sat on a fixed wooden cradle, a square white tent had been hastily erected, which swayed and shuddered in the still howling gale, like a ghostly apparition trapped inside an invisible cell.

Spying Tanner at the base of the veranda steps deep in conversation with DCI Forrester, and keen to look less like some dishevelled witness in need of sympathetic consolation and more like someone suited to her recently acquired rank of Detective Sergeant, Jenny removed her foil blanket and tucked it discreetly under her arm before heading over to join them.

'Ah, DS Evans!' Forrester said, seeing her approach. 'How're you holding up?'

With Forrester and Tanner offering her similar smiles of sympathetic concern, she returned a look of defiant resilience. 'I'm fine, sir, thank you for asking. It was just a bit of a shock, that was all.'

'Well, I'm hardly surprised. You're welcome to take a few days off, if you like?'

Determined not to be treated any differently from the male officers, Jenny met his eyes. 'As I said, sir, I'm fine, thank you!'

'Good to hear. Have you been able to give a witness statement?'

'To Constable Higgins, sir, yes.'

'OK. Right then. I suggest we head over to see how Dr Johnstone has been getting along.'

Finding their Medical Examiner consulting with a forensics officer just outside the ghost-like tent, Forrester called out, 'Any news?'

As the forensics officer ducked inside the tent, Dr Johnstone looked over at them, pushing his glasses up the ridge of his nose. 'Other than it's the putrefying remains of a human male, I'm afraid I haven't, no.'

'Do you at least know how long he's been down there for?'

'At this stage, I don't have a clue. Judging by the state of decomposition, what is clear, however, is that he must have been stored in some sort of airtight container.'

'What makes you think that?'

'The organic breakdown has been largely

anaerobic,' Johnstone replied, glancing around at them. Seeing nothing but puzzled expressions staring back, he launched into a more detailed explanation.

'Anaerobic decomposition describes the way organic compounds break down within an oxygen-starved environment. This typically has a two-fold effect. Firstly, decomposition is far slower. The second relates to the process by which the organic material degenerates. A human body is made up of about seventy percent water. Under normal conditions, this will immediately begin to evaporate into the air, leaving what's left of the carcass to begin drying out. But when left inside an air-tight container, there is nowhere for the water to escape to. Of course, that doesn't stop the process of decomposition, but what it does is slow it down; and as the solid compounds are unable to become desiccated, they instead turn into what could best be described as liquid sludge.'

With a clearer understanding of what he'd meant, Tanner stepped in to ask, 'I don't suppose there's any indication as to a cause?'

'Again, too early to say. There is, however, a sizable fracture to the skull, right down the middle of his parietal lobe.'

'And where's that?'

'About here,' Johnstone replied, lowering his head to run a finger along its top. 'Whether it happened before or after his death, I simply don't know. To be honest, at this stage, judging by the level of decomposition, I'm not sure I ever will.'

'But you will at least be able to give us some idea as to a time?'

'That neither, I'm afraid, not with any accuracy. I think the best I'll be able to do is give you an approximate year.'

As they let that sink in for a moment, Jenny entered the conversation by asking a rather obvious question, made even more so by the fact that nobody had yet thought to ask it.

'Any idea as to his identity?'

Taking her in, Johnstone replied, 'None at all, no.'

'No wallet, phone, jewellery?'

'Just the clothes on his back, I'm afraid.'

- CHAPTER FIVE -

RRIVING BACK AT their home, a much loved forty-two-foot Broads cruising yacht that they'd bought together after Tanner's original boat had been set on fire, Jenny found herself overcome by a sudden wave of exhaustion.

Leaving her to get some much-needed rest down within the small but cosy confines of their cabin, Tanner was able to spend a few pleasant hours in the boat's cockpit, listening to the wind whistling through the cracks in the canvas awning whilst pushing on with his current book, an omnibus edition of C. S. Forester's classic tale, *Hornblower*.

It wasn't until gone seven when the gale that had battered the Broads all day finally began to abate. As it did, Jenny emerged from below in search of food and a drink, both of which Tanner was able to provide in the form of a quiche and a glass of wine.

With the wind falling away to leave nothing more than a gentle whisper, together they rolled back the cockpit's awning to discover that the clouds had parted to reveal a fast setting sun. There they spent the remainder of the evening watching as it sank slowly behind Hunsett Mill, before daylight faded slowly away to reveal a billion stars scattered over the midnight blue of a cloudless night's sky.

Monday, 1st June

Come the morning, Jenny was feeling more like her normal self, the traumatic events of the previous day already beginning to slip into the darker recesses of her subconscious mind, somewhere she was happy for them to remain.

Inside Wroxham Police Station's main office, there was an unexpected buzz in the air. Instead of sitting staring at their various computer screens, hands clutched around mugs of steaming coffee, the station's staff were gathered at the far end, near the whiteboard where DI Cooper and DS Gilbert sat.

'Someone's birthday?' questioned Tanner, as he and Jenny slipped their coats off and draped them over the backs of their chairs.

Forrester's giant mass loomed in the middle of the group beside a pretty young girl with blonde hair and a pair of breasts Jenny would have happily died for. All the men crowding around seemed unable to keep their eyes off her. With condescending indifference, Jenny replied, 'Looks more like Bring your Daughter to Work Day.'

'I didn't know he had one.'

'I didn't know he had a wife!'

'Maybe that *is* his wife?'

Jenny scowled at him. 'Let's be serious, shall we?'

As a round of deep bulbous laughter rose up

from the group, they saw Forrester glance over at them with a cheerful expression, one that was very much at odds with his usual sombre demeanour.

As the group began to disperse, Tanner and Jenny remained where they were to watch Forrester place a guiding hand around the attractive blonde's shoulders to direct her towards them.

Giving Jenny a nudge, Tanner whispered, 'Mail order bride?'

Jenny forced herself to keep a straight face as the odd-looking couple reached them, and Forrester made the introductions.

'DI Tanner, DS Evans, I'd like you to meet my niece, Sally Beech. She's joining us today as our new DC.'

As Jenny's chin fell to the floor, she watched in horror as the girl gave them each a perfect smile, before batting her eyelashes up at Tanner.

Holding out one of her small delicate hands, the new girl looked up at Tanner. 'It's a pleasure to meet you.'

What about me? Jenny thought, taking an instant dislike to the girl.

Forced to stand there watching as her boyfriend took hold of the outstretched hand, her internal dialogue continued along similar lines. *If you say, "The pleasure's all mine," I'll be taking you outside to beat the shit out of you.*

Fortunately for Tanner, he said nothing in response, but from out of the corner of her eye she saw him smile down at the new DC, blushing slightly as he did, enough at least for her to know that he fancied her.

As Tanner and the new girl shook hands, staring deep into each other's eyes for what was beginning to feel like an eternity, Jenny found herself having to fight down the primal urge to force them apart and give them both a good slap.

'Sally's been working as a PC in Norwich for the last two years,' Forrester continued.

Only two? fumed Jenny, forcing a grin. It had taken her five to become a Detective Constable.

'This is her first position as a member of CID, so I trust you'll both help to make her feel at home.'

'Of course!' said Tanner. 'Welcome on board!'

Jenny cringed with embarrassment. The distinctly nautical expression seemed wholly out of place, especially coming from her boyfriend in the middle of the office. It was the sort of thing she could imagine some middle-class accountant would say, whose only experience of sailing was taking his family to France on the cross-Channel ferry.

'Anyway,' Forrester went on, 'I've decided to have her working alongside DI Cooper and DS Gilbert for the time being.'

Thank God for that! thought Jenny, letting out the breath she didn't realise she'd been holding.

'But that largely depends on what Dr Johnstone comes back with regarding the body found at Barton Broad yesterday.'

'I assume nothing's come through yet?' asked Tanner.

'Nothing yet, no,' Forrester confirmed, checking his watch. 'I think it's unlikely we'll hear anything back before lunch.'

- CHAPTER SIX -

I T WASN'T UNTIL gone three o'clock when the Medical Examiner's report finally appeared, giving Forrester reason to invite Tanner and Jenny into his office to discuss its contents.

'So, what do you think?' he eventually asked, glancing up at Tanner, who was still leafing through a printed copy.

'From what I can make out, it doesn't seem to draw any conclusions as to how he died. Neither does it say if Dr Johnstone thinks anyone had a hand in it. All it says is what he'd already told us: that the body had decomposed anaerobically, and that the only injury found was the fractured skull, something which could have occurred at any time between when he died and when his body was found. He hasn't even been able to identify him.'

'It's not exactly conclusive, is it?' agreed Forrester. 'But even if he's been unable to say what ultimately caused the man's death, and whether someone did, or did not, have a hand in it, I think we can assume that someone definitely *did* have a hand in attempting to hide it. With that in mind, I think it's safe enough for us to conclude that the circumstances surrounding it are at least suspicious, giving us both cause and reason to move forward with an investigation, which I'd like you to lead.'

'Sir,' replied Tanner, with a dutiful nod.

Forrester switched his attention to Jenny. 'Under the circumstances in which the body was found, I do need to ask if you're happy to assist?'

Before she had a chance to answer, Forrester added, 'If not, I'd completely understand. It would certainly present a good opportunity for my niece to gain some more experience by stepping into your shoes.'

Jenny sat bolt upright to blurt out a reply, tripping over the words as she did.

'I can do it, sir. I-I mean, I'm fine. Never felt better. Finding the body yesterday – it's as if it never happened.'

'Really?' Forrester sounded more than a little surprised.

'Well, obviously it *did* happen,' Jenny continued, realising how her answer must have sounded. 'It's just that I can't remember it having done so.'

Taking on the look of a concerned psychologist, Forrester leaned forward in his chair to study her face. 'To be honest, Jenny, that doesn't sound at all good. Are you able to remember anything at all about yesterday?'

'Sorry, I didn't mean that I can't remember what happened. I can, of course. I meant that I'm not thinking about it all the time, at least not anymore, certainly not to the point where I can't do my job.'

'But you *were* thinking about it all the time?'

'Well, I – er – suppose I was, for a while, but only immediately afterwards. But I'm fine now, sir. Honestly.'

She was about to tag, 'Scout's honour!' onto the end when she was finally able to regain control of her mouth, and the words that had been tumbling their way out.

Forrester continued with his observation of her for a few more moments, before leaning back in his chair. 'OK, well, if you're sure, then I suppose you can work with Tanner, as normal; but I think it's probably prudent to book you in for some counselling.'

'But I'm fine, sir; really I am.'

'So you keep saying, Evans. But just because you think you are, it doesn't mean you actually are.'

Realising she'd achieved the outcome she'd been fighting for – to remain by Tanner's side whilst keeping the new girl as far away from him as possible, given the circumstances – and doing her best to suppress a triumphant grin, Jenny shrugged her shoulders. 'I understand, sir, of course.'

Noting her sudden change of demeanour, Forrester gave her an odd look, before moving the conversation along.

'Anyway, back to the task at hand. I suppose the first thing we need to do is establish who this person is.'

'There's not much in here to help with that either,' muttered Tanner, who'd been quietly leafing through the report. 'Apparently, there wasn't any skin left to take fingerprints from, and his DNA didn't come up on the database. All we have are what's left of his clothes. I can't even find anything about a time of death.'

'Ten to fifteen years ago,' said Forrester, reading from the onscreen version, before lifting his head to gaze up towards the ceiling. 'That would put it sometime between 2005 and 2010.'

'At least we know where he died,' interjected Jenny, keen to include herself in the discussion.

'But do we?' questioned Forrester.

He was right, of course. He could have been killed anywhere, and Jenny kicked herself for having made such a stupid observation.

'But we do at least know where he ended up, which is something,' interjected Tanner. 'We also know how old he was.'

Forrester returned his attention back to the computer screen. 'Sorry, I must have missed that.'

'It says he was in his late teens, early twenties.'

'OK, so we know *approximately* how old he was.'

'Approximately, yes,' confirmed Tanner.

After a moment of silence, Forrester clicked the file closed to sit back in his chair.

'OK, I suggest you start with people who'd been reported as missing during the proposed time frame. And get forensics to send you over some pictures of his clothes. It's possible someone will be able to recognise him from something he was wearing at the time.'

- CHAPTER SEVEN -

RETURNING TO HIS desk, despite feeling like he was back on Missing Persons again, Tanner was pleased to have an investigation to focus his mind on. The past few months had been far quieter than he would have liked, and he found having to look busy all the time was probably more exhausting than actually being so.

Jenny was also pleased to have something to do, but she found it increasingly difficult to concentrate as the day wore on. Unusually for her, she felt exhausted, having barely slept the night before. Every time she'd attempted to, her mind had dragged her back to the previous day, on board the safety boat, and the putrefying green face staring out at her from inside the torn black waterproof bag. When she had been able to drift off, her dreams had been dark and disturbing, waking her up to leave her staring wide-eyed at the cabin roof, desperate to distinguish between reality and the lingering shadows of her unconscious mind.

Her ability to concentrate wasn't being helped by the intermittent sounds of snorts and giggles coming from the direction of DI Cooper's desk, where Forrester's niece, Sally Beech, had been stationed. Judging by their body language, and the cacophony of noise they were making, it was as clear as day that they were flirting with each other; or at least DI Cooper was flirting with Sally, and the girl was lapping up the attention. At the sound of one particularly loud shriek, Jenny glanced up to see DS Vicky Gilbert, seated at the same cluster of desks, giving first Cooper, then the girl a look of unamused reproach.

Catching each other's attention, she saw Vicky roll her eyes before shaking her head. Knowing they were both thinking the same thing, they smiled at each other, before another snort had Jenny on her feet, all set to tell Cooper to put a sock in it, before remembering just in time that he outranked her. Jenny was still only a Detective Sergeant, whereas Cooper was a DI, albeit a very young one.

Reining herself in, she turned to Tanner. 'Coffee?'

At his acceptance, she made a beeline for the kitchen, making sure to catch Vicky's eye as she did.

As she poured out a couple of mugs from the office's relatively new filter coffee machine, Vicky's head appeared over her shoulder.

'Have you ever seen anything like it?' she whispered, pulling a mug out from the cupboard above.

'I know!' agreed Jenny, adding, 'Unbelievable!' as she fetched some milk from the fridge. 'Does Cooper know she's Forrester's niece?'

'Uh-huh, but it doesn't seem to be stopping him

from having a go.'

'Well, he'd better be careful. With the noise they're making, Forrester's bound to hear.'

'He's been on the phone,' said Vicky. Her desk had an oblique view through their DCI's glass partition, which often proved useful.

'Anyway,' Jenny said, collecting her mugs from the counter, 'at least she seems more interested in Cooper than my John.'

Skulking back out, she swivelled her eyes over towards Cooper's desk to see that Sally Beech was staring directly at Tanner.

'Don't even *think* about it,' she fumed, only to see Tanner glance up from his monitor to send Sally what looked to be nothing short of a broad flirtatious smile.

Reaching his desk, she plonked the mug down in front of him, nearly spilling it as she did. 'Enjoying the view?' she asked, her voice thick with condescension.

'Huh?' Tanner replied, glancing up with a confused frown.

'Nothing,' she muttered, but in a way that sounded like she meant the exact opposite.

Whipping her head round towards where the new girl sat, she was shocked to find her staring back. And instead of looking away, the girl went on to offer Jenny a broad, home-baked sort of smile, one that lingered far too long for it not to be antagonistic.

So, it's war then, Jenny thought, before baring her teeth back at her.

After that, the office seemed to settle into its more

normal flow, as everyone knuckled down to their various tasks at hand. Come five o'clock, Tanner and Jenny glanced up to see Forrester lumbering towards the exit, with his niece firmly attached to one of his thick chubby arms.

Passing their cluster of desks, Forrester caught their eyes. 'I'm just taking Sally home,' he said, with a rare sheepish expression. 'Any luck identifying that body?'

'Well, we're making progress,' Tanner replied.

Jenny was attempting to bore her eyes into Sally's, but the girl was ignoring her. She was far too busy batting her eyelashes at Tanner.

Filling his niece in on what they were talking about, Forrester said, 'DS Evans here found a body yesterday, over at Barton Broad, who we're trying to identify.'

'How awful!' exclaimed Sally, offering Jenny a disingenuous look of horror.

'We've been able to narrow the possible victim down to one of six men,' continued Tanner, 'aged between fifteen and twenty-five, registered as living in Norfolk, all reported missing during the five-year time period in question.'

'Did you get the pictures of his clothes?'

'We did, sir, yes.'

'OK, so what's next?'

'We're in the process of working out who all their parents or relatives are, should they have any, with a view to arranging to meet with them; but it's going to take time, I'm afraid.'

'Can't you identify him using his DNA, or fingerprints?' Sally queried, glancing up at her uncle.

'I'm afraid we're only allowed to retain such information if the person in question was convicted of an offence,' Forrester explained.

'And even then,' interjected Jenny, 'that person is entitled to apply to have such information deleted.'

'What about dental records?' Sally asked, directing the question back up at her uncle.

'Unfortunately, there isn't a national database for such information. We'd have to contact the person's actual dentist in order to find out, which is only possible, of course, when we know who the person is.'

'But can't you just ask them all, at least those in the local area?'

'Well, we could, I suppose,' Forrester replied, sending Tanner a questioning look.

Having already asked herself that same question, when she'd been trying to help identify the body of the woman whose abdomen had been churned to a pulp by a reversing hire boat the year before, and seizing the opportunity to make the new girl look as ignorant as possible, Jenny replied, 'I think that's a great idea. After all, there are only eighty-seven dentists in Norfolk. I'm sure it wouldn't take us too long to get in contact with them all.'

Unsure whether she was being sarcastic or not, Forrester cleared his throat. 'I must admit that I didn't know there were quite so many. It's probably best if you stick to contacting the families first. Maybe start with the one who lived nearest to where he was found, and work your way out.'

Seeing his niece pout rather obviously beside

him, Forrester added, 'But of course, if that doesn't work, then I suggest you go down the dentist route.'

'Yes, sir,' said Tanner.

'Anyway, maybe you should head home yourselves, and pick this up in the morning?'

'We've already arranged to meet with the parents closest to Barton Broad, so we're going to drop round there on the way home.'

'Excellent! Good! Well, we'd better be off, but do keep me posted.'

APTER EIGHT -

ITED UNTIL they were in
S, heading over to the village of
, where the parents of the first
n their list lived, before bringing
Forrester's niece.

you think of the new girl?' she
l indifference, taking her eyes off
lickering past to examine the

ιew girl?' Tanner repeated.

Feeling her lips tighten, she glanced away from
him to resume staring out of the window. 'You
know – Forrester's niece, Sally Beech. The one with
all the hair, and the makeup.'

With a shrug, Tanner said, 'I can't say I'd given
her much thought.'

Opening her mouth like a goldfish, Jenny
rotated her head to glare at him, before returning
to the view outside. As far as she was concerned,
that was what someone would say who'd spent the
day doing the exact opposite.

'So, you don't think she's attractive?'

'She's all right, I suppose.'

'I see. Not your type?'

Tanner took his eyes momentarily off the road

to glance over at Jenny. Although her head was turned away, he could see enough of her reflection in the window to know what she was thinking.

With an amused smile, he returned his attention to the road. 'To be honest, I suspect she's *everyone's* type.'

Jenny glared back at him. 'So, you admit it then?'

'What, to finding her attractive? Well, yes; but in my defence, I am a man, and a heterosexual one at that. Personally, I think you should be more worried if I *didn't* find her attractive.'

'I'm not worried!' Jenny stated, his honesty taking her by surprise. 'But you were openly flirting with her.'

'What, by saying hello?'

'You said, "Welcome on board!"'

Still finding the conversation to be highly amusing, Tanner said, 'And that's what people say when they're flirting, is it?'

'No, it's what middle-aged wannabe yachtsmen say when they're trying to get a girl into bed.'

'I must admit, I thought it was a little cheesy when I said it.'

'So, you're saying that you weren't flirting with her then?'

'OK, maybe a little, but nothing compared to Cooper.'

A moment of silence followed, before Jenny said, 'You noticed that, did you?'

'I'm not sure how anyone could miss it. At one point I was sorely tempted to go over there to tell them both to shut up.'

'Me too,' muttered Jenny, feeling considerably

better about the whole thing.

'I'm surprised Forrester didn't come out to see what was going on.'

'He was on the phone, apparently,' she said, unfolding her arms. 'I suppose you saw the way she was looking at you?'

'Well, yes, but in fairness, who can blame her? After all, I am *exceptionally* good-looking.'

Spitting out a laugh, Jenny said, 'Oh, you are, are you?'

'Of course! Well, I would be if I looked a little more like Brad Pitt stepping out of the shower, and a little less like Bernard Manning coming out of the toilet.'

'Who?' Jenny asked, smirking.

'You know. He was in Fight Club and Ocean's Eleven.'

'I actually meant the other one.'

'Oh, Bernard Manning. Well, yes. I suppose he was a bit before your time. Anyway, as blonde as Forrester's niece is, and oh my god, she is very blonde, she isn't a patch on you.'

Smiling to herself, Jenny muttered, 'She's got bigger breasts than me.'

'Well, yes, but who hasn't?'

'Oi!'

'Just kidding!'

Staring down at them, Jenny said, 'Well, I wouldn't mind if they were a little larger.'

'To be honest, it's been so long since I last saw them, I'm not sure I can remember.'

'I suppose it has been a while. Tell you what, if you find somewhere quiet to stop, I'll refresh your memory.'

Doing a double-take between her and the road ahead, he tried to assess whether she was joking. Remembering how she'd described herself when they'd first met: a "Horning girl", one who was perpetually horny, he was forced to assume she wasn't. But either way, it was probably too late to find out.

'Sadly, we're just entering Barton Turf,' Tanner announced, as hedgerows were replaced by bungalows and red brick farmhouses. 'So unless you'd be happy to use someone's drive, it may be better to wait till we get back to our boat.'

- CHAPTER NINE -

ITH JENNY PROVIDING him with directions, they were soon pulling into an open gravel-lined driveway on which sat a modest modern bungalow with whitewashed walls and black-framed shuttered windows. Parked in the drive was an angular-shaped Land Rover Discovery and a large white dinghy lashed to a galvanised steel road trailer, its mast lowered in such a way that it lay over the top of the boat at an angle.

'They must be members of Barton Broad Sailing Club,' mused Tanner, bringing the XJS to a halt beside the Land Rover. 'It's only down the road.'

'Possibly,' Jenny replied, 'but if they are, I'm not sure why they'd keep their boat here, and not at the club.'

Stepping out, they skirted behind the Land Rover to take a closer look at the boat.

'Any idea what it is?' asked Tanner, out of personal curiosity.

'Well, it's too small to be a Wayfarer,' Jenny replied. 'And it's nothing modern, like an RS200. It could be a GP14.'

Having discussed the possibility of them buying something similar for themselves, Tanner asked,

'How much would one of those cost?'

'What, a GP14? Oh, not much. They're not the most popular class. We could probably pick one up for a grand – maybe two.'

Tanner raised one of his solid dark eyebrows. 'Sounds like a lot to me.'

'Well, yes, but that's hardly surprising, given the fact that your car's only worth about 50p.'

'You mean £50, surely!' Tanner rebutted. He'd given up trying to defend his car against Jenny's seemingly endless parade of jokes a long time before. Life was easier to simply go along with them.

'Sorry,' she replied. 'I forgot that you filled it up yesterday.'

Pretending to scowl at her, he turned to look at the bungalow. Seeing a net curtain twitch, he muttered, 'We'd probably better go in, before they call the police.'

'Now that *would* be funny,' Jenny replied, as they began crunching their way over the drive, heading for the front door.

A smaller than average man with greying hair and a thin youthful face soon answered the bell.

'Frank Boyd?' Tanner enquired, digging out his ID.

'I am, yes.'

'Detective Inspector Tanner. This is my colleague, Detective Sergeant Evans, Norfolk Police.'

'It's not about my boat, is it?' the man enquired. 'I know I haven't paid my toll fee this year, but only because we hardly ever use it.'

'It's not about your boat, Mr Boyd. May we come in?'

The man peered at them with suspicion. 'Am I allowed to ask what it's about?'

Tanner hesitated for a moment. He was never sure how best to approach such a delicate subject. If the body Jenny and her friend had discovered the day before did belong to their son, then the news was going to be a traumatic shock for him. If it didn't, they'd simply be raising false hopes that their son had at last been found.

'We may have news about your son, Mr Boyd,' he said at last.

'James!' His eyes widened in surprise. 'Have you found him?'

'That's what we'd like to talk to you about,' Tanner replied, hoping such a response would have been ambiguous enough.

But when his initial look of surprise turned to one of nervous anticipation, Tanner knew it hadn't worked.

Gesturing for them to come in, he turned his head to look up the stairs. 'Darling!' he called out. 'It's the police! They say they've got news about James.'

As footsteps thundered over their heads, Tanner attempted to correct the man. 'We *may* have news, Mr Boyd. We're not sure yet.'

'My wife will be down in a minute,' he continued, making no obvious sign that he'd heard Tanner's last remark. 'Please, do come in.'

Leading them down the hall into the living room, the man stopped beside an antique coffee table set before a large floral-patterned sofa. 'May

I get you something to drink?' he asked, wringing his hands.

'We're fine, but thank you,' replied Tanner, taking the opportunity to glance around.

'Right, well.'

As the room fell into an awkward silence, Boyd followed Tanner's gaze for a moment, before saying, 'I'd better see what's keeping the wife.'

Watching him duck out, Jenny gave Tanner a nudge to direct his attention towards a photograph taking centre stage on a sideboard behind them.

Tanner turned to stoop down and study the image of an exceptionally good-looking young man wearing a navy blue offshore sailing jacket with a distinctive yellow piping around the collar. In the background was a forest of aluminium masts, and behind those a large black building silhouetted against a low-lying sun.

'That's Barton Broad Sailing Club,' Jenny whispered.

'The jacket looks familiar too,' muttered Tanner, just as the man re-entered the room, closely followed by a small fragile-looking woman with permed grey hair.

'This is Janet, my wife,' the husband announced. 'And these are Detectives...er...?'

'Detective Inspector Tanner and Detective Sergeant Evans, Norfolk Police,' Tanner responded, smiling. 'May we sit down?'

'Of c-course, yes, sorry,' spluttered Boyd. 'Please do.'

'And may we get you something to drink?' offered Mrs Boyd, not knowing he had already asked.

'We're fine, but thanks again,' Tanner replied, as he and Jenny perched on the edge of the sofa.

Boyd stepped over to stand in front of a mantlepiece, whilst his wife sank down into an armchair to the side, her hands clasped together in her lap.

'You said you had news of our son?' prompted the husband, his eyes focussed on Tanner.

Unable to answer that question directly, Tanner replied, 'We have found someone, yes, but I'm afraid that at this particular stage, we can't be sure if it's your son or not.'

'How can you not be sure?' demanded Mrs Boyd. 'Either it is, or it isn't.'

Bracing himself, Tanner took a deep breath. 'The body of a young man was found yesterday morning. We're endeavouring to identify him.'

A cold hard silence fell over the room as the couple looked at Tanner, their eyes fixed, unblinking.

Taking a firm hold of the mantelpiece, Boyd eventually asked, 'Is it the one they said had been found at Barton Broad?'

Tanner confirmed that it was.

When they seemed to run out of questions, Tanner motioned Jenny to pass him the file they'd brought with them.

Placing it down on the coffee table, he rested a hand over the top of it to re-engage the attention of the people before him. Noticing how pale their faces had become, leaving his hand where it was he said, 'We're trying to establish his identity. We're hoping you may be able to help us – but only if you feel able to.'

With their eyes now glued to the file, Boyd croaked, 'Those aren't pictures of him, are they?'

'We found some items of clothing at the scene. It's those we're hoping you'll be able to take a look at.'

The husband and wife stared at each other, their lips pursed tight.

With memories of his daughter clouding his mind, Tanner's heart went out to them. Since Jenny had brought his attention to the photograph on top of the sideboard, he was almost certain that the body that had been found was indeed their son.

'You don't have to, of course,' he added, almost urging them not to.

'But – it would help if we did?' proposed the husband.

Tanner paused. 'It would; but only if you feel comfortable.'

After glancing at each other again, seeing Mrs Boyd offer her husband the hint of a nod, the man said, 'I think we should.'

Tentatively, Tanner half-opened the file, enough for him to remove the first photograph and to position it on the table in front of them.

Pictured was a clean pair of faded blue jeans, lying over a white worktop.

'They're not James's,' the wife stated, sitting back in her chair to give Tanner a defiant glare.

Having expected there to be a moment of denial, Tanner asked, 'How about this one?' as he slid out another photograph, this time of a threadbare t-shirt on which could be seen the brand name Lee Cooper.

With nothing more than a cursory glance, the

woman declared, 'It's not his either. You must have found someone else's son.'

'And this one?' Tanner asked, pulling out the final photograph, this time of a navy blue offshore sailing jacket with yellow piping around the collar, which looked identical to that being worn by the boy in the photograph behind them.

Tanner saw the husband bite down on his bottom lip before spinning away to the window, leaving his wife staring down at the picture as if she'd been hypnotised by it.

When no response was forthcoming, Tanner gave her a gentle prompt. 'Do you recognise it, Mrs Boyd?'

Ignoring Tanner's gaze, she lifted her eyes to rest them on the framed photograph behind Tanner's head.

Tanner watched as her eyes began welling up with tears. As they overflowed to tumble down the sides of her face, she gave a single nod before burying her head in her hands.

With the only sound in the room being that of Mrs Boyd sobbing quietly, Jenny rested her hand on Tanner's arm. Having discovered what they'd come to find out, she mouthed the words, 'We should go.'

Although he had a dozen questions he'd like to ask about their son, Jenny was right. This was hardly the best time.

He picked up the photographs from the coffee table and placed them back into the file. From over by the window the faltering voice of the father asked, 'Do you know what happened to him?'

'Unfortunately, at this stage we don't,' Tanner

replied. 'But I can assure you that it is my intention to find out.'

Handing the file back to Jenny, Tanner took the opportunity to ask, 'I don't suppose there's anything you can tell us about him that may help? Was he a member of the sailing club, for example?'

'He was,' Boyd confirmed.

Searching his mind for a question that might help them to talk more openly, Tanner looked over towards Mrs Boyd. 'Can you tell us what he was like?'

Tugging a tissue out from the sleeve of her blouse, she dabbed at her tears. Straightening herself up, she fixed her reddened eyes on Tanner's. 'He was a good boy,' she began. 'Always helpful around the house.'

'I assume he lived here?'

'He did, of course. He was halfway through his 'A' Levels, when he –'

She gripped the tissue, her gaze transferring down towards her hands.

'Did he have many friends?'

'Too many,' she replied. 'Girls in particular. He was an exceptionally good-looking young man.'

'I don't suppose you can remember when the last time you saw him was?'

'It was the evening before he disappeared. We heard him leave in the morning, but it was before we got up.'

'Did you have any idea where he was going?'

'To the sailing club, as always!' she replied, resentment ringing out in her voice.

A frosty silence fell over the room, eventually broken by the father.

'He had a passion for sailing, one which I'm afraid I encouraged.'

'You can say that again,' his wife muttered.

Mr Boyd continued to face Tanner and Jenny. 'It's true, I did, I can't deny it. I first took him sailing when he was only five. From the moment we went out, from the expression on his face it was obvious that he loved it. After that, every weekend he'd beg me to take him, no matter what the weather was like. I eventually signed him up to join in with the children's sailing, even though he was too young. They weren't supposed to start until they were eight. James had only just turned seven. It took a little persuading, but they eventually took him. The moment he sat inside one of their little Oppies, he just took off without a care in the world, heading out for the farthest side of the Broad. I remember they had to send a safety boat out after him.'

The man stared off into space for a moment, smiling to himself at the memory. 'When he was twelve, he started telling everyone that he wanted to become the youngest person to sail around the world.'

A loud snort of disapproval came from his wife.

'Obviously,' Boyd continued, 'neither of us encouraged that. It was one thing for him to sail on the Broads, but quite another for him to set off to sea, not on his own, and we didn't have a large enough boat to take him ourselves. All we had was a Wayfarer that we kept at the club, but it didn't stop him from having a go. He was just one of those people who always seemed to be searching the horizon, you know, whenever we went out. It didn't take long for him to start taking it out on his own, without letting us know. When he was fifteen, he came in one day to tell us he was going on a camping trip with his friends. We got a call later that day from Great Yarmouth Yacht Station. They'd picked him up at Haven Bridge, on the River Yare. He'd gotten into trouble with the tide whilst attempting to head out to sea, running aground in the process.'

His wife snorted again, but didn't say any more, leaving him to continue.

'It wasn't long until he seemed to discover girls. After that there was less talk about him setting sail for far and distant lands.'

'Any girls in particular?' questioned Tanner, nodding over at Jenny to take her notebook out.

'Oh, I'm not sure,' the man replied. 'As my wife said, there were quite a few.'

'I don't suppose you can remember their names?'

'Er...' Boyd glanced over at his wife.

'Kelly Fisher, for a start!' she spat, her eyes zooming in on the notebook Jenny had taken out.

Taken aback by the venomous way she'd said it, Tanner asked, 'Any others?'

'As I said, Inspector,' she said, 'there were a number, none of whom I particularly cared for, but Kelly Fisher was the one claiming to be going out with him at the time.'

'And what was she like?' asked Tanner, noticing that Jenny had only written the date and time along the top of the page, not the name they'd just been given.

'Much the same as all the others.'

'And that was...?'

'They were all tarts, Inspector – interested in one thing, and one thing only.'

'Of course, yes,' Tanner said, the woman's venomous tone arousing his professional curiosity. 'It would help if you could remember some of the other girls' names.'

'I'm afraid Miss Fisher's is the only one I can recall, but I did give a far more extensive list to the police, when we first spoke to them, after James –'

Reminded that there would, of course, be a Missing Persons file for them to reference, which should have the information he was endeavouring to uncover, Tanner was about to get to his feet to leave, when Mr Boyd said, 'If it's of any help, they were all into sailing – his friends that is. The girl, the one my wife mentioned –'

'Kelly Fisher,' chipped in Tanner, still curious to know why Jenny hadn't written it down.

'Yes, Kelly. At the time, she was one of the Broads' best junior sailors, at least as far as racing went. I think one year she may have even won the Topper Nationals.'

Knowing a Topper was a junior class racing dinghy, one Jenny had told him she used to sail, Tanner asked, 'I take it she was also a member of the sailing club?'

'Not our club, no; but I think that's where they met, when she came to take part in one of the club's open events.'

Feeling they had enough to be getting on with, Tanner pushed himself off the chair. 'Mr and Mrs Boyd, I'd like to thank you for your time.'

Seeing them stand, with an imploring look the husband asked, 'The clothes we looked at. Are we right in thinking…in thinking that –'

He didn't need to finish what he was saying. Tanner knew what he wanted to know: if the body they'd found was definitely that of their son.

As much as Tanner would have liked to be able to give them some form of closure, he was still unable to say for a fact that it was. As unlikely as it may be, it was still possible that someone else had been dressed in similar clothes. They had only identified the jacket, not the rest. It would take what Forrester's niece, Sally Beech, had suggested for them to know for sure.

Unwilling to bring up the subject of dental records, at least not then, instead Tanner said, 'I'm afraid that at this stage, we still don't know, but I can assure you that as soon as we do, I'll personally be back in touch.'

- CHAPTER TEN -

ONCE OUTSIDE, THEY began quietly making their way back over the drive, heading for Tanner's car, the only sound that of the gravel crunching under their feet.

Nearing the car, Jenny broke the silence. 'I assume the next step is for me to work out who James Boyd's dentist was?'

'Yes, but it's a little below your pay grade,' Tanner replied. 'I suggest you get one of the PCs to do it. Better still, ask Forrester's niece. After all, she was the one who suggested it.'

Keen to keep the new girl just as far away from their investigation as possible, or to be more precise, at arm's length from her boyfriend, Jenny thought for a moment. 'I'll ask Higgins. I'm assuming we're progressing on the basis that the body is that of their son, James Boyd?'

'I think so.'

'Unless someone dressed the corpse up to look like him?'

'Quite,' Tanner agreed, pleased to hear she'd considered that scenario herself. 'It wouldn't be the first time, although, in this instance, I think it's unlikely. If someone had wanted the body to be incorrectly identified, I doubt they'd have gone to so much trouble to hide it.'

'What if someone intended to vanish off the face of the Earth, leaving some dead guy behind to take their place?'

'Well, I know they told us that their son dreamt of sailing off around the world, but I doubt he'd have gone to the lengths of leaving a body behind dressed up as himself before doing so.'

'And what about the other question?'

'If he was murdered?' queried Tanner, unlocking the Jag so they could heave open the long heavy doors. 'I don't think we're any the wiser,' he said, as they climbed inside. 'All we know was that he was good-looking, was into his sailing and had a larger than average number of girlfriends; well, one in particular.'

Starting the engine, still curious to know why Jenny hadn't made a note of the girl's name, he pretended he'd forgotten. 'What was her name again?'

'Kelly Fisher,' Jenny replied, staring vacantly out of the passenger window.

Reversing the car, Tanner asked the question that had been bothering him since the name was first mentioned. 'Was there any particular reason why you didn't make a note of it?'

Jenny turned to give Tanner the briefest of glances before returning to the view outside. 'I know her,' she admitted. 'We were members of the same sailing club, when we were young.'

'I see. And at what point were you planning on telling me that?'

'I just did, didn't I?' snapped Jenny, with uncharacteristic hostility.

Taken aback by her tone, Tanner waited until they'd pulled out onto the road before asking, this time with a little more tact, 'Did you know her well?'

'Yes, years ago,' Jenny replied, watching hedgerows flicker past. 'Our parents joined at similar times. We learnt to sail together.'

When nothing more seemed to be forthcoming, Tanner prompted, 'What was she like?'

'Nice enough, I suppose.'

'It sounds like you didn't get along.'

'We did. Well, we did at first. We were the only two girls at the club, the only juniors that is, so I suppose we had a lot in common.'

'So what happened?'

'We started racing against each other.'

'Oh, I see,' said Tanner, smirking.

'We were both selected for the Junior National Squad at the same time,' Jenny continued, oblivious to Tanner's amusement, 'which meant we used to travel around the country to train with children from other clubs.'

'I assume you became more rivals than friends?'

'Something like that,' Jenny confirmed.

'Was she as good as Boyd's parents suggested?'

'She was all right, I suppose.'

Having experienced first-hand how competitive Jenny could be, especially on those rare occasions when they'd taken part in sailing races, allowing his smile to broaden, Tanner asked, 'Not better than you, surely?'

'She'd cheat!' stated Jenny, evidently still fuming at the memory. 'And not just sometimes. And she didn't win the Topper Nationals, like they said she did. She came second.'

'How about you? I assume you took part as well?'

'It wasn't my event,' she replied, with brisk dismissal.

'Oh. Well, never mind,' replied Tanner, endeavouring to suppress a patronising parental tone.

It was only then that it dawned on him what her revelation might mean. 'You didn't know James Boyd as well, did you?'

'Huh?' she said, as if being woken from a dream. 'Oh, no; at least, not that I can remember.'

'But you may have done?'

'It's possible. The Broads is quite a small community, especially for those of us who sail.'

Realising the importance of the question, she whipped her head round to stare at Tanner. 'You don't think that means I could be taken off the case?'

That was exactly what he'd been thinking.

'If you know someone who turns out to be a suspect in what is likely to become a murder investigation, and if there's also the chance that you knew the victim, then I'm afraid it probably does, Jen, yes.'

'But everyone knows everyone around here.'

'I don't think that's exactly true; not to the point where you're all old sailing club rivals.'

As Jenny's mind took two giant steps forward to realise what would most likely happen if she were taken off the case – Forrester's niece being moved in to take her place – raising her voice she declared, 'But it's not as if we went to the same school or anything. We'd just see each other at the weekends, and not even every weekend either. And I'm sure I don't know James Boyd. I'd have recognised his photograph if I did.'

Seeing the imploring look of desperation on her face, Tanner found himself wrestling with his conscience. Had he still been working down in London, and Jenny had just been some colleague he barely knew, he wouldn't have hesitated to have her re-assigned.

'OK, but I am going to have to interview her, and without you, I may add. And if it does look like she may have had something to do with whatever happened to James Boyd, then for the sake of the investigation, and for your own personal safety, I'll have no choice but to recommend that you're taken off.'

'But –'

'No buts, Jen, sorry.'

Locking her arms over her chest, Jenny bored her eyes into the Jag's wooden dashboard. As far as she was concerned, Tanner was totally over-reacting. Had he been a local, he'd have understood just how small the Broads community was. People simply weren't pulled off investigations just because they happened to know someone linked to a case. If they were, then there'd be hardly anyone left to cover the workload.

As she mulled that over, she contemplated the idea of bringing the subject up with DCI Forrester. But then she remembered two things. Firstly, that Forrester wasn't much of a local himself, insomuch as he wasn't born and bred in the Broads. Secondly, and more importantly, his niece had just landed from planet Blonde, and he'd probably see her admission to vaguely knowing one of the possible suspects as the perfect excuse to do what she was most dreading: to kick her out and give Bimbo Beech the chance to work on what seemed likely to become a murder investigation. That thought led rapidly towards what she was probably most upset about: Tanner's reaction when he'd been introduced to their new Detective Constable. Maybe the real reason behind his sudden – and most uncharacteristic – insistence for them to start working quite so rigidly to the Police Code of Ethics was because he secretly wanted the chance to work with her, not Jenny.

- CHAPTER ELEVEN -

WHAT WAS LEFT of their journey back to their boat was taken in silence. Although Jenny's mood had lightened since she'd admitted to having known one of the possible suspects, despite her best efforts she'd been unable to shake the feeling, no matter how implausible, that Tanner had become an overnight stickler for the rules purely for the chance to spend some quality one-on-one time with a girl who just happened to be, even by Jenny's admission, a drop-dead gorgeous blonde.

'What do you fancy for dinner?' asked Tanner, as they pulled into the public car park, just downriver from where their boat was moored.

'I don't mind,' said Jenny, half of her intent on making sure Tanner knew that she was still upset with him, whilst the other was keen to show him that she was mature enough not to be.

As soon as the car came to a halt, she opened her door and stepped out, just as her phone rang. Digging it out from her handbag, she glanced down to see who it was, but she didn't recognise the number. Expecting it to be an unsolicited sales call, probably from her mobile phone provider, she answered with a cautious 'Hello?'

'Oh, er, hi Jen,' came a voice that was vaguely familiar. 'It's Rob, er, Ellison?'

Having always known him by his unabbreviated name, it took a full moment for Jenny to work out who he was, which was just about long enough for a particularly nervous sounding voice to add, 'From Barton Broad Sailing Club?'

'Robert!' she exclaimed, with genuine surprise.

With the prickle of a blush, she flicked a glance over at Tanner. Seeing the back of his head emerge from the car, she spun away to continue the conversation in private.

'Sorry. I wasn't expecting to hear from you.'

'No, well. I hope you don't mind?'

'Not at all!' she stated, intrigued to know why he had called. If it was for the same reason most men did, at least out of the blue like this, then he was about to be disappointed. Despite the fact that she was currently a little upset with Tanner, she knew it was only temporary. She still loved him dearly, and had no intention of leaving him for anyone, even if that person was an old sailing friend who seemed to have transformed into some sort of Greek god since they'd known each other back when they were teenagers. Something else she was curious about was answered by his next comment.

'I got your number from your parents.'

'Who?' she replied, leaving her caller struggling for something suitable to say in response.

'Sorry,' she said, the moment she realised the joke had gone completely over his head, and for good reason. 'Just kidding,' she added. 'I must admit, it's been a while since I saw them. How are they?'

'Who? Your parents?' he questioned, apparently still unable to grasp the fact that she wasn't being serious, at least not entirely. 'Oh, er...they seem fine. I was actually calling to make sure that you were all right, after what happened yesterday.'

'Oh!' she replied, unable to help feeling a little disappointed that he'd not called to ask her out. 'I'm OK. How about you?'

'Well,' he said, 'it's not every day one finds a dead body.'

Jenny was sorely tempted to come back with, 'You're right, it's normally every other day,' but she swallowed the words to simply agree with him.

'Anyway,' he continued, 'I was calling to see if you'd like to come out for a drink sometime?'

There it is, she thought, with a relieved smile. She'd not been asked since Tanner had, and with her thirtieth birthday just around the corner, she was beginning to wonder if men still found her attractive.

With her mood lifted, she found herself saying, 'I thought you were calling to see how I was, after finding that dead body?'

'I-I was, yes,' he spluttered, 'but I – er...'

'Sorry, I was only joking – again!'

Turning to see where Tanner had got to, she asked, 'When were you thinking of?' as her mind entertained the idea of accepting. She may not be even the slightest bit interested in ending her relationship with Tanner to take up with some new man, but she couldn't see the harm in having a drink with an old friend. Besides, with Sally Beech waltzing around, batting her eyelashes so obviously at Tanner, it wouldn't do any harm to remind him that she was still effectively on the market, insomuch as he'd yet to put a ring on her finger. The best he'd done so far was a bracelet, and not a particularly expensive one at that.

'How about tomorrow night?'

Jenny stopped where she was. In her mind that was far too soon. If she was going to accept, she'd been thinking more along the lines of the coming weekend.

'Unless you've got something else planned?' he said. 'I thought it would be good to talk about what happened – what we found yesterday, when we righted that boat.'

Before he said that, she'd not given a second thought to the psychological impact such a horrific discovery would have had on him: not only him, but also the two senior sailors they'd been in the process of rescuing.

'Hold on,' she said, lowering her phone to wrap her hand around its base. If she was going to agree, she knew she'd have to clear it with Tanner first.

Approaching their boat, she called out, 'John? Are you there?'

'Hello!' came his muffled but cheerful response, from somewhere deep within the cabin.

'I've got Robert Ellison on the phone. You know, the guy we met at the sailing club yesterday.' When there was no reply, she added, 'The one who was driving the safety boat.'

'Uh-huh.'

'He'd like to go out for a drink with me tomorrow night. It sounds like he needs to talk about – about what happened.'

'OK, no problem.'

'Are you sure?'

Tanner emerged into the cockpit, his head appearing from behind the white canvas awning that was still waiting to be rolled back.

Offering her a warm benevolent smile, he said, 'It's not a problem, Jen. You hardly ever go out, and I've got more than enough to keep me busy.'

That was a lie. He hadn't. He'd nearly finished his current book and didn't have another to start on. But he didn't want to give her the impression that he'd be jealous of her going out with some "old friend" who was far better looking than him, and of most concern, at least fifteen years younger.

- CHAPTER TWELVE -

Tuesday, 2nd June

THE FOLLOWING MORNING, after arranging to meet Kelly Fisher, the girl they'd been told had been James Boyd's girlfriend at the time of his disappearance, and having flicked through the original Missing Persons report, Tanner drove his XJS over to the Norwich-based recruitment agency where she worked.

Despite Jenny's renewed protests, Tanner had left her at the station to help Constable Higgins track down Boyd's dentist, enabling them to formally identify his remains, and then to go through the Missing Persons report in more detail.

Waiting in one of the agency's small meeting rooms, it wasn't long before he was joined by an attractive, immaculately dressed woman with mesmerising green eyes and dark red hair, scraped back into a ponytail.

'You must be Detective Inspector Tanner,' she said, entering the room with a distinct air of confidence.

'I am,' Tanner confirmed, pushing himself up from the modern armchair he'd been sitting in to present her with his ID. 'I assume you're Kelly Fisher?'

The woman nodded. 'You mentioned on the phone that you wanted to talk about James Boyd?'

'That's correct,' Tanner replied, exchanging his ID for his little-used notebook.

'Despite what I told you – that I'd been through all this with the police about two decades ago?'

'That was in 2006?' questioned Tanner, referring to his notes.

'OK, so not two decades, but either way, you have to admit that it was a very long time ago.'

'I'd have to admit that, yes,' agreed Tanner. 'Shall we sit down?'

'Has he been found?' she asked, ignoring the offer. 'Is that what this is about?'

'That is what I'd like to discuss with you, Miss Fisher,' Tanner confirmed, gesturing to a seat as he resumed his own.

With an impatient look, she tugged at her rather short skirt to plonk herself down on the chair opposite, crossing one of her bare tanned legs over the other as she did.

Doing his best not to let her smooth long legs distract him, Tanner referred to the notes he'd made before the meeting.

'So?' Miss Fisher demanded, dragging Tanner's eyes up from his notebook.

'We believe we have found him, yes, but we're still awaiting final confirmation.'

The lady took to clenching her hands together on her lap. 'You mean –? Is he –?'

'A body was discovered at the bottom of Barton Broad on Sunday,' Tanner stated. 'You may have heard about it?'

Staring down at the carpet, in a more subdued tone she replied, 'I-I hadn't, no, but I rarely watch the news these days.' Raising her head, she caught Tanner's eyes. 'Do you know how he –? Do you think someone – ?'

'We don't know for certain, no, but we are treating it as suspicious.'

As her focus returned to the floor, Tanner went on, 'We met his parents yesterday. They mentioned that you were his girlfriend at the time.'

Casting a wary eye over him, she said, 'I was, yes.'

'Looking through the original Missing Persons report, we found statements given by some of his friends saying that he'd broken up with you the day before he went missing.'

'I assume you also read that the police at the time seemed to be under the impression that I may have had something to do with his disappearance?'

'I'm sure they were keeping an open mind,' Tanner remarked.

'Well, it didn't seem like they were, judging by the number of questions they kept asking.'

'You told the police you were with your parents at the time.'

'That's correct.'

'Did you mention to them that he'd only just broken up with you?'

'Sorry, but I can't remember.'

'Are you able to remember why he did?'

'Why he broke up with me? I really can't, no.'

'Can you at least recall how you felt about it at the time?'

'I was probably a little miffed.'

'A little miffed,' Tanner repeated, looking down to make a note of the word.

'Miffed as in slightly upset, as opposed to "miffed" as in losing it completely to end up bashing him over the head with my hairdryer.'

'...hairdryer,' Tanner repeated, as he continued to write.

Realising he was taking down everything she was saying, with a look of unamused horror, she said, 'I was only joking.'

Tanner stopped his note-taking to glance up at her. 'Sorry, so you're saying that you *didn't* bash him over the head with your hairdryer?'

She gave him a dirty look. 'May I ask if this is a formal interview?'

Tanner pretended to look puzzled. 'Sorry, but how'd you mean?'

'I mean, aren't you supposed to tell me that I have the right to remain silent and that I shouldn't talk to you without having spoken to a lawyer first?'

'Oh, no, I'm not arresting you, Miss Fisher. I'm simply asking you a few questions.'

'Then can you please stop writing down everything I say as if it's some sort of admission of guilt for having killed James Boyd.'

'Nearly finished,' Tanner replied, returning to his notes.

Hearing her huff rather loudly, he eventually re-engaged eye contact. 'Can you think of anyone else who may have wished him harm?'

'What do you mean, anyone else?'

'Sorry, my fault. Let me rephrase the question.

Can you think of someone else who may have wanted him dead, apart from yourself, of course?'

'I think I've had just about enough of this,' she muttered, pushing herself up from her chair.

'Carol Mortimer, for example?' interjected Tanner, his attention still focussed on his notes.

Hearing the name, the woman sank back into her chair. 'I know Carol, yes.'

'She was in your class at school?'

'That's right.'

'Can you tell me a little more about her?'

'There's not much to tell, really.'

'According to her statement,' Tanner said, looking up to catch her eyes, 'she was also going out with James at the time of his disappearance.'

'What utter rubbish!'

'So, it's not true then?'

'Of course it isn't!'

He raised an eyebrow. 'But why would she lie about something like that?'

'Because she fancied the pants off him, just like all the other girls. She'd have given anything to have actually gone out with him.'

'I assume that when you use the term "going out" you actually mean having sexual intercourse?'

Miss Fisher didn't answer, but instead gave Tanner a look of disdain.

Referring back to his notes, Tanner continued. 'His parents seemed to think that he had a string of girlfriends.'

'Girl *friends*, maybe, but I was the only one he was going out with.'

'You mean, having sex with?'

The woman shifted uncomfortably in her chair.

'I could be wrong, Inspector, but I believe the act of making love does form part of most adult relationships.'

'Yes, of course: which reminds me. How old were you at the time?'

'I was sixteen, Inspector, which I believe made me legally old enough.'

'So, you weren't aware that he was sleeping with someone behind your back.'

'He wasn't!' Fisher insisted, fixing her eyes on Tanner's, as if trying to convince him.

'If you say so,' Tanner replied. 'But had he been, and you'd found out, I suppose you'd have been, what was that word you used again? Oh yes, that's right: a little miffed?'

'No doubt I would have been, but he wasn't.'

'Despite what this Carol Mortimer said.'

'Uh-huh.'

'I see. May I ask what makes you so sure that she wasn't?'

She shrugged. 'Woman's intuition, I suppose.'

Tanner offered her a thin smile. 'I understand James was a keen sailor.'

'You could say that.'

'As were you?'

'At the time.'

'Not anymore?'

'Not since I graduated, no.'

'That's a shame. I've been told you were quite good.'

'I was OK.'

'Weren't you in the Junior National Squad?'

'I was, yes,' she replied, with a surprised look.

'And one year you won the Topper Nationals?'

'I came second,' she corrected, looking none too pleased to be reminded.

'Still, that's very good though, isn't it?'

'My father didn't seem to think so, but there we go.'

'Yes, well, I suppose parents can be a little over-demanding sometimes.'

'Sometimes, yes,' she replied, in a way that gave the impression that hers had always been.

'Did you ever go sailing together – you and James?'

'Occasionally, but he was more into cruising. I did try to get him interested in racing, but it just wasn't his thing.'

'According to his parents, he left very early on the morning of his disappearance. Do you have any idea where he was going?'

'The plan had been that he was going to take me to the Isle of Wight Festival in his parents' boat, but that was before we broke up.'

'Do you know if he was going to take anyone else instead?'

'I've no idea.'

'Carol Mortimer, perhaps?'

She shrugged a response.

'Was there anyone else he may have considered going with?'

'Not that I'm aware of.'

'But he must have had other friends who were into sailing.'

'I suppose.'

With Jenny in mind, Tanner went on, 'What about the other members of the Junior National Squad? I understand there were one or two who came from around here?'

'There were quite a few, yes, but we didn't know each other all that well. I don't think any of us went to the same school, or anything.'

'Did any of them know James?'

'I've no idea. But if you're thinking that any of them were going out with him behind my back, then you're barking up the wrong tree.'

'And why's that?'

'They were all men, Inspector – well, boys, back then.'

'All of them?'

'Well, there was one girl.'

'And who was that?'

'Jenny Evans.'

Deliberately keeping her name out of his notes, Tanner asked, 'And this Jenny Evans: did she know James?'

'I would have been surprised if she didn't.'

Having had Jenny tell him the exact opposite, with an uneasy feeling Tanner asked, 'And what makes you say that?'

'Because *everyone* knew James; at least all the girls did.'

'Did you ever talk about him with this Jenny Evans girl?'

'I must have done.'

'Can you remember specifically if you did?'

'I can't *specifically* remember, no, but he was always a key talking point, so again, I'd have been surprised if I hadn't.'

- CHAPTER THIRTEEN -

WHEN THE MEETING was over, as he headed back to Wroxham Police Station there was only one thing dominating Tanner's mind, and it wasn't the investigation; at least not directly.

Assuming James Boyd had been killed, intentionally or otherwise, as far as Tanner was concerned Kelly Fisher was most definitely going to have to remain a suspect. Her alibi, that she'd been at home during the morning of his disappearance, could only be corroborated by her parents, hardly the most impartial of witnesses. More importantly, if what Boyd's mother had said at the time was true – as corroborated by Carol Mortimer – that her son had been seeing more than one girl, and if Fisher had somehow found out, then she had motive. In Tanner's experience, crimes of passion were by far the most common causes of murder. She'd openly admitted to having had a fight with him the night before, but despite it having led to James Boyd ending the relationship, it was remarkably odd that she couldn't remember what it had been about. Had she been a boy, then maybe: they didn't tend to take those sorts of things quite so seriously. But if Miss Fisher had been anything like his daughter, then she'd probably have been able to play back the argument in her head, almost word for word, even fifteen years later.

As interesting as all that was, it wasn't the problem Tanner's mind was wrestling with. He was trying to decide what to do about Jenny. She knew the suspect, there was no question about that; and even though she didn't seem keen to admit it, or possibly she simply couldn't remember, there was an above average chance that she knew the victim as well. Under such circumstances, as the senior investigating officer, he had a duty to put in a formal request to his superior that she be transferred to another investigation. But in this case, it wasn't quite that straight forward; not when they were going out with each other. If he did, he knew what she'd say, and it wouldn't be, 'thank you'. He wasn't even sure if Jenny was incorrect in her assertion that personal knowledge of those involved in an investigation wasn't as significant as it was in the Met. He knew that Wroxham, for example, had a population of less than two thousand, most of whom had been born and bred there. So it was hardly surprising that everyone seemed to know each other. The question was, should he tell Forrester, and what would be his reaction if he did? If he ordered Jenny to be re-assigned, what would she say to him, when they got back to their boat?

'How'd it go?' asked Jenny, as Tanner nudged his way past her chair to his desk.

'Oh, fine,' he replied, his dilemma still unresolved.

'Do you think she had anything to do with it?'

'I'm not sure,' he replied, dropping his coat over the back of his chair. Keen to change the subject, he asked, 'How've you been getting on?'

'I've just finished going through the original Missing Persons investigation, but I couldn't find anything else, at least nothing that stood out.'

'Did you get a chance to ask Higgins to ring round the local dentists?'

'I did, yes. He's already found the right one. He emailed Boyd's x-rays over to them about half an hour ago. Hopefully we'll hear back any minute.'

Tanner glanced down at his watch. 'OK, well, I suppose I'd better give Forrester an update.'

'Do you want me to come?' Jenny asked, attaching a look of hopeful expectation.

'No, you're OK,' Tanner replied, with casual dismissiveness. He may not have decided if he should tell Forrester about Jenny's relationship with one of the suspects, but he did at least know that he didn't want her included in the discussion, were he to start one. 'Could you look up that other girl, the one who also said she was seeing James Boyd?'

'Carol Mortimer?'

'That's the one. Try to find out where she works and ask if we can pop round. Hopefully we'll be able to see her when I'm done.'

- CHAPTER FOURTEEN -

'MAY I COME in?' asked Tanner, having rapped on the door.

'Of course,' Forrester replied, waving vaguely at him to do so, the bulk of his attention still focussed on his monitor.

Tanner hovered over the threshold, half in, half out. 'I just thought I'd give you an update on how we've been getting on with that body we found on Sunday.'

'Good, yes, well...come in then,' Forrester repeated.

Closing the door behind him, Tanner stepped inside to take up a rather rigid pose behind one of the two chairs facing Forrester's desk.

'At this stage, we're fairly sure it's James Boyd,' he began, 'a seventeen year-old who went missing back in 2006.'

Forrester finally gave Tanner his full attention. 'Was that whose parents you met with on your way back home yesterday?'

'It was,' Tanner confirmed. 'They were able to identify the jacket he was found in.'

'Have we had dental confirmation?'

'Not yet, no, but we're expecting to hear back from them any time now.'

'I assume you've been through the original Missing Persons report?'

'We have, and I've just returned from interviewing the girl highlighted as having been the last person to see him: Kelly Fisher.'

'Sorry, but I thought you said that we're still awaiting official confirmation that the body is that of James Boyd?'

'Well, yes, sir, but –'

'And yet you've already started interviewing suspects?'

'I know, sir, but –'

'Without even knowing who the victim is?'

At that point, Tanner decided that it was probably best to keep his mouth shut. He'd been so pre-occupied with what to do about Jenny knowing Kelly Fisher that he'd neglected to follow the most basic of procedures.

'You're a bit keen, aren't you?'

'Perhaps, sir, but I really do think that the dental confirmation is just a formality.'

'But a necessary one, though, don't you think?'

'Yes, sir. Of course, sir.'

Fortunately for Tanner, since the arrival of his niece, Forrester had been in a far more cheerful frame of mind than was to be normally expected.

'OK, well, no harm done I suppose. But please remember in the future that we need a formal identification before we can start going around interviewing suspects.'

'Absolutely, sir.'

'So anyway, what did she have to say for herself?'

With his mind still bogged down with what he

was going to do about Jenny knowing the suspect under discussion, Tanner replied, 'Sorry, who sir?'

'The woman you interviewed, Tanner! Who else?'

'Of course, yes. Pretty much what she'd said in the original Missing Persons report.'

'Which was?'

'That they'd been going out with each other and that he was planning on taking her to a music festival on the Isle of Wight, using his parents' boat, but the night before they were due to leave they had an argument, leaving her with the impression that he was going to go on his own.'

'Any idea what the argument was about?'

'She said she couldn't remember.'

Seeing Forrester raise an eyebrow, Tanner continued. 'James's parents – well, his mother at least, seemed to be of the impression that he had a string of girlfriends. In the original report, one of them claimed that she'd also been seeing Boyd at the same time as he was going out with Kelly Fisher.'

'I assume you're thinking that that's what the argument could have been about?'

'The thought had crossed my mind, sir, yes.'

'And your next step?'

Tanner pulled out his notebook. 'To have a chat with the other girl, Carol Mortimer, to find out whether what she says now is the same as what she said back then. For all we know, she could have been playing out some teenage fantasy that she had been seeing Boyd, when in fact the opposite was true, and her feelings towards him had been unrequited.'

'OK, sounds good,' said Forrester, returning his attention to his monitor. 'Let me know how you get on.'

Surprised that Tanner didn't move, he looked back at him. 'Was there anything else?'

This was the moment for Tanner to tell Forrester that Jenny knew Kelly Fisher, possibly James Boyd as well. But now that the time had come, he found himself hesitating, his mind re-engaging itself in the same back and forth discussion. Did it really matter that she did, and how much damage would it do to their relationship if he asked for her to be removed from the investigation, which was effectively what he'd be doing if he told Forrester?

With his DCI boring holes into his face, Tanner plumped for the easiest option – which was simply not to bother. After all, what possible difference could it make?

Already regretting his decision, Tanner said, 'Sorry, nothing sir. I'll let you know how we get on with Carol Mortimer.'

With Tanner heading for the door, Forrester called out, 'But not before you've had official confirmation back from the dentist!'

- CHAPTER FIFTEEN -

'SO, WHAT'S THE verdict?' asked Jenny, watching Tanner sit down behind his desk.

'The verdict?' Tanner replied, logging into his computer with the pretence of nonchalant ambivalence.

'I assume you told him that I knew one of the suspects. That *was* why you went in there, wasn't it?'

'Oh, that! I'm sure it won't be a problem.'

'What – so, you didn't tell him?'

'It didn't come up in the conversation, no.'

Her face displayed both confusion and surprise. 'But – don't you think it should have?'

With a bemused look, Tanner turned to say, 'Sorry? I didn't think you wanted to be taken off the investigation?'

'Well, no, but, even so, I think it would have been prudent to have told him, don't you?'

With mounting frustration, Tanner said, 'Well, it's too late now.'

'You can go back in, can't you?'

'What, and say, "Sorry, sir, but I forgot to mention that DS Evans just happens to know the prime suspect, seeing that they used to sail together when they were young"?'

'Yes, and? Why not?'

'Because he's going to be mighty curious to know why I didn't think to mention it before!'

'Then you should have told him, shouldn't you!'

'Unbelievable,' muttered Tanner under his breath, just as PC Higgins approached.

'Sorry – am I disturbing you?' he asked, exchanging concerned glances between the two officers.

Tanner forced a smile. 'Not at all, Higgins. How can we help?'

'News back from the dentist, sir. They've confirmed that the records we sent over to them do belong to James Boyd.'

'Well, that's something, at least.'

'Yes, sir,' replied the young uniformed officer, standing to attention, as if waiting to be dismissed.

'Whilst you're there,' Tanner said, 'can you do me a favour and pop in to tell DCI Forrester?'

Watching him turn to do so, Tanner mumbled to himself, 'At least that will keep him off my back about that.'

Pleased that at least one burden had been lifted from his shoulders, he turned to offer Jenny a calming smile. 'Listen, let's not worry about you knowing Miss Fisher, for now at least. I can always bring it up with Forrester later.'

'But how will you explain to him why you didn't tell him before?'

Shrugging his shoulders, Tanner replied, 'Hopefully it won't come up.'

'And if it does?'

'Then I'll just tell him that you simply didn't realise that it was the same person. It does happen.

After all, it was a long time ago. Anyway, now we definitely know who the body is, we need to arrange to meet up with Carol Mortimer. Were you able to track her down?'

'I was, yes. She's a veterinary assistant in Hoveton, just down the road.'

'OK, great. Give them a call, ask if she's in, and if we'd be able to have a quick chat.'

- CHAPTER SIXTEEN -

PARKING NEARBY, THEY were soon stepping into the quiet reception area of a small veterinary practice with a tiled grey floor and cute pawprint-design wallpaper.

Behind the desk sat a young girl, grinning at them. 'Hello!' she called out, with near sycophantic cheerfulness.

Noticing an elderly woman to the left, occupying the middle of three fixed plastic seats with a cat basket parked on her lap, Tanner stepped up to the desk to lean over the counter with his ID. 'Is Carol Mortimer in?' he asked, keeping his voice low. 'We called earlier.'

'I'll just check for you,' the girl replied, the smile remaining fixed in place.

Pushing herself away from the desk, she crossed to one of two doors behind her. After poking her head around the nearest one, she returned a moment later.

'She'll be out in just a minute. Would you like to take a seat?'

With the choice to sit each side of the old lady or to remain standing, Tanner replied, 'We'll wait over here,' before drifting away with Jenny to spend the time taking in a series of pet photographs scattered over one side of the wall, each one with an odd sort of name scrawled underneath.

A less cheerful woman soon emerged through one of the doors, her skin as white as her ill-fitting lab coat, both of which were in stark contrast to her jet-black hair.

'You wanted to see me?' she asked, fixing Tanner and Jenny with a look of professional intent.

'We do,' Tanner replied. 'Is there somewhere we can talk?'

Glancing over to the receptionist, she said, 'I'll be outside for a moment,' and led Tanner and Jenny back through the entrance.

Out on the high street, with the vet's door firmly closed, Tanner made the formal introductions.

'I'm Detective Inspector Tanner. This is my colleague, Detective Sergeant Evans, Norfolk Police.'

'Yes, and –?'she said, studying the two IDs.

'I take it you are Carol Mortimer?'

With narrowing eyes, as if selecting each word with deliberate consideration, she replied, 'I am. Why? What's this about?'

'We understand you used to know someone by the name of James Boyd.'

Her eyes widened as her weight shifted from one foot to the other. 'I did, yes; but that was back at school, before he disappeared.'

'I'm sorry to have to tell you that a body was found at the weekend.'

'Is it – is it him?' she asked, her mouth left hanging open, waiting for a response.

'We've officially identified it as being him, yes,' confirmed Tanner.

The woman looked away, blinking at the appearance of unexpected tears.

'I'm sorry,' she apologised, wiping at them with her lab coat's oversized sleeves. 'I wasn't expecting that.'

'And I'm sorry for being the bearer of such unfortunate news,' Tanner responded.

After a momentary pause, he said, 'We understand you spoke to the police, at the time of his disappearance.'

'They came around to my parents' house,' she responded with a nod.

'Can you remember what you told them?' questioned Tanner, looking to find out if she'd be able to confirm what she'd said back then: that she'd been in a relationship with the deceased.

'I really can't, I'm afraid,' she replied, regaining her former stone-like composure.

'We understand you went to school together?'

'We were in the same year, yes.'

'Did you know him well?'

'Better than most.'

'Would you be able to describe your relationship?'

'We were seeing each other, if that's what you mean.'

Tanner raised an eyebrow. 'What about Kelly Fisher?'

'What about her?'

'We've been led to believe that she was his girlfriend.'

'Well, officially, I suppose; but he didn't love

her.'

'He was in love with you instead, was he?'

'That's what he told me.'

'What else did he say?'

'That he was going to dump Kelly to go out with me instead.'

'So you were seeing each other behind Kelly's back?'

'That wasn't my choice. I kept telling him to break up with her.'

'And did he?'

'I don't know. He promised he would, after school that day, but I never saw him again.'

'How about the sailing trip to the Isle of Wight. Did you know anything about that?'

'Of course. He'd been telling everyone he was going to go for months. He told me that he was going to break up with Kelly and take me instead. He was supposed to call me to let me know when he had, to arrange to meet me at his sailing club the next morning, but he never did.'

'Did you try to call him?'

'I didn't, no. I just assumed she'd managed to persuade him not to break up with her, like she always seemed able to.'

The sudden blast of a car horn distracted them.

Glancing over to see a man apologise to the driver who'd almost run him over as he bounded across the road, Tanner returned his attention to the veterinary assistant.

'What was Kelly Fisher like?'

'She was a sporty type. Very competitive. Not very bright, though.'

'Anything else?'

'She was captain of the hockey team, or she was for a time.'

'Why, what happened?'

'She was accused of attacking a hockey player from another school during an away game. Broke her collar bone, apparently.'

'Was she suspended?' Tanner asked, thinking he'd be able to confirm the story by checking with the school records.

'I don't think so, but I do know that she was kicked off the team. I also remember that she denied it, and told everyone that she'd quit because she'd been selected for some special sail training thing.'

With that tying in with what Jenny had told him about the Junior National Squad, he moved the interview on. 'I don't suppose you can remember what you were doing, the night James Boyd disappeared?'

'I was at home, with my parents, waiting for him to call.'

As that also corroborated her original statement, Tanner decided to bring the conversation to a close.

'Miss Mortimer, thank you for your time,' he said, digging out his card and handing it to her. 'If you remember anything else that you think may be of help, please feel free to give either myself or DS Evans here a call.'

'No problem,' she replied, taking it out of his hand to read what it said, 'but I can't imagine what that would be.'

'Well, you never know.'

As Tanner led Jenny away, Mortimer called

after him, 'Mr Tanner! Sorry, but may I ask what happened to James? I-I mean, how did he –?'

Tanner turned back to face her.

'We're not one hundred percent sure yet, Miss Mortimer, but that's what we're intending to find out.'

Heading back to the car, Tanner said to Jenny, 'That all seemed to tie in with what we've learnt from the original Missing Persons investigation.'

'Her description of Kelly Fisher certainly rang true – at least from my experience.'

A moment of silence followed, before Jenny said, 'You never told me what Kelly said, when you spoke to her.'

'Pretty much what she said at the time,' came Tanner's rather curt response.

'Would it be worth re-checking their alibis?'

'After such a long time, probably not. Both said they were with their parents, which makes sense, given that they lived at home.'

'What about asking their brothers and sisters? I know Kelly had a younger brother.'

'We could, I suppose, but I doubt it would make much difference, whatever they came out with.'

'Not if they mentioned something that contradicted what their parents had said.'

'Perhaps, but it wouldn't alter the fact they they'd still be members of the same family. The emotional ties they have to the suspects are just too strong to make them reliable witnesses. A court would simply assume they'd say whatever they had to in order to protect their siblings.'

Reaching the car, parked on the side of the road,

Jenny stopped on the kerb. 'So, what do we do now?'

'I think we're just going to have to keep ploughing our way through the original list of people interviewed at the time, and hope that someone comes out with something that doesn't correspond with their original testimony.' With his hand tucked under the door handle, he checked his watch. 'But as it's gone half five, I suggest we head back to our boat. Maybe something will come to us over a bottle of wine.'

'Oh, shit!' Jenny stared down at her own watch.

'What's up?'

'I'm supposed to be meeting Robert Ellison. I'd forgotten all about it.'

'What time?'

'We said we'd meet at the Red Lion at eight, the one just down the road.'

'OK, well, no problem,' Tanner replied, with deliberate nonchalance. 'Plenty of time for us to get back for something to eat before you go.'

- CHAPTER SEVENTEEN -

ALAN DICKSON'S PULSE quickened as he turned his BMW 7 Series into a quiet tree-lined car park, just off the edge of Ludham village. Beside him, with her office skirt riding tantalisingly high up her smooth naked thighs, sat a girl he barely knew. Her name was Lorna Edwards, she worked in accounts, and she was married. She was also devastatingly attractive and had a body he'd happily die for, figuratively speaking of course. Apart from that, he knew little else about her. One thing he did know was that he fancied the pants off her. He had done since the day she'd ambled past his desk one insipidly dull Monday morning, just two months before. At that stage he'd not seen her face, just her perfectly formed heart-shaped bum, as it swayed first one way, then the other, like a hypnotist's pendulum. When he discovered her face to be as attractive as the rest of her, possibly more so, he knew he had to have her. Finding out later that same day that she was married was, for him at least, irrelevant. After all, so was he. He'd tied the knot a few years earlier. Surprisingly, it had made little difference to the way he found himself constantly chasing after women, even more than he had before he'd proposed. He knew he shouldn't, but he didn't seem able to stop himself. It wasn't that he didn't love his wife. He did, very much. The problem was that he didn't find her as attractive as he had done before they got married. He'd no idea why. She hadn't changed, not physically; he just found himself with a constant yearning to be with other women.

Fortunately, he'd been blessed with above-average height, rugged good looks, and a razor-sharp sense of humour. The combination of all three allowed him to have just about any girl he set his sights on. Perhaps that was his problem? He'd become so used to being able to do so, that by the time he decided to marry, he found himself unable to break the habit. For him, having sex with women he barely knew was a drug like no other; one that gave him such a high, he was left with little choice but to do it over and over again, each time with a different woman. The more challenging the girl proved to be, the greater the rush he'd receive in return.

That was where Lorna came in. She was possibly the most attractive woman he'd ever met; the fact that she was married made her doubly desirable. But it soon became clear that the challenge was far greater than he'd originally anticipated. Not only was she married, but she was happily so. However, after a few after-work trips down the pub with everyone else, where he'd plied her with alcohol whilst listening to her niggling little marital problems, he was soon able to persuade her otherwise; and more importantly, that she deserved better.

A few weeks later and they were going out on their own together, and a goodbye kiss soon turned into more. But despite his very best efforts, she'd never allow him to go all the way with her; not in the back of his car, nor in any of the other places he suggested, forcing him to think of something a little more adventurous.

Seeing the deserted, dimly lit car park he'd brought her to, she whipped her head around to glare at him. 'You told me you were taking me somewhere special!'

'I am,' he replied, offering her a disarming smile.

'Well, I'm not doing it here,' she snapped, locking her arms over her designer leather jacket.

'Don't worry, I'm not asking you to.'

'I'm not doing it up against a tree, either!'

Turning the engine off, he swivelled around in his seat to face her.

'Listen, I've always said that I'd never ask you to do anything you don't want to do.'

'And I've always said that I'm not doing it in the back of a car, and that extends to where you park one!'

'I know. Now, come on. I've got something to show you. If you don't like it, I'll take you straight home.'

Lorna took a moment to study his face, which she'd become increasingly fond of over the last couple of months. 'Promise?'

'I promise,' he replied, pushing open his door. 'Come on. It's not far.'

Following his lead, Lorna stepped cautiously out, staring about, her eyes searching the shadows that seemed to be lying in wait for them beyond the thick line of trees.

Noticing her apprehension, Alan skirted around the car to close the door for her, before tugging open the one behind. Reaching in, he pulled out a small backpack. 'Look, I've even bought refreshments.'

Nudging the door closed with his elbow, he opened the bag to reveal a large green bottle nestled up against two long thin champagne glasses.

'What are we celebrating?' Lorna asked, already sounding more relaxed.

'Us!' he stated, with a reassuring smile.

Closing the bag, he took her by the hand to lead her towards a gap in the trees, locking the car behind them as he did.

Entering what was the narrowest of footpaths, they began following it, ducking their heads under a tangled web of overhanging branches. The further they went, the darker it became, until they eventually emerged into a clearing strewn with empty beer cans, discarded fast-food packaging and other unsightly human detritus.

'I sincerely hope this isn't what you dragged me all the way out here for?' Lorna questioned, staring about with disgust.

As a shadow began creeping its way over the clearing, Alan glanced up to see a dense grey cloud rolling its way over their heads. *Please don't rain*, he begged, just as Lorna began tugging her jacket around her waist.

'It's just over here,' he said, the words tumbling out. Having come so far, he was desperate not to have to turn back now.

Taking her hand once more, he led the way through a thicket of shrubs and trees until they suddenly found themselves standing at the edge of a wide expanse of flat open water, stretching out as far as the eye could see. There they stopped to stare out towards the horizon beyond, where a dazzling array of orange and red exploded out from a fast-setting sun, like an atom bomb, scorching the sky above.

Hearing Lorna gasp, Alan smirked to himself. The stunning sunset was a most welcome addition to the scene he'd only previously been able to imagine.

'There's a rowing boat over here,' he said, guiding her eyes towards a tarpaulin covered boat tied up to an old wooden jetty.

'Is it yours?' she asked, still feeling hesitant.

'It belongs to a friend,' Alan lied, something which came naturally to him.

Someone from work had told him about it. Neither knew who owned it.

'But we can take it out?' she queried, gazing back out over the Broad.

'He said we can,' Alan replied, picking his way over towards it.

Following, Lorna watched as Alan placed a careful step on the blackened wooden jetty. 'Is it even safe?'

'Should be,' he replied, cautiously planting his full weight down onto it to begin creeping along, feeling the structure move underfoot. As much as his body yearned to be inside the girl standing just a few steps behind him, his mind was beginning to have serious doubts about this being the best method to go about it. He'd never so much as set foot on a boat before, let alone a small rowing-type one. But how hard could it be?

Realising Lorna had stopped where she was, he called back, 'It's quite safe.'

'It doesn't look safe,' she replied, placing a tentative step onto the dilapidated structure.

Endeavouring to take her mind off the fragility of the jetty on which they were both now standing, looking down at the boat, Alan said, 'If you can untie it, I'll unhook the cover.'

Lorna turned her attention to the rope she could see leading from the boat to the post nearest to her. The entire length was covered in green slime, and the knot around the post looked like it had grown there.

'I'm not touching that!' she stated, sending Alan a mutinous look.

Doing his best to suppress a world-weary sigh, Alan replied, 'Tell you what, if you unhook the cover, I'll try to undo the ropes.'

Crouching down to have a go, Lorna muttered to herself, 'This better be worth it.'

Overhearing, Alan's heart picked up a beat. As far as he was concerned, her remark meant that she'd finally agreed to have sex with him, on the condition that he'd be able to get the boat out. He wasn't concerned by the same remark's veiled threat. He knew he wouldn't be able to perform to a satisfactory standard. Not the first time. But it would hardly matter. From experience he knew the hardest part was the initial persuasion. After that, it would be easy enough. All he'd have to do would be to whisper a time and place into her ear whilst passing her in a corridor, or when making themselves a coffee.

'I can't undo these stupid hooks either!' Lorna complained, standing up to fold her arms in protest at having to do anything that could be seen to be helping Alan to have his way with her.

Having undone the first of two mooring lines, Alan crouched down to start unclipping a series of elasticated hoops from half a dozen metal hooks embedded along the top of the hull, just beneath the lip of the boat. With the side nearest to him done, he reached over to begin removing the first few on the other side, placing his free hand on the edge of the boat in order to do so. With the whole thing tilting precariously towards him under his weight, hoping Lorna wasn't losing her patience, along with her mood, he called out, 'Nearly there,' in a cheerful, overly optimistic tone.

With the first few far side hooks unclipped, he heaved back a section of the tarpaulin to clamber on board, using his feet to shove what he assumed to be oars underneath over to the side. Kneeling on one of the bench seats, he stretched himself out over the rest of the boat to unclip the last of the hooks before finally being able to pull the cover off.

There, underneath, lay the body of a man; his eyes closed, his skin deathly white, the tip of a tongue protruding out through thin purple lips.

The shock of seeing him there sent Alan staggering back, rocking the boat violently beneath him as he frantically clambered out.

From the jetty, staring down, Lorna lifted her hands to cover her mouth, watching the body's head roll first one way, then the other, as the boat lifted and fell.

With the boat finally beginning to level out, the head came to an eventual rest at an odd sort of an angle, facing up towards them.

'Is he –?' queried Lorna, her voice barely loud enough for Alan to hear.

'He must be,' stated Alan, as if certain of the fact.

Lorna didn't reply, but instead turned to send Alan a questioning look.

'Can't you see it?' Alan asked, leading her eyes down with his own.

There, curving over the man's chest was a thick steel rod, the lower half of which was buried deep into his stomach, out from which oozed thick, half-congealed blood.

Lorna gagged, the foul taste of bile forging up into her throat.

Just as her mind accepted the fact that they were staring down at a long-dead corpse, the tip of its tongue disappeared inside its mouth, and its eyes blinked open to stare up into her own. Only then did she let out an ear-bleeding scream.

- CHAPTER EIGHTEEN -

TANNER WAS JUST beginning to contemplate the idea of having an early night when the call came. A body had been discovered inside a rowing boat, moored up on the banks of Hickling Broad.

Making a note of the location, he was soon on the phone to Jenny.

'Sorry to interrupt,' he began, lifting his voice above the noise of a busy-sounding pub.

'What's up?' came her somewhat jaded response.

'A body's been unearthed, over near Catfield Common. Forrester wants us to take a look.'

There followed a momentary pause, before her voice came back over the line. 'OK. If you can text me the location, I'll meet you there.'

Ending the call, Tanner took a moment to thumb out a message giving the details before grabbing his keys and coat and hurrying over to his car.

Arriving to find Jenny climbing out of her Golf, and giving her a half-wave through the windscreen, Tanner pulled up alongside.

'Sorry to have ruined your evening,' he apologised, closing his door.

'Hardly your fault,' Jenny replied, taking in the dimly lit car park, along with the dense line of trees that seemed to be crowding in around them. 'We were running out of things to talk about anyway.'

The sudden blast of a siren made them both jump.

Staring towards the entrance, they each held up a hand to shield their eyes from the headlights of the squad car swinging into the car park.

Nodding over to acknowledge their arrival, Tanner turned his attention back to the task at hand.

'Any idea how to get to the Broad from here?'

'There must be a path that leads down to it somewhere,' replied Jenny, glancing about. Pointing to where a nondescript car could be seen, with two white faces staring out through steamed-up windows, she said, 'That could be it, over there.'

Following where he was being directed, Tanner could just about make out a narrow gap in the trees, just past the car.

As the two police officers slammed their doors closed, Tanner called over to them, 'We're going to try to find the body. You two stay here for now; have a chat with the couple in the car. Find out how long they've been here, and if they've seen anyone come or go, preferably with a description.'

Seeing them nod their understanding, Tanner allowed Jenny to lead the way towards where the car was parked, and the space between the trees beyond.

Doing their best to ignore the couple, who'd stopped gawping out of the window to begin frantically pulling on their clothes, Tanner and

Jenny dug out their phones to access their torch apps. With beams of light bathing the way ahead, they ducked through the gap to begin picking their way along a footpath through the trees.

Crossing a rubbish strewn clearing, they skirted past a series of shrubs. A moment later Hickling Broad loomed into view, its gently rippled surface glistening in the afterglow from the long-set sun.

Scanning the area with their torch lights, it was Jenny who saw the small wooden rowing boat with its cover thrown back, most of which lay half-submerged in the surrounding water.

'It must be in there,' she called back to Tanner, a few feet behind.

Placing a tentative foot on the jetty, being careful not to touch anything with her hands, she lifted herself up and shuffled her way along, shining her torchlight down into the boat as she did.

'It's here all right,' she said, glancing over her shoulder to watch Tanner approach.

Returning her gaze to take in the man's face, her breath caught in her throat.

'Christ, John,' she muttered, barely loud enough to be heard. Raising her hand to her open mouth, she added, 'I think – I think I know him.'

'What was that?' queried Tanner, who'd only just reached the jetty.

Jenny's eyes remained fixed on the body's pale drawn face. 'I know him!' she repeated, that time with more certainty.

Tanner didn't know quite how to respond. Instead he focussed his attention on where he was placing his feet, as he crept over the sagging jetty to where she was standing.

'It's Craig. Craig Jenkins,' she continued, seeing Tanner appear besides her. 'He used to be in our junior sailing squad.'

'The same one Kelly Fisher was in?' questioned Tanner, staring down at the body lying sprawled on its back, attempting to work out what had been hooked into the upper half of its abdomen.

'The very same,' Jenny confirmed, unable to take her eyes off the face that seemed to be staring up at them, its eyes partially open.

It was then that she saw him blink, at least she thought she did.

'Jesus Christ!' she exclaimed, stumbling forward to begin clambering on board. 'I think he's still alive!'

'Wait – what?'

With the boat rocking violently under her weight, she scrambled over the body towards his head. Once there, she knelt down to press two fingers against the side of his neck.

'It's faint, but I think there's a pulse.'

With the same hand, she peeled back the eyelids to shine her phone's torchlight down into them.

'And his pupils are dilating. He's definitely alive. Can you make sure an ambulance is on its way? Then head back to get a medical kit from the squad car.'

'But – he can't be,' came Tanner's somewhat delayed response.

Realising he'd still not moved, Jenny whipped her head around to glare at him.

'For Christ sake, John. NOW!'

- CHAPTER NINETEEN -

ABOUT HALF AN hour later, Tanner was standing beside Jenny back in the car park, a comforting arm wrapped around her thin narrow shoulders.

Emerging through the gap in the trees they saw their Medical Examiner, Dr Johnstone, the dull glow from an overhanging lamp lighting his face.

Jenny opened her mouth, about to call over a question to him, but seeing his drawn morbid expression, she snapped it closed again. The answer was obvious enough.

'I'm sorry,' he said, coming to a halt in front of them. 'I'm afraid there was nothing anyone could do.'

Jenny returned a single nod of solemn acceptance.

'But at least we have a fair amount to go on with this one,' he continued, in a more upbeat tone of voice, 'especially as the murder weapon was left in place.'

Tanner spoke up. 'Am I correct in thinking that it's a rhond hook?'

'I believe it is,' Johnstone confirmed, pushing his glasses up the bridge of his nose. 'From my initial observation, it looks to have been driven through the victim's stomach, possibly piercing his liver as well. Neither injury was immediately fatal. The fact that it was left in place meant that it effectively plugged the wound, which would go a long way to explain how he was able to last as long as he did.'

The headlights from a car sliding into the car park made them all glance around.

Seeing it was DCI Forrester's BMW, Johnstone apologised once again, as if the man's death was somehow his fault.

'I'll aim to have a report over to you by tomorrow lunchtime.' With that, he sent Jenny a kind smile before turning to make his way back to where a group of overall-clad officers appeared to be waiting for him.

Removing his arm from Jenny's shoulders, Tanner stood a little taller as they shuffled around to face the lights of their DCI's incoming car.

Whilst waiting for him to park, Tanner leaned in towards her to ask, 'How're you holding up?'

'I'm OK,' Jenny replied, her voice level, if a little stilted.

It was clear that he was going to have to tell Forrester about Jenny knowing the victim, and that he'd been a member of her junior sailing squad, the same one as Kelly Fisher. 'Are you absolutely sure it was your old friend, Craig Jenkins?'

'About as sure as I can be.'

'I assume he knew Kelly Fisher?'

Jenny nodded her response, as they watched Forrester reverse his car into a narrow space between the forensics van and an ambulance.

'I don't suppose you know if they were seeing each other, back then?'

'Who? Craig and Kelly?' queried Jenny, as if appalled by the very idea.

'May I take that as a no?'

'Well, if they were, nobody told me about it.'

'Do you have any idea if Craig Jenkins knew James Boyd?'

'I don't think so, but I can't be sure.'

'You don't know if they were at school together?'

'They may have been, I suppose.'

'What about Carol Mortimer? Did Craig Jenkins know her?'

'I'm sorry, I've no idea.'

'OK, that's fine.'

Seeing Forrester lumbering his way over towards them, keeping his voice low, Tanner decided it was best to tell Jenny his intentions.

'Unfortunately, I'm going to have to tell Forrester about this – that you knew the victim; probably about you knowing Kelly Fisher as well.'

Jenny replied in a similar hushed tone, albeit one marred by a strong undercurrent of resentment. 'I suppose you're going to recommend that I'm kicked off the case?'

'This one, definitely, I'm afraid. Sorry. I don't know about the Boyd investigation. I suppose it depends if we decide that they're linked.'

'But they must be, surely?'

'I'm not so sure. At the moment, the only thing that seems to connect the two is that both victims knew Kelly Fisher.'

'And me, of course.'

'Well, yes. Quite! But I think that unless some

form of physical evidence is unearthed to indicate that Kelly Fisher had a hand, along with some sort of a motive for her having done so, then any link is tenuous at best; at least that's what I plan to tell Forrester. Hopefully, that way he'll allow you to remain on the Boyd investigation, if only in the background.'

'And then I suppose he'll assign that niece of his to work with you on this one.'

'That's up to him. Anyway, you'd better let me have a chat with him on his own. Maybe you can find out what that couple in the car had to say for themselves?'

'Fine,' muttered Jenny.

Tanner watched in silence as she stomped away, heading over to where he could see the two officers who'd arrived shortly after them chatting to each other, just inside the car park's entrance.

With Jenny gone, he turned his attention to his approaching boss.

'Evening, Tanner,' he heard Forrester call out, still a few feet away.

'Sir.'

'So?' the DCI said, coming to a halt and catching his breath. 'I hear we have another body on our hands?'

'A white male, sir, in his late twenties,' Tanner confirmed.

'Any idea of the cause?'

'It looks like someone impaled him with a rhond hook.'

'A rhond hook?'

Before he'd arrived in Norfolk, some eighteen months earlier, Tanner's response to the item in question would have no doubt been very similar. However, as he now had no less than three of them stored in the bow of his boat, he was able to give a suitably informed response.

'They're similar to an anchor, in size and weight, but instead of being used to catch on the sea floor, they're designed to secure a boat to an embankment.'

'And what makes you so sure he was killed by one of those?'

'Because it was left inside him, sir.'

'Fair enough,' Forrester replied, glancing over Tanner's shoulder, as if searching for the body to be able to confirm what Tanner had said.

'Time of death?'

Tanner looked down at his watch. 'I'd have to check with Johnstone, but I'd say it was probably only about ten to fifteen minutes ago.'

Seeing Forrester raise a curious eyebrow, Tanner sought to clarify his comment. 'He was alive when we found him, although barely.'

'Any theories as to why the murder weapon was left behind?'

'It's possible that it may have been to deliberately extend the time it took for him to die, as it effectively helped plug the wound. The only other alternative I can think of is that whoever stabbed him with it was unable to take it out afterwards.'

Forrester cast his eyes around the car park whilst massaging the heavy jowls of his jaw.

'Which *could* indicate that it was a woman,' postulated Tanner, 'lacking the strength to take it out. Or whoever did it just didn't care.'

'I don't suppose there's any indication if he was attacked where he was found?'

'Nothing so far. Forensics are going over the scene as we speak.'

'Do we know who he is yet?'

'Actually, sir, I need to talk to you about that.'

Forrester turned his head to glare over at Tanner. 'Please don't tell me he's someone famous.'

'Nothing like that, no.'

'Well, thank God for that!'

'It's Jenny Evans, sir. She thinks she knows the victim.'

'*Thinks* she knows?'

'She seems confident that she *does* know him, sir.'

'Not a family member, I hope?'

'No, sir. She's fairly sure it's someone from her old junior sailing squad. Craig Jenkins.'

'Then it's probably best if she gives this one a miss.'

'Probably, sir, yes,' Tanner agreed. 'Which leads me onto something else.'

'Go on.'

'Kelly Fisher, sir.'

'The suspect in the James Boyd case?'

Tanner nodded, before continuing. 'I'm afraid she was in the same junior sailing squad.'

'The same one as Jenny?'

'And the victim here as well, sir, yes.'

Forrester took to boring his round little eyes into Tanner's face. 'I see! And just exactly when were you intending to tell me that?'

Tanner shifted uneasily from one foot to another.

'Well, sir, she wasn't sure, at first; after all, it was a long time ago.'

'It wasn't *that* long ago, Tanner!'

'Perhaps not.'

After glaring at him for a moment longer, Forrester turned to look away.

'I suppose this means that we're going to lose her from *both* investigations.'

'That's if they *are* two investigations, sir.'

Forrester returned to cast a wary eye over him. 'Let me guess, Tanner. You're about to tell me that they're linked.'

'I was only going to suggest that it was a possibility.'

'The connection being this Kelly Fisher girl, I suppose?'

'And Jenny as well, I'm afraid.'

Forrester returned to massaging his jowls. 'The problem is, Tanner, that this isn't London.'

'I am aware of that, sir.'

'It's the Norfolk Broads,' Forrester continued, 'the population of which is far smaller.'

'Again, I'm –'

'Which means that half the time, everyone seems to know everyone else.'

'That's not *exactly* true, sir, is it.'

'Of course it isn't, Tanner, but you get my point.'

'I understand that the Broads is a much smaller community, if that's what you mean, sir, yes.'

'It's also far less transient, in that people have a tendency to neither leave nor to move here; present company excepted, of course. So just because someone happens to know two people who died some fifteen years apart, it doesn't automatically mean we have a serial killer on our hands.'

'I completely agree, sir.'

After doing a double-take between Tanner's face and the space he'd been staring at whilst making his case, Forrester took Tanner's words in with some caution. 'You do?'

'Absolutely, sir, which was why I said that it was only a possibility.'

'OK, good,' Forrester replied, relaxing his stance. 'We've had enough serial killer investigations around here recently to last us a lifetime!'

'Which is also why I don't think Jenny happening to know one of the suspects from her childhood is necessarily all that important, sir.'

Realising that he'd not only been led up the garden path, but brought back down it again, Forrester narrowed his eyes at Tanner.

'I take it that means you're of the opinion that DS Evans shouldn't be taken off the investigation?'

'No, sir. For her own safety, I think she should be. It's the other one I thought she might be able to remain working on – in the background, at least; and only if the two continue to remain separate.'

Forrester took a moment to think about that, glancing around at the various emergency vehicles. When he saw Jenny, over by the entrance, deep in discussion with the two uniformed officers, he looked back at Tanner.

'If I agree, I assume you'd be happy for me to give DI Cooper the lead on the Boyd case, with DS Evans working underneath him?'

Tanner had failed to consider that scenario as being a possibility, and found himself immediately fighting back against the idea. He'd grown used to working with Jenny. The idea of her being assigned to someone else jarred against his system, especially as every fibre of his being told him it *was* a murder investigation, one that was now to be led by someone as young and inexperienced as Cooper. Under such circumstances, how would he be able to keep an eye on her? She'd had enough close calls already, and that was when he'd been about. Then he remembered what had happened to his former counterpart, DI Burgess, the Easter before, stabbed to death in some godforsaken windmill.

'To be honest, sir, I'm not sure that would be a good idea.'

'And why's that, may I ask?'

'It's Cooper, sir. He doesn't have enough experience to lead a murder investigation.'

'I wasn't aware we'd reached the conclusion that James Boyd had been murdered?'

'Well, no, sir, but you know what I mean.'

'Unfortunately, Tanner, I don't. Besides, even if it is murder, Cooper needs the experience. And as it's effectively a cold case, I think it would be an excellent place for him to start.'

Tanner now regretted persuading his DCI to keep Jenny on either investigation; but unable to give Forrester the real reason for him not wanting Jenny to work under anyone else but him – that he didn't trust Cooper to take proper care of her – he was left with no choice but to simply say, 'Yes, sir.' The best he could do now was to prove that the two cases were one and the same. That way he'd at least be able to get her off both.

'Meanwhile,' continued Forrester, beginning to

look decidedly pleased with himself, 'I'm going to assign Vicky to work with you on this one, Sally as well.'

'Of course, sir.' Tanner's shoulders slumped as his face visibly sagged. *Jenny will be delighted!* he thought, already dreading the fallout.

'That's settled then!' declared Forrester, as if he'd just won a landmark case in court. 'And whilst you're at it, you may as well swap desks with Cooper.'

'Swap desks?' Tanner repeated, his mouth falling open.

'Of course,' the DCI continued, seemingly oblivious to the bombshell he'd just dropped. 'There's hardly much point in working alongside Vicky and Sally if you're stuck all the way over on the other side of the office, now is there?'

- CHAPTER TWENTY -

Wednesday, 3rd June

TANNER WAS RIGHT to have worried about Jenny's reaction to the news that she'd been re-assigned to work with Cooper. But it was nothing to how she reacted when told that Sally Beech would be working underneath Tanner. And that was before he told her that Forrester had ordered him to swap desks with the junior DI, which meant that not only would Tanner be working with Sally, but he'd be sitting right next to her as well.

Telling Jenny that he was convinced Forrester had done it more to keep Cooper away from his niece, than him away from Jenny, did little to lighten her mood. She spent the rest of the evening making sure Tanner knew exactly how she felt about the whole situation, by saying as little to him as was humanly possible.

Come the morning, the atmosphere between them remained frosty, with Jenny being unable to shake the feeling that Forrester hadn't split them up to get Cooper away from his niece, but more to get his niece wedged up alongside Tanner, no doubt at her request. After all, a girl like Sally wouldn't be interested in the junior DI, not if there was the chance for her to have the senior one instead. And she could imagine Forrester jumping at the chance for his niece to get between them. He'd never liked the fact that they'd been seeing each other. For all she knew, he'd been searching for just such an opportunity to break them up, ever since he'd found out that they were an item.

If Jenny wasn't happy with the situation, it was obvious DI Cooper wasn't too pleased about it either. As Tanner and Jenny pushed through the double doors into the main office, they saw him standing by his desk, removing various items from one of the drawers to drop down into a box, looking every bit the sulking toddler who'd been told to put his toys back into the pram, having only just thrown them out.

Sally, meanwhile, was perched on the edge of her chair, typing away with great gusto, as if giving an enthusiastic piano recital of Beethoven's Ode to Joy.

'You'd have thought Cooper would have been pleased to have his own murder investigation,' posited Tanner.

'He's probably more upset that he won't be able to continue with his endeavours to climb into Little Miss Beech's pants, which is what you're no doubt looking forward to.'

'Oh, come on, Jen!' Tanner protested.

'I'll put the coffee on, shall I?' Jenny replied, sending him a smile that was as wide as it was fake before spinning away to the kitchen, leaving him staring hopelessly after her.

With most of Tanner's morning spent moving from one desk to another, leaving everyone else to begin making their own psychological adjustments to the new office dynamics, it didn't seem long before the post-mortem report for the body found inside the rowing boat came through.

After a brief consultation with Forrester, Tanner was soon standing alongside him in front of the whiteboard, ready to begin an office-wide briefing.

'If I can have everyone's attention?' the DCI called out, his robust voice carrying effortlessly to the back of the room.

He waited a moment for the various conversations surrounding him to subside.

'As I'm sure you all know by now, the body of a man was uncovered yesterday evening over by Hickling Broad. He's since been identified as Mr Craig Jenkins, and the post-mortem report has concluded that he was murdered. So I'm afraid it's all hands on deck, once again.

'The reason for shuffling personnel around a little this morning is because DS Evans knows the victim. It's for that reason that DI Tanner will be working on this investigation with DS Gilbert and DC Beech. DI Cooper has been re-assigned to cover the investigation into the body found at Barton Broad over the weekend. And before anyone brings it up, yes, I'm fully aware that the two cases share a connection in the form of...' Forrester cast his eyes over at Tanner, asking for the name.

'Kelly Fisher, sir.'

'Kelly Fisher,' repeated Forrester, 'who we

believe knows our most recent murder victim *and* the young man found at Barton Broad; but apart from that, at this stage there's nothing to suggest the two cases are linked. So, for the time being at least, DI Cooper is continuing the investigation into what happened to James Boyd, with the support of DS Evans. Everyone else will be focussing on the murder of Craig Jenkins.'

Seeing his niece raise her hand, Forrester hesitated for the briefest of moments before saying, 'You have a question, DC Beech?'

'Isn't Kelly Fisher one of the suspects in the investigation into James Boyd, the body found at Barton Broad?'

'I believe she is, yes. Why?'

'Doesn't DS Evans know her as well?'

The question sent a wave of muttered comments flying around the room, as Jenny blushed with furious indignation.

Forrester, raising his hands in a bid to placate his audience, nodded. 'I'm told she does know the suspect,' he confirmed, 'but only from her childhood.'

'But still,' continued his niece, revelling in the moment. 'Shouldn't she be taken off that case as well?'

Forrester narrowed his eyes over at her.

'In an ideal world, perhaps; however, with two serious investigations on-going, we're short-staffed as it is.'

Finding Jenny in the audience, perched on the end of her desk with her arms folded, and seeing the furious colour of her face, and how her eyes seemed to be endeavouring to drill holes in the carpet, Forrester thought it wise to help bolster her spirits. 'On top of that, DS Evans is a damned fine detective, one whose services have proved invaluable over the last couple of years. Consequently, she's someone who, quite frankly, I'm not prepared to do without.'

A ripple of agreement followed. There were few people in the office who didn't like Jenny, whilst the opposite was beginning to prove true of Forrester's niece.

Sally closed her mouth rather abruptly, allowing her uncle to continue.

'So anyway, I'm going to hand you over to DI Tanner, who'll be briefing you on what we know so far in relation to Craig Jenkins. Tanner?'

'Thank you, sir.' Tanner stepped forward. 'At around half-past nine yesterday evening, we received a call that a body had been found hidden inside a rowing boat, near a public car park on the banks of Hickling Broad. The call was placed from a nearby public phone box by a woman who, despite being asked several times, refused to leave her name. Furthermore, judging by the quality of the call, it's considered likely that she was attempting to disguise her voice. For both reasons, we're treating the call itself as suspicious, and have sent the recording off to forensics for analysis. With any luck, they'll be able to give us some sort of an idea as to the caller's identity, at least her age and social demographic.

'As DCI Forrester has already mentioned, we know the victim to be twenty-nine-year-old Craig Jenkins. A wallet belonging to him was found at the scene, and his dental records have confirmed his identity.'

Tanner turned to gesture up towards the top of the whiteboard. There a photograph had already been fixed; that of a young man wearing a formal black tie, his hands wrapped around an elaborate trophy whilst he beamed a victorious smile at the camera.

'Mr Jenkins was an architect working for a company called Harris & Atwood, based over in Norwich. Recently married, thankfully with no children, he lived with his wife down the road in Horstead.

'DS Evans and I were first to arrive at the scene, where we found him half-hidden inside a seemingly disused rowing boat.'

Taking a file out from under his arm, he pulled out a photograph, graphic in nature, that had been taken looking down at the body, still lying inside the boat. Fixing it to the whiteboard, directly underneath the one of him carrying the trophy, Tanner stood back to allow everyone else to see, whilst taking a moment to study it for himself.

'This, here,' he said, directing everyone's attention to a curved metallic object which hovered vertically over the body's chest, 'is a rhond hook; an item similar to an anchor, normally used to secure a boat to a riverbank. The item had been passed through his stomach, puncturing his liver to the left. As you can see for yourselves, the weapon was left in place.'

Whispered mutterings circled the room.

'We don't know exactly why,' Tanner continued, 'but the post-mortem report says that it was wedged in with such force, it may have been difficult for the assailant to remove.'

More muted conversations could be heard.

'As I can hear some of you suggesting, that *could* tie in with the anonymous caller being a woman, who *may* have found herself unable to pull it out again. However, at this stage, such ideas are pure speculation. It could equally have been left there for a purpose, which leads to my next point.'

Tanner purposefully paused for a moment, allowing the room to fall silent again.

'Despite the seriousness of the injuries, when DS Evans and myself arrived at the scene, he was still alive.'

An audible gasp rose up from the floor.

'The post-mortem concludes that the weapon, having been left inside him, effectively plugged the wound. And as it punctured neither his heart nor lungs, or any major arteries, it is believed he could have been there for several hours before succumbing to his injuries. Whether or not the assailant had that in mind is, at this stage, unknown. If they did, then it's possible the killer had enough medical knowledge to know how to inflict such an injury, and that leaving the weapon where it was would allow him to remain alive long enough to be found. Again, that could tie in with the anonymous phone call. However, it could equally be that the killer had no particular idea what they were doing and, as mentioned before, was simply unable to remove the weapon. We've yet to hear back from forensics, but hopefully they'll be able to give us more of an idea about that. We also don't yet know if he was attacked where we found him, or somewhere else, but forensics should be able to throw some light on that as well.'

Seeing Constable Higgins raise his hand, Tanner gestured over at him. 'You have a question?'

'I was just curious to know if the car park near where he was found was the one at Catfield Common?'

Tanner glanced over towards Jenny, seeking confirmation. Realising she wasn't paying attention, but had taken to scrolling through some application on her phone, he returned to the young constable. 'I believe it was, yes.'

'It's just that the car park does have a certain reputation, sir.'

'So I've been told.'

'So I was just wondering if it could have been sexually motivated, sir?'

'As in...?'

'As in Craig Jenkins may have lured a girl there to forcibly have his way with her, and she fought back.'

'With a rhond hook?' questioned Tanner, doing his best not to belittle what he considered to be a possibility bordering on the ridiculous.

'Well...' continued the young constable, going decidedly pink around the edges, as everyone began turning to look over at him, 'maybe the man had one in the back of his car, and that was what came to hand? It would at least explain why the call from the girl was anonymous.'

Realising it wasn't as stupid as he'd first thought, Tanner raised an eyebrow. 'You know, that's really not a bad idea.' Out of habit he glanced back over at Jenny, hoping she'd be making a note of it, before remembering she wasn't working with him anymore, making it unlikely that she would have done. Judging by the way she was staring at her phone, he wasn't even sure she'd heard it.

Unable to find Vicky, his eyes fell on Sally Beech instead, hoping that catching her attention would be enough for her to know that he wanted her to write Higgins' suggestion down. But all it did was to earn him another of her now all-too familiar flirtatious smiles.

Tanner looked back at Higgins. 'Maybe you could make a note of that for me, Constable?'

A surprised look followed, after which the young constable began scrabbling around for his notebook.

Leaving him to it, Tanner turned his attention back to his audience, at least those within it who were listening.

'So, whilst we wait to hear back from forensics, I want us to find out all we can about our victim; in particular what he was doing near the car park. Did he drive himself? If so, where's his car? If not, who did?'

Finally seeing Vicky's face, he caught her attention to say, 'DS Gilbert, I want you to work with uniform to find out who his family and friends were. Then you need to arrange to speak to them all; at least those he'd been in contact with during the last few days.'

'DC Beech, start a background check on the victim, maybe with Higgins' help,' he added, wondering if she even knew what a background check was. 'We need access to his phone, mobile, email, social media and financial accounts.

Meanwhile, I have the joyful task of telling his wife. And I don't need to remind you all to keep your mouths shut, especially to the press.

'OK, that's it for now.'

As if doing the opposite of what he'd just asked them to do, a cacophony of noise erupted from the floor, as everyone began talking freely amongst themselves whilst making their way back to their desks.

Turning around to face the white board, Tanner folded his arms to rest his hand on his chin. A gentle tap on his shoulder had him spinning around to find Sally Beech standing behind him, all lipstick and teeth.

'I was just wondering if you wanted me to come with you,' she asked, peeling a perfect blonde curl away from one of her incandescent blue eyes, 'to speak to the victim's wife?'

'Oh, um...' Tanner began, only to see Jenny glaring over at him as she sat down at her desk. 'Thanks, but I think it would probably be more beneficial if you were to stay here to crack on with that background check.'

As if from nowhere, Forrester appeared at his other shoulder.

'Ah, Tanner, I assume you're taking Sally with you to visit the wife?'

Feeling like he'd been caught between a rock and a hard place, almost literally, shifting his gaze from the uncle to the niece and back again, he said, 'I was actually thinking DC Beech should stay here, sir, to push on with the background check into Craig Jenkins.'

'I think Higgins can handle that. Besides, Sally

could do with the experience.'

With Tanner unable to come up with any other reason for Sally not to come with him, he heard Forrester say, 'Excellent! Right then. Let me know how you get on,' before marching off, leaving Tanner wondering what Jenny was going to say to him when they got back home, after she'd watched him stroll out of the office, with the new girl no doubt endeavouring to attach herself to his arm.

- CHAPTER TWENTY ONE -

'IS THIS YOUR car?' Sally asked in a surprised tone, as she followed Tanner over the car park.

Suppressing the burning desire to tell her that it wasn't, and that he'd stolen it on his way into work, Tanner bit his tongue. 'It is, yes,' he replied instead, leaving him curious to know what she'd say in response; after all, he couldn't imagine it was the sort of thing she'd like.

'It's...' she began, her eyes dancing erratically over the bodywork, as if unable to rest themselves on any one part. 'It's beautiful!' she eventually announced, before turning to look over at him as if her complimentary remark deserved some sort of special prize.

The words may not have stuck in Sally's throat, but they certainly jarred in Tanner's mind. He'd heard the occasional flattering comment made with regards to his car over the years, but nobody had ever been quite so generous to describe it as beautiful before.

'Really?' he asked, the word coated in doubt.

'I had a boyfriend once who had a Jag,' Sally continued. 'But it wasn't as nice as this.'

Unlocking it, Tanner replied with casual

indifference. 'Is that so.'

'To be honest, I think I prefer yours,' she added, sending Tanner a sugar-coated smile.

Attempting to grimace something similar back, Tanner tugged open the driver's door to climb inside. Sally may be exceptionally pretty, but he knew her type – and it wasn't his. She was a trophy seeker, one desperate for attention; the sort of girl who used her looks to entrap men of financial means or social status, before discarding them underfoot the moment another came into view. Her interest wasn't in him as much as being able to prove to Jenny, and everyone else in the office, that she could have him, should she so choose.

Having spent the first part of the journey enquiring into Sally's professional experience, which was virtually non-existent, Tanner used the remaining time to brief her as to how best to relay the news to someone that a loved one had died. During the discussion he briefly touched on what psychologists termed the five stages of grief, which such distressing news had a tendency to evoke, after which he outlined what he expected of her.

Arriving at their destination, a quiet cul-de-sac on the outskirts of Norwich, Tanner found somewhere suitable to park and climbed out.

Regretting not having Jenny alongside him, Tanner reminded Sally of her duties as they made their way over towards the door.

'So, just to recap, should we be able to get to a stage where we can ask her some questions, if you could be ready to take notes, that would be useful.'

'And what if she's too upset?'

'Then we simply tell her how sorry we are and make our excuses. Our main objective is to let her know about her husband.'

Stepping up to the door, Tanner pressed the bell before turning back to the new girl. 'It depends how she takes the news.'

Hearing the sound of approaching footsteps, Tanner pulled out his ID, gesturing Sally to do the same.

The door soon opened to reveal a woman with a long thin face, staring out at them through a pair of deep-set brown eyes.

'Mrs Jenkins?' Tanner enquired.

'I am, yes.'

'My name's Detective Inspector Tanner. This is my colleague, Detective Constable Beech. Norfolk Police.'

Clinging to the edge of the door, Mrs Jenkins took a moment to examine their respective IDs.

'We were wondering if we could come in?'

'Is it about my husband?'

'It is.'

The woman looked directly into Tanner's eyes. 'Is he...OK?'

'If we could come in?'

'Of course, sorry,' she apologised, spinning around to lead them down a gloomy hallway.

'May I get you something to drink?' she asked, calling over her shoulder as they followed her into a small dark kitchen with unfashionable wooden units and a cheap Formica worksurface.

'Nothing, thank you,' Tanner replied.

Despite his answer Mrs Jenkins asked, 'Tea or coffee?' whilst lifting the kettle to begin filling it up.

Forced to assume she'd not heard him, or possibly that their presence, and the news they had concerning her husband, had left her desperate to keep her mind focussed on something else, Tanner waited for her to turn the tap off.

'Coffee, thank you,' he eventually replied, gesturing over at Sally to say the same.

Instead of following suit, Sally muttered, 'Nothing for me, thanks,' whilst staring about the somewhat grotty kitchen with a disapproving air.

With cupboards and drawers being frantically opened and closed, Mrs Jenkins persisted. 'Milk and sugar?'

'Just milk, thank you,' Tanner replied, pleading with his eyes for Sally to stop staring about as if the entire kitchen was crawling with maggots.

'You said you'd heard from my husband?' the woman asked, raising her voice over the steadily rumbling kettle.

Reaching the conclusion that it might be easier for her to hear the news whilst keeping herself busy, Tanner drew in a breath.

'Mrs Jenkins, I'm afraid we have some upsetting news for you.'

With the woman showing no signs of responding, he continued by saying, 'Yesterday evening, a body was discovered over at Hickling Broad.'

Tanner watched as she leaned over to open a fridge door and pull out a bottle of milk.

Beginning to wonder if she could hear him over the noise of the kettle, he raised his voice slightly to say, 'Mrs Jenkins, we have reason to believe the body is that of your husband, Craig Jenkins.'

Ditching the bottle on the side, Tanner saw her hand reach up to a cupboard above her head to grab the door's handle. But instead of pulling it open, she took hold of it as if for support, her head rolling forward as she did.

With the kettle now boiling furiously, the thermostat finally clicked itself off, leaving the room to descend into an oppressive silence.

She remained where she was, her outstretched hand latched on to the cupboard's handle, like an exhausted climber, catching her breath.

Unsure what to say next, Tanner happened to catch Sally's eye; but all he got in response was an ambivalent shrug.

Tanner was about to ask Mrs Jenkins if she'd like to sit down, when she lifted her head to resume the task of opening the cupboard to remove a large jar of sugar.

Leaving it on the side, she poured the contents of the kettle into two mugs.

'Did you say one sugar or two?' she asked, her voice a façade of cheerful hospitality.

Tanner knew she was only asking to deflect the news.

'I am truly sorry, Mrs Jenkins.'

'Of course – you said milk, no sugar. How stupid of me.'

Turning to face them, a mug in each hand, with lines of mascara running down the sides of her face, it was obvious she'd been crying in silence.

As she approached, her attention focussed on the mugs, one of her knees buckled underneath her, sending steaming coffee cascading over the sides.

Rushing forward, Tanner rescued a mug with one hand whilst using the other to guide her into the nearest chair.

Leaving the mug on the table, he pulled out the only other chair to sit down opposite her, leaving Sally standing awkwardly behind him.

Just as he was about to say again just how sorry he was, Mrs Jenkins suddenly blurted out, 'He'd started having an affair with someone, you know.'

Curious to find out more, Tanner leaned over the table towards her. 'What makes you think that?'

'It was his phone. It had started bleeping all the time. Before then, you wouldn't have known he even had one. And then, last night, it rang, just as he was walking in the door. He said it was work, but took the call outside. He'd never done that before. And then, when he came back in, he said he'd left something important back at the office and had to go back for it.'

'By car, I assume?'

Seeing her nod, Tanner asked, 'I don't suppose you could tell us the make and model?'

'It was a Saab. I've no idea what type.'

'Colour?' Tanner glanced up at Sally, hoping to see her taking notes.

Seeing she was doing nothing more productive than craning her neck to peer out of the kitchen window, he fished out his own notebook, shaking his head as he did.

'Dark blue,' the woman continued. 'When he didn't come home, I thought – well, I suppose I thought he'd left me for someone else. That's why I didn't call the police.'

'I don't suppose you were able to overhear any part of his phone conversation?'

'I only heard him say that he'd be there in ten minutes. That's how I knew he'd lied to me about having to go back to the office for something.'

'Do you have any idea who the caller might have been?'

'I don't, no.'

'And the time?'

'It must have been around about half-past six. Maybe a little later.'

Tanner thought for a moment. 'Did he have any interests, outside of work?'

She shook her head. 'He's never been much of a one for going out. He's always been happy enough to spend his evenings in front of the TV.'

'What about sailing?'

The woman glanced up with a confused frown.

Realising he was going to have to clarify his question, Tanner added, 'We understand he was quite keen, when he was young?'

'Oh, you mean dinghy sailing. Yes, well – that was before we met. He hadn't been for years. Not since we got engaged.'

'I don't suppose you know if he'd kept in contact with any of his friends from back then?'

'I've no idea. Maybe online?'

'But not in person?'

'As I said, he hardly ever went out.'

'But he did occasionally, though?'

'Well, occasionally, yes, but not for a long time.'

Tanner took a moment to collect his thoughts.

'We understand your husband was an architect.'

Staring at the contents of her mug, she nodded. 'May I ask what you do?'

'Me?' she asked, looking up.

'Do you work?'

'No, not anymore,' she replied, lowering her head once again. 'I used to, of course, but then I became...'

She stopped mid-sentence; fresh tears welling up in her eyes. 'Our circumstances changed,' she eventually continued, wiping them away with the back of her hand, 'and I was forced to leave. When it came time to return, the company I worked for had gone into administration. I've not been able to find anything since. Nothing suitable, anyway.'

'I'm sorry to hear that.'

'Don't be. I never much cared for what I did.'

'May I ask what that was?'

'I was a legal secretary,' she replied. 'Incredibly dull, but I suppose, I suppose I'll have to start thinking about...' she said, her voice trailing away with her eyes, over to the far side of the table where sat a pile of mostly unopened letters.

- CHAPTER TWENTY TWO -

BACK OUTSIDE THE house, as Tanner made a beeline for his car, his thoughts were interrupted by Sally, calling out behind him, 'Do you think it was her?'

'Do I think it was who?'

'The wife? Mrs Jenkins?'

Feeling it should be obvious to anyone with half a brain that she wasn't a suspect, he replied, 'I really don't, no.'

'Why not?'

Realising he'd forgotten what he'd been thinking about, reaching the car he let out a heavy sigh. 'Because she doesn't have a motive, for a start.'

'What about the affair he was having?'

'She *thought* he was having,' Tanner corrected.

'Yes, well, in my experience, woman are normally right about such things.'

In your experience, mused Tanner, but only to himself.

'And she certainly seemed upset about something, other than having just been told that her husband was dead.'

Tanner was about to tell Sally the reason he thought the lady had been emotionally compromised, when he remembered what he'd been thinking about, before she'd opened her mouth.

'I need to call the office,' he announced, hoping to bring what he felt to be a pointless conversation to a rapid close.

Feeling that her thoughts weren't being sufficiently appreciated, Sally went on, 'And she didn't seem too keen to go back to work, either.'

Deciding to humour her, Tanner stopped to ask, 'And why would that make her suddenly want to murder him?'

'Maybe he'd been going on at her to get a job, and she just got sick of it.'

'Maybe, yes,' agreed Tanner, turning his head away whilst rolling his eyes, digging out his phone as he did.

'Maybe they were having money troubles,' Sally continued, apparently unperturbed, 'and she'd taken out a life insurance policy on him?'

'So you're saying she did it for the money?' queried Tanner, working hard to keep a straight face.

'Exactly!' exclaimed Sally, with triumphant glee.

Tanner pulled open the car door for her. 'Hold that thought,' he said, gesturing for her to climb inside. 'I have to give the office a quick call, but we can continue this on the way back to the station.'

Waiting for her to climb in, he closed the door before stepping away to make the call, without being overheard doing so.

After dialling the number, it wasn't long before he

was put through to the person he was hoping to speak to.

'Vicky, it's Tanner. We've just finished talking to Craig Jenkins's wife.'

'How'd it go?'

'About average, I suppose. Listen, she said someone had been in frequent contact with him in the days leading up to his murder.'

'Does she know who?'

'No, but the way he was behaving, she assumed it was the start of some sort of affair. Anyway, the night he went missing, he got a phone call, just as he walked in the door from work. Afterwards, he told his wife he'd left something behind and had to go back; but she'd already overheard him saying that he'd meet whoever had called him ten minutes later.'

'So you're thinking that whoever called is the one who killed him.'

'I'd have thought it likely, yes. Even if it wasn't, we need to find out who it was. Can you make it a priority to dig up his phone records? The last call was made at around half past six yesterday evening.'

'OK, got it.'

'Another thing. She said he *drove* off. As his car wasn't where we found him, it's looking increasingly likely that whoever killed him took the vehicle away and dumped it somewhere.'

'Couldn't they have met somewhere else, and the murderer drove him there?'

'It's possible, but if that was the case, then I think we'd have found his car keys on him. After all, why leave his wallet but take his keys? If that is what happened, and the killer did drive his car away, then his or her DNA could be all over it.'

'I'll have a chat with the council, to ask them to keep an eye out for it. Do you know what it is?'

'It's a Saab – dark blue. We'll need to contact the DVLA for its registration.'

Tanner paused, giving her a chance to make a note of all that, before going on to ask, 'I don't suppose there's been any news from forensics?'

'Nothing yet, no.'

'OK, well, hopefully they won't be too much longer.'

Tanner thought for a moment.

'Is Jenny around?'

There was a short silence from the other end of the line.

'I can't see her. Shall I ask her to call you?'

'No, don't worry. We're on our way back now anyway.'

- CHAPTER TWENTY THREE -

ARRIVING BACK AT the station, Tanner caught Vicky's attention at the far end of the office before scanning the room, searching for Jenny. Despite seeing DI Cooper, sitting behind what had been Tanner's desk just the day before, she was nowhere to be seen.

He was about to ask Cooper if he knew where she was, when he saw her emerge from the kitchen, a steaming mug held in each of her hands.

Catching her eye, he smiled at her. It wasn't reciprocated.

Intercepting her before she reached her desk, trying to be discreet Tanner asked, 'Can I have a quick word?'

Stopping in front of him, she caught his eyes to say, 'Sorry, I'm a bit busy at the moment.'

'It's about the investigation, I-I mean, your investigation. I have a small favour to ask.'

'Can't you ask Cooper?'

'I'd rather not.'

'Oh, go on then. Let me dump these, then we can talk in the kitchen.'

A minute or so later, Jenny joined Tanner beside the coffee machine, as he poured himself a drink.

'Right, what's up?' she asked, leaning against the fridge with folded arms.

'I just wanted to ask if you've accessed Kelly Fisher's phone records yet?'

'We have, yes, why?'

'If I gave you a phone number, would you be able to check it against her outgoing calls?'

'I assume you want to know if she's been in contact with Craig Jenkins?'

'Well, I've just got back from speaking with his wife –'

'And not just you, either,' Jenny interjected, driving home her veiled accusation through a thin smile.

Ignoring the remark, Tanner pushed on.

'She mentioned that someone had been making regular contact with her husband in the days leading up to his murder. Also, that someone had called him that night, who she overheard him say he'd meet in ten minutes. If it was Kelly Fisher, then we have ourselves a prime suspect. That would also suggest the two investigations are one and the same, which would mean we'd be able to get back to working together again.'

'OK, I'll take a look.'

'Great, thanks. I'll email the number over to you.'

'Anything else?' she asked, pushing herself off the fridge.

'There was one more thing.'

'Well, hurry up. My coffee's getting cold.'

'I was hoping you'd be able to give me a list of all the people who were in your junior national sailing squad; those from around here, at least?'

'And why would you want to know that?'

'To see if it was any of them who'd been in contact with Craig Jenkins.'

Jenny thought for a moment. 'I'll have to see what I can find out.'

'Can't you remember, off the top of your head?' questioned Tanner, thinking that there couldn't have been all that many.

'There were a few,' Jenny replied, glancing over at her desk.

Unconvinced that she wouldn't be able to remember them all, there and then, Tanner pushed her by asking, 'OK, who can you recall for now?'

Jenny returned to look at him. 'Well, there was Kelly Fisher, and Craig Jenkins.'

'Anyone else?'

'A guy called Marcus Hall.'

Tanner fished out his notebook. 'Which club was he from?'

'I've no idea.'

'Was that it?'

'Another guy called Chris Street. He was from Hickling Broad Sailing Club. I think that was all, from around here at least; apart from me, obviously, and Rob, of course.'

Tanner stopped to stare at her, his pen poised over his notepad.

'You mean Rob as in Robert Ellison?' he eventually asked. 'Your friend from Barton Broad?'

'That's the one – but I'd already told you that.'

'Er...I don't think you had.'

'Er...yes, I definitely did. When we first met him, at the sailing club.'

'You said you used to sail together, when you were young. You've never said anything about him being in the same sailing squad as Kelly Fisher and Craig Jenkins.'

'Well, anyway. He was only in it for a while.'

'Do you have any idea why he left?'

'He probably got kicked out. He was never all that good.'

'What was his sailing club?'

'I've no idea.'

'Is there any chance he knew James Boyd?'

'I doubt it.'

'But it's possible, though?'

'Of course, but as I've said before, just about everyone around here...'

'...knows everyone else,' finished Tanner.

'Well, they do,' Jenny concluded, with an ambivalent shrug.

Tanner took a moment to make a note of his name. As he did, somewhat absently, he added, 'Anyway, you won't be able to see him again.'

'I beg your pardon?' challenged Jenny, planting her hands firmly down on her hips.

'Robert Ellison,' Tanner repeated, glancing up with a bemused frown. 'You won't be able to see him again; at least not until the investigation is over.'

'How dare you tell me who I can and cannot see!' fumed Jenny, her face and neck flushing with blood.

'Er...I'm sorry Jen, but he's a suspect in a murder investigation.'

'Since when?'

'Since the body of Craig Jenkins turned up in a

rowing boat, with a rhond hook sticking out of him.'

'Oh, I see. So I suppose everyone living on Planet Earth who just happens to know Craig Jenkins has suddenly become a suspect in his murder?'

'If they were in your national sailing squad, then I'd have to say yes, they are.'

'And it's got nothing to do with the fact that he's an exceptionally good-looking man who's recently asked me out, and who just happens to share my interest in sailing?'

'Don't be stupid.'

The moment he said it, he knew he shouldn't have.

'What did you say?' Jenny demanded.

'Sorry,' Tanner said. 'You know I didn't mean that.'

'Please, don't be. After all, I must be, for going out with you all these months.'

'Jen, I...'

'And if I want to see Rob again, there's not a damned thing you can do about it. To be perfectly honest, at this precise moment, I'd far rather be hanging out with him than you. At least he doesn't go around calling me stupid all the time.'

'I'm not disturbing anything, am I?' came Vicky's hesitant voice, just outside the kitchen's entrance.

'Literally nothing, no!' stated Jenny, spinning around to storm out, her head facing the floor to prevent Vicky from seeing just how upset she'd become.

Vicky faced Tanner. 'I can come back?'

'No, it's fine,' he replied, his face pale and

drawn. 'What's up?'

'It's just that I've found out where the call came from, the one that was made to Craig Jenkins's mobile, before he went missing.'

With his mind already busy replaying the argument he'd just had, only half listening, he said, 'Go on.'

'It was from a public phone box.'

'Uh-huh.' He looked over Vicky's shoulder to watch Jenny plonk herself down behind her desk.

Endeavouring to garner a little more of his attention, Vicky added, 'It was the same one used to call in about the body of Craig Jenkins.'

'The same what?' asked Tanner, his full attention finally turning to the Detective Sergeant standing before him.

'The same public phone box.'

As his mind wrapped itself around what that could mean, Vicky continued, 'It can't be a coincidence.'

'It could be, but I'd have to agree with you. It does seem unlikely. I assume you know which one it is?'

'It's the one in Catfield.'

'That rings a bell.'

'It's the village next to where Craig Jenkins was found – near Hickling Broad.'

'I suppose that would lend itself to the idea that our mystery lady caller had simply stumbled over the body, and that was the nearest pay phone.'

'But it wouldn't explain why the person who'd called him, just before he disappeared, happened to use the exact same one.'

'No, I suspect you're right. It's more likely to

have been the same person.'

'Do you think it's worth getting forensics down there, to check for prints?'

'What – inside a public phone box?'

Vicky shrugged. 'It's a long shot, I know, but they can't be used all that much. Not these days, at least.'

'OK, it's worth a go, I suppose. I think it would also be worthwhile sending a couple of uniforms down, to ask the local residents if they saw anyone using it at around half six yesterday evening, as well as whenever it was that the anonymous call was made, but I'm going to have to clear all this with Forrester first.'

- CHAPTER TWENTY FOUR -

'AH, TANNER!' EXCLAIMED Forrester, seeing his senior DI's head appear through the door. 'I was just about to call you over. The forensics report has come in for that body you found in the rowing boat.'

Tanner stepped inside, closing the door behind him. 'Anything of interest, sir?'

'Actually, yes, there is,' Forrester replied, returning to his computer screen.

With Tanner standing behind one of the chairs in front of his desk, Forrester looked up at him to ask, 'Is there any particular reason why DS Evans's prints and DNA have been found plastered all over the body?'

Recalling the moment they found Craig Jenkins, Tanner jumped in with, 'That's because of what we discovered, sir, when we arrived at the scene.'

'I think you're going to have to clarify that statement, Tanner.'

'If you remember, sir, he was still alive.'

'I see. And that explains why her prints and DNA were found all over him, does it?'

'Well, it does, and it doesn't.'

Forrester looked at him, awaiting clarification.

Tanner thought for a moment as he tried to think of how best to describe what happened, in a way that would keep the blame off Jenny, along with himself for that matter.

'Go on,' prompted Forrester, with a look of growing impatience.

'Well, sir, when we arrived, Jenny thought she recognised him, and when we realised he wasn't dead, she climbed on board the boat to try and help him.'

Forrester glanced back at his computer screen. 'But the report says they even found her prints on the murder weapon?'

'Then she must have touched it, when trying to help him.'

'The guy had an anchor buried inside his chest, Tanner. What, exactly, did she think she'd be able to do? Pull it out and stick a plaster over it?'

Deciding that it probably wasn't the best time to correct him – that the murder weapon was a rhond hook, and it wasn't buried inside his chest but had been driven into the man's stomach – still endeavouring to come to Jenny's defence he replied, 'I think it was just an instinctive reaction, sir, given that she knew him, and everything.'

'That's all well and good, Tanner, but by doing so, not only has she contaminated the crime scene, but she managed to do so in such a way as to make it look like she killed him.'

'Yes, well, in hindsight, sir, it probably wasn't the most sensible thing for her to have done.'

'In hindsight, Tanner, you bloody well should have stopped her!'

'Yes, sir, of course. But it all happened very

quickly.'

'Couldn't you have at least told her to put gloves on first?'

'Again, sir, it all...'

'...happened very quickly. So you said, Tanner. And now we're stuck with a murder victim who not only does Miss Evans know, but has her DNA and fingerprints all over him.'

More than a little perturbed to hear him refer to Jenny without her rank, Tanner blurted out, 'It was my fault, sir. As you said, I should have stopped her.'

'Yes, well, at least we had the good sense to take her off the case, I suppose.'

Realising Forrester was probably thinking more about how he was going to explain the situation to his own superiors, Tanner sought to further reassure his DCI that they'd taken the correct measures by adding, 'And as soon as we found out she knew the victim as well, sir.'

'Quite! However, she still knows the woman who remains the main suspect in the cold case she's working on with Cooper. What was her name again?'

'Kelly Fisher, sir.'

'Which is beginning to make me a little nervous.'

'I'm sure that isn't an issue, sir.'

'Unless the two cases do turn out to be connected, of course,' muttered Forrester.

'But there's still nothing to suggest that they are.'

'You mean, apart from Kelly Fisher knowing James Boyd and Craig Jenkins, and Miss Evans knowing Craig Jenkins and Kelly Fisher?'

The time had come for Tanner to tell Forrester what he'd found out just a few minutes earlier – that Jenny also knew another man he felt compelled to consider as being a suspect in the investigation into the murder of Craig Jenkins: the oh-so handsome Robert Ellison. But against his better judgement, instead of doing so, he found himself saying, 'I think if Jenny had known James Boyd as well, sir, then I'd probably have to agree with you. But as things stand, the connection remains tenuous at best.'

'OK, well, I hope you're right, for all our sakes.'

Tanner kicked himself. There was a voice inside his head screaming at him that the opposite was true, in that the two cases were one and the same, and that Jenny was stuck in the middle of both.

'Anyway,' Forrester continued, 'how've you been getting on with our most recent murder investigation? I assume that's why you came in here?'

'We seem to be making progress, sir. Vicky's just found out that the anonymous caller who phoned in about finding the body of Craig Jenkins used the same public phone box as whoever it was who called him the evening he went missing.'

'That sounds encouraging. Whereabouts is the phone box?'

'Catfield, sir. So I was hoping to be able to send a couple of uniforms over there, to ask some of the locals if they saw anyone using it at the times in question.'

'Makes sense.'

'I was hoping to be able to send a forensics team down there as well, sir, to give the phone box the quick once over.'

'A *public* phone box?' queried Forrester, without sounding convinced.

'Well, yes, sir; but in this day and age, it's unlikely to have been used much since then, if at all.'

Forrester considered that for a moment, before reaching a similar conclusion. 'OK, let's hope you're right. Otherwise, all we're going to get is about fifty years' worth of fingerprints from just about everyone who's ever stepped foot inside the bloody thing.'

'Yes, sir.'

'And what about suspects?'

'Sorry, what about them?'

'Do we have any?' Forrester demanded, glaring over at Tanner.

With his mind turning to Kelly Fisher, he replied, 'It's a little too soon, sir.'

'There must be someone you have in mind. How about his wife?'

'She seemed to lack motive, sir,' Tanner replied, wondering if his niece had been talking to him.

'I've been told otherwise.'

With his suspicions confirmed, Tanner asked, 'Would that have been DC Beech, by any chance?'

Forrester shifted uncomfortably in his chair. 'She did mention something to me about it, yes.'

'Well, sir, if I'm correct, Sally's theory is that she murdered her normally stay-at-home husband because they were having money troubles, fuelled by her suspicions that he'd started an affair. So she took out a life insurance policy against him, drove to the public phone box in the middle of Catfield, somehow managed to persuade him to meet her at the car park next to Hickling Broad, plunged a rhond hook into his stomach before hiding his body inside a rowing boat, returned to the same public phone box to let everyone know what she'd done, and then drove home to await our call; none of which is the most likely explanation I can think of, sir.'

'That's as maybe, Tanner, but Sally said she thought Mrs Jenkins was hiding something important, and that there were a pile of unopened letters on the kitchen table which she thought looked like unpaid bills.'

'I think that was about her baby, sir.'

'Her baby?'

'Yes, sir. I suspect she'd lost it either during, or shortly after its birth. That would explain any money troubles they'd been having, as she was struggling to find the motivation to start working again. But that's no reason to murder her husband.'

'I see. You're sure about this baby thing?'

'Well, sir, she didn't say so specifically, but it was implied. In fairness, had Sally not spent the entire interview staring out of their kitchen window, instead of taking notes as I'd asked her to, she'd have probably picked up on it as well, sir.'

Speechless for once, Forrester did nothing but glower.

'So, in answer to your question,' Tanner continued, 'no, I don't think Mrs Jenkins murdered her husband.'

'Well, fair enough; but you still haven't answered my original question.'

'Sorry, sir. What was that again?'

'Who did, Tanner?'

'Well, as I said before, sir, it's too early to tell.'

'But you must have some idea?'

Tanner's mind returned to Kelly Fisher, and the list of people Jenny had just given him. That was where he intended to start. But if he told Forrester that, he'd no doubt start going on about how the two murder cases must therefore be linked, and that Jenny should subsequently be taken off both.

'I need to do a little more digging, sir,' he stated, 'before I'm willing to draw up a list of suspects.'

Forrester let out a heavy sigh. 'Then you'd better get on with it, hadn't you,' he said, before returning his attention to his computer screen.

- CHAPTER TWENTY FIVE -

BACK IN THE main office, seeing Sally Beech sitting opposite Vicky Gilbert, doing nothing more productive than her nails, Tanner stepped over to catch Sally's eye. 'I don't suppose you could make me a coffee?' he asked, attaching an amorous smile onto the end.

Looking surprised to have been asked, Sally jumped up, saying, 'Of course!' before slinking her way over to the kitchen.

'I thought you didn't like the way she made your coffee?' Vicky commented.

'I don't, but I can't trust her not to go telling her uncle everything I say and do. So, from this point forward, I want her kept out of the loop, as best we can at any rate.'

'Fine by me,' agreed Vicky, suppressing a smirk.

The moment Sally disappeared inside the kitchen, Tanner took his seat to begin whispering to Vicky.

'OK, first up, Forrester's agreed for us to send forensics over to that public phone box, and for a couple of uniforms to start asking the locals if they saw anyone using it at the times we know it was.'

'Easily done.'

Tanner retrieved his notebook to open it to the

most recent page. Handing it over to her, he said, 'Then I want us to arrange to meet with these people.'

Vicky glanced down the list. 'Who are they?'

'They're Jenny's friends from her junior sailing squad days.'

'OK, no problem; but why the secrecy?'

'Because I don't want Forrester finding out.'

'But – why not?'

'Forensics found Jenny's prints and DNA all over Craig Jenkins' body.'

'You mean – he thinks Jenny murdered him?

Tanner shook his head. 'Nothing like that, no. She managed to contaminate the crime scene when she recognised him and went to help, for which I can hardly blame her. But it was a mistake, nonetheless. Mine as well, for that matter. And I get the distinct impression that Forrester is looking for an excuse to have her kicked off her current investigation as some sort of punishment. So I'm very keen for him not to reach the conclusion that Cooper's case and mine are one and the same, else he will.'

'Am I to assume you think they are?'

'To be honest, I'm finding it difficult not to, especially as just about everyone involved in both knows everyone else, and all from the same place as well.'

'Where's that?'

'Jenny's old junior sailing squad. It's not exactly helping that she's decided to get chummy with one of them, either.'

Vicky glanced down the list, leading Tanner to point out the name. 'Robert Ellison. We met him at

Barton Broad sailing club on Sunday. He was the one who drove the safety boat, when they found the body of James Boyd. They've already been out for drinks together.'

'Is that what you two were arguing about earlier?'

'I told her she wouldn't be able to see him again,' Tanner replied, allowing his eyes to drift over to where Jenny was sitting, scowling at her monitor.

'I bet that went down well.'

'No, well. Probably not my finest hour,' Tanner conceded, 'So anyway, if we can keep it under wraps for now, that would be useful.'

'OK, but I'm not sure how we're going to do that? If we're not at our desks for days on end whilst we go around interviewing all these people, Forrester's soon going to wonder where we are.'

'I was thinking that if we can arrange to meet them within the shortest time period possible, I'd conduct the interviews and you could stay here, to cover for me.'

'And what am I supposed to say when he asks where you are?'

Tanner shrugged. 'Just tell him I've broken down somewhere. Judging by the poor opinion everyone around here has of my car, I suspect that would be believable enough.'

Seeing Sally tottering her way back towards them, a steaming mug clasped in each hand, Vicky nodded towards her. 'What about Little Miss Beech?'

'I suggest we send her down to the phone box in Catfield, to oversee forensics and help with the door to door enquiries. That'll keep her out the way, for now at least.'

'Here you are,' Sally announced, reaching Tanner's desk. 'Just the way you like it.'

Peering down his nose at it as she placed it on the desk in front of him, Tanner replied, 'Looks great! Thanks Sally.'

As she took her seat, he asked, 'How are you getting on with the background check into our victim?'

'Craig Jenkins?' she asked, as if having to remind herself.

'That's the one,' Tanner replied, doing his best to keep any hint of sarcastic condescension from his voice.

'I've just been given access to his email and social media accounts, but I'm still awaiting his phone records.'

'OK, let me know when you have. Then I've got a little job for you.'

- CHAPTER TWENTY SIX -

WITH BEECH BEING kept busy in Catfield, Gilbert took over the job of conducting Craig Jenkins's background check, leaving Tanner free to drive over to Norwich to meet with one of the people from Jenny's list: Marcus Hall.

'Thanks for taking the time to see me,' said Tanner, on being invited into a large empty boardroom.

'Not a problem,' replied the tall, gaunt, balding man holding the door open for him. 'It's not often we get the police in here.'

'I'd have thought, being a divorce lawyer, you'd have them in every other week!'

'Our clients rarely become that emotional,' Hall chuckled, closing the door. 'Anyway, how can I help?'

'Last night we found the body of someone who we believe you may know.'

Raising an intrigued eyebrow, the man gestured for Tanner to take a seat.

Doing so, Tanner waited for his host to follow suit. 'His name was Craig Jenkins.'

'Good god! I've not heard that name in a while.'

'I understand you used to sail together, when

you were young.'

'Well, we were in the same squad, if that's what you mean. Separate boats, mind. But that was years ago.'

'I don't suppose you can remember when you saw him last?' asked Tanner, digging out his notebook.

'Crikey! I'm not sure. Not recently, I know that much. Probably not since the training. I can't remember seeing him after that.'

'How did you two get along?'

'Oh, OK, I guess. We didn't know each other all that well. We only saw each other when we were sailing.'

'And how often was that?'

'Most weekends. Even if there wasn't an official training event, we'd often meet up, as we both lived in the Broads area.'

'I understand there were others in the squad who came from around here?'

'There were, yes.'

'Can you remember who they were?'

Gazing up to the ceiling, the man thought for a moment. 'From memory, Craig Jenkins, Chris Street, Robert Ellison, Jenny Evans and Kelly Fisher.'

'How about James Boyd?'

'James Boyd,' he repeated, turning the name over in his mind. 'I can't say I've ever heard the name before. He certainly wasn't in our squad, not in my time.'

'You mentioned Kelly Fisher. Can you tell me what she was like?'

'Much like the rest of us, I suppose.'

'We've been told she could be quite aggressive.'

'On the water, perhaps, but then again, I think we all were, to a degree.'

'And how did you all get on when you *weren't* on the water?'

'Oh, fine,' Hall replied, with a dismissive shrug.

'No fights or arguments?'

'Only about incidents that took place during the racing.'

'How about relationships?'

'Sorry, how d'you mean?'

'If there were four boys and two girls, there must have been something going on between some of you.'

'Oh, that! Well, I suppose we did occasionally talk about Jenny and Kelly in that way, as boys have a tendency to. I've no idea if they did the same.'

'But there was nothing going on between any of you?'

'Not that I was aware of.'

Taking a moment to make a note of that, Tanner asked, 'I don't suppose you happened to stay in contact with any of them?'

'Not since I stopped sailing, no.'

'And when was that?'

'When I went to university.'

'So you haven't seen any of them since?'

'Not in so many words.'

Tanner glanced up from his notes. 'Does that mean you have?'

'Well, I *thought* I saw one of them recently. A few times, actually.'

Poised with his pen, Tanner leaned over the

table. 'And which one was that?'

'Jenny.'

'Jenny, as in Jenny Evans?' queried Tanner, unable to hide his surprise.

'Well, it looked like her.'

'And when was that?'

'On two or three occasions over the last couple of weeks, when I was out in the evening.'

'But you didn't speak to her?'

'To be honest, I wasn't sure if it was her, after all these years. And each time I saw her, I was too far away to say hello.'

'Far away, as in...?'

'She'd be sitting on the other side of whichever pub I happened to be in. And when I thought I might wander over, she'd gone.'

'But if she was that far away, how did you know it was her?'

'Because she was staring at me, as if she knew who I was.'

'Maybe she didn't know who you were, but was simply a girl trying to catch your eye?'

'I'd be so lucky,' the man smiled, revealing a row of misaligned stained teeth. 'Even if that was so, the same girl, three times, at three different places?'

'Are you suggesting she's been following you?'

'I'd not thought of it like that, but thinking back, it was a little odd. And it wasn't as if she was surrounded by a group of friends, either.'

'How d'you mean?'

'There was nobody else with her, Inspector. Every time I saw her, she was on her own.'

- CHAPTER TWENTY SEVEN -

HAVING MADE A note of the dates, times and places where Marcus Hall had thought he'd seen Jenny, Tanner emerged from the legal firm's offices with concern creasing his forehead. He didn't think for a minute that the woman Hall thought he'd seen was Jenny. What was troubling him was that someone must have been doing their best to make it look like it was.

The conversation he'd had with Forrester crashed into his mind, about how Jenny's prints and DNA had been found all over the body of Craig Jenkins. He had to forcibly remind himself that she'd definitely placed them there herself. It hadn't been someone else. He'd even watched her do it.

Heading towards his car, he wondered who could have been pretending to be Jenny. Retrieving his notebook to check the address of the next suspect on his list, he glanced down at his watch. The person lived on the other side of the Broads, on the outskirts of Great Yarmouth. With it approaching rush-hour, it was going to take him a while to get there, but at least the journey home would be shorter.

He contemplated calling Jenny, to let her know what he was up to, and what time he might be back, but thought better of it. She'd only ask him who he was going to see, and at that stage, he wasn't prepared to tell her. He didn't particularly want to call Vicky either, not if it meant having to say that the man he'd just spoken to seemed to be under the impression that he was being stalked by Jenny. Nevertheless, he felt he had to touch base with her, just in case Forrester had been asking after him, but also to find out if there'd been any news from Sally Beech, over in Catfield.

Swapping his notebook for his phone, he leaned against his car to call the office.

'Vicky, it's Tanner.'

'Hi, Tanner. How'd you get on with Marcus Hall?'

'OK, I guess. I'm about to head over to Chris Street's house, but he lives near Great Yarmouth, so I could be a while.'

'No problem. I can't see myself leaving anytime soon.'

'Has Forrester been asking after me?'

'Not yet, but I've seen him look this way a few times.'

'How about DC Beech. Any news?'

'She's on her way back now.'

'What, already?'

'She said she had to leave at five.'

'Then she clearly doesn't understand how this job works.'

'Well, no, but that's hardly surprising.'

'Did she say anything?'

'Only that forensics have finished with the phone box, and that they were able to dig up a couple of witnesses who saw it being used at the given times.'

'Description?'

'Neither got a good look, but both said something similar.'

'And what was that?'

'That it was a young woman with shoulder-length dark hair, blue jeans and a brown leather jacket.'

'What – both times?'

'Both times, yes.'

'Shit,' cursed Tanner, under his breath.

'Why, what's up?'

'Oh, nothing,' he replied, his earlier concern mutating into more of a feeling of anxious dread. 'Is Jenny there?'

'She is, yes. Do you want a word?'

'No, it's all right. Can you just tell her that I might be back a little late?'

'I assume you don't want me to tell her where you are?'

'I'm not sure that would be a great idea, no.'

'OK, no problem.'

'And how about you? Anything of interest cropping up from Craig Jenkins's background check?'

'Only that he didn't seem to have much of a life.'

'OK, well, keep going. Look out for any contact he may have had with his junior sailing squad friends – and that's going to have to include Jenny as well, I'm afraid.'

- CHAPTER TWENTY EIGHT -

I T TOOK TANNER nearly an hour to reach Chris Street's house, far longer than he'd been expecting, after getting lost on the way.

He parked on the kerb outside a small detached town house, set back from a busy road. Heaving himself out, he made his way over a short narrow concrete drive, its surface cracked and lined with weeds. Edging past a bland Ford Mondeo, he stepped up to the door, rang the bell and waited.

There was no response.

Standing back, he checked the windows, looking for signs of life.

There weren't any.

He glanced down at his watch to see that it was nearly six. Hoping he'd not had a wasted journey, he was about to have a look around the back when he saw a car begin reversing into the drive, coming to a halt in front of the Mondeo.

A smartly dressed woman stepped out and scowled at him. He pulled out his ID and headed over to meet her.

'Mrs Street?' he called out.

'I am, yes,' she replied, her hand resting on the still open door. 'And you are?'

'Detective Inspector Tanner, Norfolk Police,' he

said, holding his ID aloft. 'I'm looking for your husband.'

'Is he not in?' She glanced over his shoulder, first at the car, then at the house behind him.

'There was no answer, no.'

Closing the car door, she narrowed her eyes at him. 'What's it about, anyway?'

'Nothing to worry about. I just had a few questions for him. Any idea where he might be?'

'He's probably taking the dog for a walk.'

'And how long does that normally take?'

'About an hour.'

'I don't suppose you could give him a call for me, to let him know I'm here?'

With a frown of disapproval, Mrs Street dug her phone out from the depths of her handbag.

She waited for a few moments with the phone pressed to her ear. 'He's not picking up. I'll have to leave him a message. What did you say your name was again?'

'Detective Inspector Tanner, Norfolk Police.'

- CHAPTER TWENTY NINE -

L EAVING THE WOMAN his card, Tanner made his way back to his car. There he waited for a few minutes, hoping Mr Street wouldn't be long. With time to kill, he decided to check something that had been playing on his mind since his earlier meeting with Marcus Hall.

Fishing out his phone and his notebook, he found the dates and times the divorce lawyer had told him he'd seen Jenny, or someone he thought looked like her, watching him. He then opened up the calendar on his phone. The dates he'd been given correlated exactly with when Jenny had been taking part in Barton Broad's weekday evening racing. Although she'd not been on their boat with him at the time, at least it meant that someone at the club should be able to vouch for her presence.

Struck by a sure-fire way to prove she had been there, and not stalking some guy in Norwich, he searched up the sailing club's website, looking for its racing results page. Jenny had shown them to him after she'd taken part in her first race, whilst bemoaning how rusty she'd become over the years.

He clicked open the link entitled Summer Evening Race Results and ran his eyes along the top, searching for the dates in question, only to realise that it hadn't been updated for over three weeks.

Frustrated, he scrolled to the club's contact page, found a number and dialled it; but the phone just rang endlessly without being answered. It didn't even switch to answerphone.

He contemplated the idea of driving over to see if there was anyone around to ask, before realising that he was over-reacting. Jenny had definitely been at the club on the evenings in question, and there would, of course, have been someone there who'd be able to vouch for her. Even if nobody could remember if she'd been there or not, the race results would be around somewhere; they just hadn't been uploaded onto the website yet.

With his phone still in his hand, he put a call through to the office.

'Vicky, it's Tanner. Any news?'

'Nothing much to report, I'm afraid,' she replied. 'I've just finished going through Craig Jenkins' social media and email accounts, but haven't found any sign of him being in contact with anyone from the junior sailing squad.'

'What about his phone records?'

'I've not started on those yet.'

'Finances?'

'I'm still awaiting access.'

'I don't suppose forensics have come back with anything from that public phone box?'

'Er, not yet, but in fairness, they only finished there a couple of hours ago.'

'Of course, yes, sorry. How about Forrester. Has he been asking after me?'

'He did, but only on his way out the door. I just

told him you were chasing a possible lead.'

'OK, good.'

Tanner paused for a moment.

'I don't suppose Jenny's still there?'

'Cooper gave her a lift home about an hour ago.'

'Well, fair enough,' Tanner replied, checking the time on his dashboard to see that it was gone seven o'clock.

'How about you?' Vicky enquired.

'Mr Street wasn't in, but his wife says he should be back soon, so I'm waiting in the car for him to appear. I suggest you call it a day, and I'll see you first thing tomorrow.'

As he ended the call, something caught his eye in his side-view mirror. In the early evening light he could clearly see a man charging up the road behind him, desperately holding on to a large dog on the end of a straining lead.

Remaining where he was, Tanner watched as the man was dragged past his car. Ducking his head to try and catch a glimpse of his face, he was about to step out when he saw him continue past the Streets' drive without stopping.

It couldn't be him.

Coming to the conclusion that he could end up waiting there half the night, he gave up, started the engine, pulled his seat belt on, and indicated to start making his way home.

- CHAPTER THIRTY -

L EAVING HIS CAR in the public car park, near to where his boat was moored, Tanner continued on foot, his mind consumed with thoughts about Jenny, the most immediate being how she was going to react to seeing him again. They'd not spoken since their argument in the office earlier that day, and he was expecting an icy reception.

Taking a moment to enjoy the view of his boat, with Hunsett Mill beyond, silhouetted against a warm evening sun, he heard Jenny's voice call out from inside the cockpit, 'Hello, stranger. Fancy seeing you here.'

Relieved to hear her sounding like her normal cheerful self, Tanner did his best to respond in a similar amicable vein.

'Hey, Jen! Good to hear you – even if I can't actually see you.'

'Sorry,' her voice came again, closely followed by her head, poking out through the closed canvas doorway. 'I've only just put the awning back on.'

'Having an early night?'

'I was actually about to head off to the club.'

'What, sailing?' Tanner questioned, stopping where he was.

'No, rock climbing,' Jenny replied, in her familiar sarcastic tone. 'Apparently, Norfolk's famous for it.'

Tanner scowled. 'To be honest, I'm not sure that's a great idea, not this evening.'

'Normally, I'd have to agree with you, especially as I've never done it before. But as I think the tallest cliff face around here is less than three feet high, I think I'll be OK.'

'Please be serious, Jen.'

'Fine! But I'm not having you tell me that I can't go sailing just because you think Rob's going to be there.'

'It's got nothing to do with him, at least not specifically.'

'What is it then?'

'It's...well, it's...' He was struggling to decide how much he should tell her about what he'd uncovered during the course of the day.

'I'm sorry, but you saying "It's...it's" isn't actually an answer, John. That's just you repeating the same word twice.'

'It's just that I think someone may be trying to implicate you in the murder of Craig Jenkins.'

'Oh, come on! Now who's trying to be funny?'

'I'm serious, Jen. The forensics' report came back from the crime scene, and your prints and DNA were found all over it.'

'That's hardly a surprise, is it? After all, I was there at the time, trying to save the poor man's life.'

'That's as maybe, but we've also found a couple of witnesses who've said that they saw the person who made the call from the phone box at Catfield at the specific times we know it was used.'

'Sorry, but did you just say that you've found a couple of witnesses who've confirmed that the phone box was being used when you already knew it was?'

Doing his best to ignore her glib sarcasm, Tanner pushed on, 'The person matched your description, Jen, all the way down to your leather jacket.'

'Then I suppose that's just my bad luck that I'm the only person in the whole of Norfolk who owns a brown leather jacket.'

'There's more, I'm afraid.'

'What – even more than my fingerprints being found on the body of someone I was trying to help, and that a girl wearing a brown leather jacket was seen using a public phone box?'

'I met Marcus Hall this afternoon.'

Jenny stopped to eye Tanner with wary suspicion. 'Go on.'

'He told me that on three separate occasions over the last few weeks, when he was out after work in Norwich, he thought he saw you, sitting on your own, staring at him.'

'OK, I must admit that does sound a little creepy, but I'm not sure how it proves that someone is trying to frame me for the murder of Craig Jenkins.'

'Because Marcus Hall was in the same junior sailing squad as you, and Jenkins, along with Robert Ellison, Chris Street and Kelly Fisher, the person under suspicion for having murdered James Boyd.'

'Who wasn't even in our squad!' Jenny reminded

him.

'I'm not talking about James Boyd, Jen, or anyone else for that matter. I'm talking about you; and how at every turn in my investigation into Craig Jenkins' murder, your name seems to keep cropping up.'

'Oh, hardly.'

'And when I checked the dates and times when Marcus Hall said he'd seen you watching him, each and every time you were at the sailing club.'

'Well, there you are then. It wasn't me!'

'I'm not saying it was you, Jen.'

'Er...it does sound a bit like you are.'

'I'm saying it sounds like someone is doing their very best to make it look like it was you.'

Jenny shrugged. 'Well, if they are, they're not doing a very good job of it. I freely admit to having touched the body of Craig Jenkins, so it's hardly as if someone had to go to the trouble of planting any evidence. As for the person using the phone box, I seem to remember I was out with Rob at the time, which I'm sure he'll be happy enough to corroborate, along with about half the people in the pub. And even if Marcus did think he saw me following him around Norwich, there are going to be about a dozen or so people down at the sailing club who'll say I couldn't have been, as I was taking part in the same race they were.'

'I get all that, Jen, and I agree with you. My concern is: what do we do if the worst thing happens – that you're accused of murdering Craig Jenkins? What then?'

'But that's just ridiculous.'

'Perhaps, but if the case ended up in court, how

would the jury see it?'

'Just as I described.'

'What – that you personally know everyone involved, your prints and DNA were all over the crime scene, you were seen using the phone the victim was called from, before he was killed – and then afterwards, alerting the police – and that you've been seen stalking another member of the same junior sailing squad?'

'And my defence will be able to provide a long list of witnesses who'll be able to testify that I couldn't have been at the phone box on the occasions in question, nor could I have been stalking Marcus Hall, as I was nowhere near Norwich at those times.'

'And what happens when those witnesses are cross-examined?'

'They'll say the same thing.'

'But will they, Jen? You know what it's like.'

Turning to the side, Tanner began to act out the part of a prosecuting attorney cross-examining a key defence witness.

'Are you sure the witness was with you at the time?'

'Absolutely.'

'There's not a single element of doubt in your mind?'

'Well, I'm fairly *sure she was there, yes.'*

'I see, so you're only fairly *sure?'*

Tanner turned back to Jenny. 'If your innocence comes down to whether or not someone only *thought* you were at the same place as them at the time, then your case will come crashing down around your ears, especially when the prosecuting attorney shows them a picture of a rhond hook embedded inside the stomach of one of your old sailing chums, one that has your fingerprints plastered all over it.'

'But what about motive?' Jenny demanded. 'You're always telling me that's what lies at the heart of every investigation.'

'When there's hard physical evidence to back up the prosecution's case, I'm afraid motive tends to fall by the wayside. Anyway, look, with all that aside, what I'm really concerned about is why someone seems to be trying to implicate you in the first place. What motive could *they* have, and to what lengths are they prepared to go?'

'That's *if* someone is trying to implicate me,' Jenny argued.

'Look, Jen, all I'm asking is for you to stay close, either to me or our colleagues at work, just until this investigation is over. At least that way I know you'll be safe, and that you can't be implicated in anything else.'

Jenny studied Tanner's face for a moment. 'So, this has nothing to do with me spending time with Robert Ellison?'

'No. Why, is he racing tonight?' Tanner blurted out, without thinking.

'Nice try,' Jenny scoffed, ducking her head back inside the cockpit.

'You're not still going, are you?'

Emerging back through the gap, this time carrying a large holdall, Jenny jumped down off the boat to join Tanner on the towpath.

'I'll only be a few hours, and besides, I'll be surrounded by loads of people. I'll be quite safe –

and look,' she added, glancing at the reeds over on the far side of the river, 'it's not even windy, so you really have nothing to worry about.'

'But Jen...'

'I'm sorry, John, but I'm not going to stop sailing just because you've come to the rather sad conclusion that I'm having an affair with Robert Ellison.'

'I don't think you're having an affair with Robert Ellison.'

'Then you won't mind if I go sailing then, will you?' she said, barging past him to begin stomping her way along the towpath, heading for her car.

- CHAPTER THIRTY ONE -

TANNER WAS RELAXING on the bench seat in his cabin cruiser's open cockpit, a book in one hand, a glass of wine in the other, when his phone rang on the table beside him.

With the sun sinking fast and Jenny still not back, he automatically assumed it was her, letting him know that she was going to be late.

Exchanging the glass of wine for his phone, he raised an eyebrow as he saw that it wasn't Jenny calling, but DS Gilbert.

With an unsettling feeling in the pit of his stomach, he answered the call.

'Hi, Vicky. What's up?'

'Sorry to disturb you so late, but I've just had Forrester on the phone. Another body's turned up.'

'Where?' asked Tanner, staring over at his half-empty glass of wine, calculating how much he'd had to drink.

'At the entrance to an industrial estate, on the banks of the River Bure.'

Wracking his brains to picture an industrial estate anywhere near the River Bure, he heard Vicky add, 'Just outside Great Yarmouth.'

Pushing himself up straight, Tanner pressed the phone against his ear. 'Please don't tell me it was a man out walking his dog.'

'It was a man, yes, and a dog has been found at the scene. How did you know?'

'Police intuition,' Tanner sighed. 'Has he been identified yet?'

'Not as far as I know.'

'And I suppose Forrester wants me to head over there?'

'He's asked us both to go.'

'OK, if you can text me the location, I'll meet you there.'

Ending the call, he stood up, turned his book over to leave it upside down on the table, and called Jenny's mobile.

Cursing when it rang through to voicemail, he tried again, hoping she'd simply not been able to reach it in time. When it still wasn't answered, he felt he had no choice but to leave her a message.

'Jen, hi, it's John. Vicky's just called. Another body's been found, in Great Yarmouth. I'm going to head over there now. I think – I think it might be Chris Street.'

He paused for a moment, choosing his words carefully.

'Assuming it is,' he said, 'I don't think you should come back here tonight. Not when I'm not around. It may be better if you stayed with...' he was about to say a friend, when he realised that by doing so he'd be inviting her to stay with Robert Ellison. Instead he came up with, '...with your parents. Anyway, look, I'll give you a call when I've finished in Great Yarmouth. Maybe you could text me when you get this? OK, got to go. Speak soon.'

- CHAPTER THIRTY TWO -

A LITTLE OVER an hour later, his eyes tired and strained, Tanner rumbled his XJS down an uneven stretch of badly tarmacked road. Up ahead was a dazzling array of blue flashing lights, ricocheting off a high steel security fence. Beyond that stood a series of misshaped warehouses, corrugated roofs jutting awkwardly up into an ever-darkening sky.

Expecting to spend the journey mulling over the investigation, instead he'd found himself doing nothing more productive than worrying about Jenny, and checking his phone every five minutes. He'd delayed leaving their floating home for as long as possible, hoping for the chance to see her, but there'd been neither sight nor sound. She hadn't responded to his message either, forcing him to leave without knowing if she was intending to come back, or was in the process of doing what he'd asked her to: driving over to stay with her parents.

Bumping his car up onto the kerb to park alongside the normal eclectic mix of emergency vehicles, he turned the engine off and rubbed at his eyes. Peeling his fingers away he glanced up to see Vicky approach, forcing him to push open the door and drag himself out.

'What've we got?' he asked, with perfunctory professionalism.

'You'd better see for yourself.'

'Can't wait.'

Closing the door, he followed her along the road, past the other vehicles, towards a large sign he could see hanging above a cluster of industrial-sized wheelie-bins. The sign read Great Yarmouth Industrial Estate, underneath which were listed a dozen or so obscure company names, none of which he could be bothered to read. Behind that stood the security fence, three rows of barbed wire lining the top. Past the bins was a thin blue line of Police Do Not Cross tape, strung out over the estate's main entrance.

Tanner stopped near to where an unfamiliar uniformed police officer stood, just outside the line of tape. He didn't need to go any further. It only took a moment or two for him to know what he was looking at.

Propped up against one of the two thick square wooden posts which supported the sign above was a man wearing a suit but no tie, his head leaning back against the post behind. At first glance, Tanner thought he was just some guy, watching them. But then he saw that only one of his eyes was there. In place of the other was a hole, from which oozed blackened congealed blood that had run down his face, creeping into his half-open mouth before dripping down onto his opened-collared shirt.

Against the opposite post, in line with the man's head, was a small dog; a blue lead dangling down from its collar, the end of which lay on the ground below, coiled in a pool of glistening blood.

Tanner was abruptly awoken out of a trance-like state by the cold hard flash of a camera.

'Clearly someone wanted him to be found,' Vicky said, as they watched an overall-clad forensics officer begin circling the scene, taking photographs as he did. 'Else they'd have dumped him in one of the wheelie bins, or better still, shoved him into the river.'

Tanner didn't answer. Her remarks were obvious enough.

He took a moment to glance around. 'Who found him?'

'A man out jogging.'

'Did he see anything?'

'Only what's here. He said that at first he thought it was just some weirdo, leaning up against the base of the sign. He only stopped when he saw the dog. Do you want to speak to him?'

'Has he given a statement?'

'He has.'

'Then I think we can send him home.'

She was about to head off when she stopped to look back at Tanner. 'From what you asked on the phone about it being a man out walking his dog, I assume you already know who it is?'

'The guy I came down here to see earlier,' he replied, his voice lifeless and monotone.

'Christopher Street,' Vicky confirmed. 'I recognised his name from the list you gave me, when we found his wallet.'

Tanner dug out his phone. Jenny still hadn't been in contact.

'I can call the other people on the list, to warn

them,' she suggested.

'I think that would be sensible.'

'And Kelly Fisher?'

'Her as well, but you'd better let Cooper know first. I don't want him accusing us of trampling over his investigation.'

'What about Jenny?'

Tanner tucked his phone away. 'I've already told her to stay at her parents. Hopefully she will.'

Seeing the concern etched over his face, Vicky replied, 'I'm sure she will. She's not stupid.'

'Well, no, but she can be infuriatingly stubborn at times.'

'Can't we all,' she mused, before walking away.

Spying a familiar face, near to where the body of the dog hung, Tanner exchanged his phone for his ID, holding it up for the police constable to see.

Ducking under the tape, he turned back to call after Vicky.

'When you speak to those people, don't give away too much. Just tell them that it may be prudent for them to stay at home for a few days, ideally with family or friends. Meanwhile, I'm going to have a quick chat with our Medical Examiner.'

'Ah, Tanner!' exclaimed Dr Johnston, glancing up from his notes. 'DS Gilbert said to expect you.'

'Evening, Doctor. So, what are we looking at?'

'I'd have thought that was rather obvious,' Johnstone stated, with his usual mild condescension. 'One man and his dog, although they won't be mowing any meadows, not after being nailed to the base of a rather large sign.'

'Weapon?'

'I'm presuming some sort of nail gun.'

'I assume death would have been instantaneous?'

'For the man, definitely. Not sure about the dog, though.'

'Any sign of a struggle?'

'None that I can see. It looks like someone just pushed him against the post and pulled the trigger. Same story with the dog. Anyway, I've nearly done, for now at least. If it's as straightforward as it looks, I should have something for you by lunchtime tomorrow.'

- CHAPTER THIRTY THREE -

DUCKING BACK OUT from the cordoned off area, glancing around for Vicky, Tanner pulled out his phone. Seeing there was still no word from Jenny, he dialled her number and waited, desperate to speak to her. When it clicked through to voicemail, he let out a frustrated sigh. Drawing in a calming breath, he left her another message, this time asking her to call him as soon as possible.

With the sense that it had become imperative that he talk to her, he did something he really didn't want to do: he put a call through to her parents.

After only a couple of rings, Tanner heard Jenny's mother answer, leaving him clearing his throat to say, 'Hi, Mary, it's John. John Tanner.'

'Oh, hello, John! We were only just talking about you.'

Relieved to hear Jenny was there, he asked, 'I don't suppose I could have a word with her?'

'Have a word with who, my dear?'

'Er, Jenny.'

'Oh, Jenny's not here. I was speaking about you with Fred. We were wondering when the two of you were going to come over to see us again?'

'Jenny's not there?' he repeated, the knot in his stomach tightening.

'No, why? Were you expecting her to be?'

Not wishing to worry them, he spluttered, 'Oh, no – well, sort of, but not really. She said she might pop by. That was all. Not to worry, I'll give her a call on her mobile.'

'I would do if I were you. So, anyway, what do you think?'

With his mind racing, Tanner asked, 'Think about what?'

'When you're going to come over? It would be lovely to see the two of you.'

'Oh, er...' he said, keen to end the call, 'I'd better ask Jenny. Can I get back to you on that?'

'How about for lunch on Sunday?'

'Yes, OK, sounds good, but I'll need to check with her first. Anyway, I'd better go. Lovely to talk to you, and we'll, er, hopefully see you on Sunday.'

'Really looking forward to it, John.'

'Great. Me too!'

'And you don't need to bring anything. We'll do all the cooking.'

'That's very kind. So...see you then.'

'Yes, bye for now, and give my love to Jenny.'

'Will do.'

Before she had the chance to say goodbye again, he ended the call.

'Shit, Jen!' he said out loud. 'Where the hell are you?'

Doing his best to remain calm, he put the phone away and scanned the area for Vicky.

She was on the other side of the road, helping a scantily clad old man into the back of a squad car.

As she closed the door, Tanner caught her eye. 'I assume that was our jogger?'

'It was,' she replied, stepping clear as the car pulled away. 'He said he was happy to run home, but I thought it would be better to have him driven back. It didn't look like he'd make it otherwise.'

'Did you manage to get hold of those people?'

'Only Marcus Hall and Kelly Fisher.'

'Not Robert Ellison?' Tanner's mind flashed back to Jenny. If they had met up at the sailing club, she could easily have ended up going back to his place.

'I left him a message.'

Shaking his head clear of the jealous thoughts he could feel slithering their way into his mind, he remembered the woman he and Jenny had interviewed outside the vets the day before.

'What about that other girl?'

'Who, *Jenny?*' Vicky queried, confusion furrowing her forehead.

'Of course not Jenny!' he snarled, digging out his notebook. 'It was Carol somebody,' he muttered, flicking through the mainly blank pages.

Vicky began doing the same.

'I don't have anything about a Carol.'

Remembering how she'd been a part of his original investigation into James Boyd, and that Vicky wouldn't have heard of her, he put his notebook away.

'Don't worry. I'll have to ask Cooper about her tomorrow.'

As his mind created the scene of Jenny, snuggled up on a plush cosy sofa with Robert Ellison draping a seductive arm over her shoulders, he blurted out, 'I think we should pay Ellison a call.'

Vicky hesitated. 'Shouldn't we see Christopher Street's wife first, to tell her what's happened?'

She was right, of course, but Tanner was now desperate to find Jenny, and was certain she was with Ellison. That was why she'd not called him. There was only one other reason he could think of, and he wasn't prepared to entertain that thought, not for a single moment.

'OK, but one of us needs to find Ellison, to warn him. Would you mind going to see Mrs Street on your own?'

'Well, I could,' she replied, in a way that made it clear that she neither wanted to nor thought she should.

With the feeling he had to say more, Tanner added, 'To be honest, Vicky, I need to find Jenny. She's still not answering her phone.'

'Why didn't you tell me before?'

'I thought she'd be with her parents, but I just called them, and she's not there.'

'Do you have any idea where she might be?'

'Well, as you know, she's been seeing Robert Ellison recently. I think she might be staying with him.'

'Then why don't I come with you? I can get someone from uniform to let Mrs Street know.'

'No, I think one of us needs to do it. She may know something useful that uniform wouldn't pick up on.'

'OK, then I'm happy to see her. You go and find Jenny!'

- CHAPTER THIRTY FOUR -

IF TANNER HAD found himself becoming increasingly jealous of Robert Ellison before seeing where he lived, he was far more so afterwards.

The house was a vast red brick Edwardian mansion, located upriver of Wroxham Police Station, on the edge of Coltishall village.

As he steered his car around the wide spacious drive, circling the remnants of an old stone fountain, the headlights lit up the monstrously proportioned building which dominated the view ahead.

Seeing no sign of Jenny's car, he pulled up alongside three others, all parked along the front of the house. He stepped out and peered around. Without the headlights, the estate was eerily quiet and distinctly dark, the only illumination coming from a small leaded lamp positioned to the side of a large arched wooden front door.

He stood back to cast his eyes up, searching the many windows for signs of life. But there weren't any. All he could see were three security cameras, each with a small red light bleeping from the top, two of which were mounted high up on the corners of the building. The third was located just above the front door, and he couldn't help but notice that it was rotating slowly around to face him.

Curious to know who was watching him, and from where, he continued to glance around. Over to his right, in the shadow of one of many overhanging trees, was what looked to be a stable, with three barn-sized doors set against a dark timber-framed structure, and unlit dormer windows poking out from the slated roof. It was only when he noticed a series of tyre tracks in the gravel, leading in and out of each door, that he realised that it was a triple garage.

Curious to know if Jenny's car had been left inside one of them, Tanner began crunching his way over the drive to take a look, when a voice called out to him from a shadow to the side of the Edwardian pile.

'Can I help you?'

Turning to face the voice, his eyes attempting to penetrate the darkness, Tanner dug out his ID. 'Detective Inspector John Tanner, Norfolk Police. And you are?'

The figure emerged into the yellowing light cast by the lamp.

'Oh, hello, John. Sorry, I didn't recognise you. It's Rob – Robert Ellison. Jenny's friend from the sailing club.'

Recognising his face, Tanner strode over to meet him.

'Mr Ellison, we've been trying to call you.'

'On my mobile?'

'It's the only number we have.'

'OK, well, sorry about that. The reception here has always been rather poor. Too many trees, so

I'm told. Anyway, how can I help?'

Coming to a halt in front of him, Tanner put away his ID, taking a moment to glance up at the imposing building.

'Is this yours?'

'No, not exactly. It belongs to my parents.'

Tanner raised an eyebrow. 'They must be doing rather well for themselves.'

'Hardly! Old money, I'm afraid, which is why it's in such a state. Anyway, I assume you didn't come all the way out here at such an inhospitable hour to see where I lived?'

Still seeing no sign of Jenny, and unwilling to ask if she was there, instead he said, 'Actually, I came to warn you that it may be wise to stay with some friends for a while, maybe even family, but I see that you already are.'

'May I ask why?'

'I've just come from Great Yarmouth. We found a body there earlier, someone who I believe you may know. Christopher Street?'

'A body?' Ellison repeated. 'You mean –?'

'I'm afraid it would appear that someone murdered him, Mr Ellison.'

A look of abject horror crossed the man's face.

'Murdered! But – why?'

'To be honest, we're more concerned with *who* at the moment, especially taking in mind what happened to Craig Jenkins.'

'You're saying Craig Jenkins has been killed as well?'

'The body of Mr Jenkins was found yesterday evening,' Tanner explained, carefully observing the man's expressions. 'On the banks of Hickling

Broad.'

'Jesus Christ!' Ellison exclaimed, taking a faltering backwards step.

Tanner continued to take him in, watching as the man's eyes began frantically searching the many shadows that surrounded them.

'Why hadn't anyone told me?'

'Unfortunately, it took us a while to find out that you all knew each other.'

'Only when we were young.'

'I understand you were in the same sailing squad?' Tanner elaborated, digging out his notebook.

'That's right.'

'Jenny as well?'

'Jenny as well, yes,' the man confirmed, meeting Tanner's eyes. 'She's all right, I hope?'

'To be honest, Mr Ellison, I was about to ask you something very similar.'

'Me?'

'You *have* been seeing her recently, haven't you?'

'We had a drink together the other day, if that's what you mean. But not since then, no.'

'What about at the sailing club?'

'Only on Sunday, when we went out in the safety boat together, before we found...' His eyes glazed over to stare off into space.

'The body, hidden at the bottom of the Broad,' finished Tanner, his own eyes never leaving Ellison's.

'That's right, yes. I must admit, I've been struggling to shake the image from my mind ever since. Did you ever find out who it was?'

'James Boyd,' Tanner replied, in a matter-of-fact tone. 'He was a teenager who went missing back in 2006. I don't suppose the name rings a bell?'

'Not that I can recall. Why? Should it?'

'Not particularly. I just thought you might have known him, seeing that you'd have been a similar age, as well as the fact that you were members of the same sailing club.'

'I may be a member of Barton Broad now, but I wasn't back then.'

'I see. May I ask where you *were* a member?'

'Horsey Mere. They closed down a few years ago.'

Tanner thought for a moment. 'Would you be able to confirm who else was in the Junior National Squad from around here, other than Craig Jenkins, Christopher Street and Jenny Evans?'

'That was about it, I think.'

'How about Kelly Fisher?'

'Yes, sorry. Her as well.'

'And Carol Mortimer?'

'Er, no. She wasn't into sailing.'

'But you do know her, though?'

'From school, yes, why? Don't tell me she's been murdered as well?'

'Nothing like that, no.' Changing tact, Tanner continued by asking, 'What can you tell me about Kelly Fisher?'

Ellison shrugged. 'What do you want to know?'

'What was she like? We've been told she could be quite aggressive.'

'You don't seriously think it's her, doing all this?'

'Not at all. I'm simply asking what she was like.'

'Well, I wouldn't describe her as aggressive; at

least I never saw her being so.'

'But she was competitive, though?'

'Well, yes, of course, but they all were.'

'Not you?'

Ellison shrugged. 'Not so much. I think that's probably one of the reasons why I left.'

'You left, or you were asked to leave?'

'Probably a little of both,' he replied, with just the hint of a smirk. 'I can't say I was really into it. Not like the others. They all seemed to take it so seriously.'

'What about Jenny?'

'Oh, she was totally into it. Super aggressive! Always shouting at everyone around the course. And if she didn't win, she'd either fume with rage, or sulk: one or the other. Fortunately, she seems to have matured since then.'

'And that was Jenny?' Tanner queried. To him it sounded more like Kelly Fisher.

'It wasn't only her, but I'd definitely say that she was the most competitive.'

Tanner glanced around. 'And you haven't seen her?'

'Not since we went out for that drink.'

'And that was yesterday, at the Red Lion?'

'That's right.'

'May I ask what time you were there from?'

'Oh...' Ellison stared up into the blackness of the sky. 'I think we were due to meet at eight.'

'Yes, but what time were you there?' Tanner repeated.

'Sorry. I probably got there about ten minutes before that. I have a thing about not being late, which does tend to mean I end up being early rather a lot. But as is often the case, I didn't need to be, seeing how late Jenny was.'

Wracking his brain as he tried to remember what time Jenny had left their boat that night, Tanner asked, 'What time did she arrive?'

'I'm not sure, exactly, but I'd already had a couple of drinks by then and was beginning to think she was going to be a no-show.'

'And this was at the Red Lion?

'That's right.'

'When was the last time you saw her, before that?'

'Excluding that time at the club on Sunday, not for years.'

'Can you be a little more specific?' asked Tanner, busily taking notes.

'Probably not since we were in the junior squad together; although, saying that –'

Tanner glanced up from his notepad with a shot of alarm.

'Saying what?'

'Well, I can't be sure, but I thought I'd seen her a few times more recently.'

'Recently, as in?'

'Over the last few weeks, before we met on Sunday. We didn't say hello, or anything. I wasn't even sure it was her. She was sitting too far away. But I must admit, it did make me start thinking about her, which was probably why I recognised her so quickly, when we met at the club.'

- CHAPTER THIRTY FIVE -

WITH THE CONVERSATION coming to a close, Tanner wandered back to his car with only two things on his mind; who'd been going around pretending to be Jenny, and more importantly, where the hell was she?

He cupped his hand under the car's chrome door handle, then glanced back at the house, half expecting to see Ellison still standing there to see him off the premises.

Thankfully, he wasn't.

The security camera remained where it had been before, and hoping that Ellison wasn't watching him from some darkened room, Tanner stepped away to sneak past the fountain, over to where the converted stables lurked in the shadows. There he attempted to find a way to peer inside, but there were no windows in the barn-sized doors. The only ones were built into the roof, and there was no obvious way to reach them.

Noticing that there was a good half-inch gap around the edge of each door, he pulled out his phone and accessed its torch function. Making sure he didn't light up the entire estate, he flattened it against one of the gaps before turning it on to peer inside. There was definitely a car in there. By the looks of it, it was some sort of old Rolls Royce, or a Daimler. It wasn't Jenny's Golf.

After glancing back over his shoulder, he proceeded to the next door to do the same, before moving on to the last. From what he could make out, behind the doors were two cars and an old wooden motorboat, sitting on a trailer. Jenny's car wasn't there, neither was there any reason for it to be, other than the unsubstantiated and wholly irrational feeling of jealousy he'd been harbouring towards Ellison, ever since they'd first met.

Give it up, John, he said to himself. *She's not here.*

With that, he skulked back to his car, opened the door, climbed inside and drove quietly away.

- CHAPTER THIRTY SIX -

PULLING INTO THE car park close to their moorings, it was immediately obvious that Jenny's car wasn't there either, but by that stage he wasn't really expecting it to be.

During the journey from Ellison's palatial mansion, the focus of his attention had turned from worrying about where Jenny was to contemplating what he should do about it. He'd made a rough mental calculation that she'd been missing for about six hours, which by police standards wasn't any time at all. Had he been a husband, wandering into Wroxham Police Station to report that his wife had been missing for such a short period of time, he'd have been laughed out of the building. Jenny wasn't even his wife – just a girl he happened to be living with on board a boat.

At that moment he made a vow to do something about that. He loved her. That was beyond doubt. Thinking about it then, he wasn't sure why he'd not proposed to her before. They'd been going out long enough. He couldn't imagine finding anyone else more compatible, certainly nobody who was as intelligent and attractive, someone who even shared his rather odd sense of humour.

But deep down he knew why he hadn't. The

subject had never come up, but he had a feeling that Jenny would want to have children. Tanner really wasn't sure he'd be able to. Not again. His daughter, Abigail, had been brutally murdered, just as she was entering the prime of her life. He'd no idea if he'd be able to have another, so having to spend the rest of his life living in constant fear that the same thing might happen again. He also felt that having another child would almost be disrespectful to Abigail's memory, as if she were nothing more than a family pet who'd died, and he was out shopping for a replacement.

As he ambled down the towpath towards his boat, his mind leapt from one disjointed question to another, never able to rest on one for long before latching on to the next. Where was Jenny? What possible reason did she have for not calling him? Who'd been going around pretending to be her? Was it the same person who'd called from the public phone box, the night they found Craig Jenkins? And why had she been so late to meet Ellison, on the very same night? Was someone trying to frame her, or was Jenny the one who'd –?

Baulking at the very thought, he shook his head, furious with himself for having allowed it to penetrate his conscious mind. He should be more concerned for her safety than contemplating the ridiculous notion that she could have anything to do with what was going on. For all he knew, her body was floating face down in a river at that very moment, waiting for a reversing boat to suck her into its propeller, as had happened to that other poor girl, all those months before.

He clambered on board the yacht, calling out,

'Jenny? Are you here?'

His voice disappeared into the darkness, nothing coming back in response but the distant boom of a bittern, echoing out over the Broads.

An unwelcome shiver crept down his spine.

Stepping over to the cockpit's brass gas lamp, he lit it with the lighter kept beside it. As a comforting yellow light pushed gently at the darkness, he lifted the starboard side bench seat to reach down and retrieve the bottle of rum he kept there, along with a glass tumbler. Filling the glass, he downed the contents and stood for a moment, enjoying the sensation of the smooth burning liquid sliding down into his stomach.

Was he really going to have to turn in for the night without knowing where she was? Shouldn't he at least make the effort to start contacting her friends?

With the rum already having the required effect, he reminded himself that it really hadn't been all that long since he'd last seen her. If she wasn't at work the following morning, he'd launch a county-wide search for her. Until then, he had no choice but to stop worrying and turn himself in for the night; but not until he'd had another drink.

- CHAPTER THIRTY SEVEN -

Thursday, 4th June

FEELING AS IF he'd hardly slept, Tanner emerged into consciousness long before his alarm went off. As he lay in bed, his mind already entangled in the same web of thoughts he'd been so consumed with the night before, he searched around for his phone.

Finding it under his pillow, he woke it up. It was just after seven. He checked to see if anything had come through from Jenny. Nothing had. No text, no call, no email.

With a dull ache spreading out behind his eyes, knowing it was unlikely he'd be able to sleep again, he rolled out of bed to begin scrabbling around for some painkillers.

Arriving late at work, peering through the circular holes in the main office doors, his heart stopped when he saw Jenny's chair was empty. Bursting through them, he was about to demand if anyone had seen her, when she stepped casually out of the kitchen, still wearing her coat, a mug of steaming hot coffee in each hand.

Catching his eye, she said, 'It's not for you,

sorry,' nudging past as she did.

He was about to ask where the hell she'd been, and why she'd not bothered to return any of his calls, but instead found himself calling after her, 'What's not for me?'

'The coffee,' she replied, turning her head to acknowledge him with a brash smile.

Following her to her desk, where she placed one of the mugs in front of DI Cooper, with as much discretion as possible Tanner asked, 'Where have you been?'

Setting her own mug down, she slipped out of her coat. 'When, last night?'

'Yes, of course last night,' he replied, forcing himself to keep his voice down.

'I stayed with Sam, but I told you that.'

'You *told* me?'

'Well, I texted you.'

'But – I...' he spluttered, dragging out his phone, '...nothing came through.'

Jenny shrugged, draping her coat over the back of her chair. 'Well, I definitely sent it.'

Tanner scrolled through his texts for what must have been the twelfth time since he'd sent her the message. There was still nothing there.

'But why didn't you pick up, when I called again?'

'The battery on my phone died, and I didn't have my charger. Why? Were you trying to get hold of me?'

'Yes, of course I was trying to get hold of you.'

'Well, I'm sorry, but how could I have possibly known that?'

Desperate to vent his frustration, with his brain

shifting to finding out who her new boyfriend was, he demanded, 'Who's this Sam, anyway?'

'Samantha Cummings. My old friend from school.'

The name rang a vague bell, but the discovery that it was a girl hardly helped him feel better.

'Well, next time you decide to go away for the night, may I suggest you take your phone charger with you.'

'Hey! You're the one who told me to stay with a friend. It wasn't my choice.'

'I told you to stay with your parents.'

'No, you *suggested* I stayed with my parents. And before I get really pissed off, who the hell are you going around telling me where I should and shouldn't be staying? My dad?'

With all that he'd been thinking about the night before, the comment hit Tanner like a sledgehammer to the chest.

Instantly regretting the remark, Jenny took a moment to rein herself in.

'Anyway, unless you want to continue this outside, I suggest you stop accusing me of whatever it is that you think I've done, and leave me alone to get on with my day.'

- CHAPTER THIRTY EIGHT -

TANNER SPENT HIS morning doing his level best to be grateful for Jenny turning up unharmed, but without much success. Instead, he found himself wallowing in a mire of bitter resentment. As far as he could make out, she'd made it abundantly clear that she didn't give a shit how much he'd been worried about her. And the whole "dad" remark left him feeling like some sort of pervert, seeing that she was actually young enough to be his daughter. Perhaps unsurprisingly, he didn't have a particularly productive morning, and was about to sneak out for an early lunch, on his own, when he saw Forrester beckon him into his office.

'What now?' he muttered, dragging himself out of his chair.

A minute later, Tanner poked his head through the door his DCI had left half-open for him.

'You wanted to see me, sir?'

'Take a seat,' Forrester replied, without looking up from his computer screen. 'And make sure the door's closed.'

Tanner didn't like the sound of that, and he did as he was told.

With his attention still focussed on his screen,

Forrester said, 'I assume you haven't seen Johnstone's post-mortem report from last night?'

'Not yet, sir, no.' He'd noticed it in his inbox a couple of minutes earlier, but had been hoping to take lunch before ploughing his way through it.

'Then you won't know that we appear to have ourselves a problem,' Forrester stated, dragging his eyes off his screen to sit back in his chair and frown at his senior DI.

Tanner shifted uncomfortably in his seat, his stomach tightening.

'I don't suppose there's any chance DS Evans was with you last night?'

'I'm afraid she was out, sir,' he replied, cursing under his breath.

'Did she tell you where she went?'

'She went sailing, at her club. They have evening races during the summer; every Tuesday and Wednesday.'

'Does she sail in the same boat as someone else?'

'No, sir. She sails a Laser. It's a single-handed dinghy.'

'OK, well, hopefully somebody there will be able to verify that.'

There was a momentary pause, before Tanner dared to ask what he'd already suspected. 'Am I to assume by your question that Jenny's DNA was found at last night's murder scene?'

'Her prints as well,' Forrester confirmed, his voice quiet and distant.

'Then I'd have to agree with you, sir. We do have a problem, and it's one that appears to be growing more serious by the day.'

Forrester turned his head to look over at him.

'I managed to speak with two potential suspects yesterday,' Tanner continued, 'both of whom were in Jenny's junior sailing squad: Marcus Hall and Robert Ellison.'

'Go on.'

'Well, sir, they both told me the same thing – that they'd seen Jenny during the weeks leading up to the murder of Craig Jenkins.'

'That doesn't sound so bad.'

'They said they thought they'd seen her sitting on her own, watching them from a distance.'

Forrester clenched his hands together on the table. 'Did you find out *when* they saw her?'

'Robert Ellison couldn't remember, but Marcus Hall was able to give me the dates and times.'

'And did you compare them against her whereabouts?'

'She was at the sailing club again, sir.'

'In her Laser?'

'I believe so.'

Another pause.

'I don't suppose they have CCTV?'

'They don't even have a working phone, so I think that's going to be unlikely.'

'There must be a way for us to prove she was there, without having to resort to asking if club members can remember whether or not she was.'

'Well, sir, there will be results from the races she's been taking part in. They post them up to their website.'

'That's something, I suppose.'

'But they do tend to be published on a rather ad hoc basis, and the ones we need aren't up yet.'

'Then we're just going to have to dig them up,

aren't we?'

'There's something else as well.'

'Don't tell me you've discovered a nail gun, hidden under her bed?'

'Er, no, sir.' Forrester may have meant it as a joke, but with the way things were going, it was probably worth him taking a look; for that, or anything else someone may have decided to plant there. 'It's what I found out when I spoke to Robert Ellison last night. He met Jenny in a pub for a drink, the night we found Craig Jenkins.'

Seeing the look of frustration on his DCI's face, Tanner quickly added, 'It was before Ellison was a suspect, sir.'

'Go on.'

'Well, sir; he said that they were supposed to meet at eight o'clock, but that Jenny was late.'

'And...?'

'He was suggesting that she was *very* late, sir. On top of that, we have witnesses who've said that they saw a woman matching Jenny's description using the public telephone in Catfield, both at the time a call was made to Craig Jenkins, the one we believe lured him out to where he was murdered, and when the 999 call was made, alerting us to the fact.'

'You're not seriously suggesting it was Jenny?'

'Of course not, sir. But someone is clearly going to some lengths to make it look like it was her.'

Forrester leaned back in his chair. 'Have you spoken to Jenny about any of this.'

'Only about someone matching her description using the payphone.'

'So you don't know why she was late for her

meeting with Ellison?'

'*If* she was late, sir.'

Forrester narrowed his eyes at Tanner. 'I take it by that you think this Ellison character is lying about Jenny being late as part of some sort of elaborate scheme to frame her for the murders of Craig Jenkins and Christopher Street?'

Tanner shrugged. 'Well, he could be.'

'Yes, but on that basis, the other guy who said he'd seen her staring at him could be as well, as could the people who said they saw her using the public phone. In fact, just about everyone living in Norfolk could be!' Forrester postulated, his temper rising.

'Not everyone, sir.'

'Perhaps, Tanner, but only because you haven't asked them yet!'

Silence fell over the room, as Tanner took a moment to consider how best to respond.

'He'd need some sort of a motive as well,' the DCI continued.

As Tanner remained silent, Forrester let out an exasperated sigh. 'OK – say it was this Robert Ellison guy. Are you sure he'd have been able to murder Craig Jenkins, and to have made all the phone calls, given that he was having a drink with DS Evans at the time?'

Tanner dug out his notebook to flick through its pages. 'I believe it's possible, yes, sir. The call from the phone box to Jenkins, the night of his death, was made at six thirty-four in the evening, giving Ellison plenty of time to meet him in the car park, stab him with the rhond hook, dump his body in the rowing boat, and then use the same public phone to report the body on the way to the pub.'

'But I thought witnesses said that they saw a woman using the phone box, one who looked like Jenny?'

'He could have dressed up like her.'

'Seriously?' Forrester said, with unhidden incredulity.

'Well, again, it's possible, sir.'

'Possible, perhaps, but hardly likely. And what about the two witnesses who said they saw her watching them? I suppose that was him dressed up as her as well?'

'In fairness, if it *was* Robert Ellison pretending to be Jenny, then we only have one witness who thought they saw her, the other being Ellison himself.'

'And the recording of the 999 call: wasn't it a woman's voice?'

'It sounded like one, yes, but forensics have yet to confirm it.'

'So, again, you'd better chase them up.'

'I'd also like to go over to the Red Lion, the pub where Ellison met with Jenny, to see if anyone remembers seeing either of them. They may even have CCTV.'

'If you must, Tanner.'

'Yes, sir. Thank you,' he replied, pushing himself up.

'And don't forget to chase up those race results for Jenny,' Forrester added. 'I'd hate to see her being caught up in this any more than she already is.'

With a nod, Tanner turned to leave, just as someone knocked at the door.

'Come in!' called Forrester, returning to his monitor.

'Sorry to disturb you,' said Vicky. 'The forensics report has come back from their examination of the public phone box.'

'And...?' Forrester prompted, glancing up.

She peered over her shoulder, before stepping inside to push the door closed. 'It's DS Evans, sir,' she continued, lowering her voice. 'Her fingerprints have been found all over it.'

- CHAPTER THIRTY NINE -

'I THINK YOU'D better come and join us,' said Forrester to Vicky, exchanging disturbed glances with Tanner as he resumed his seat. 'And make sure the door's closed properly.'

As she pulled out a chair, Forrester leaned forward. 'Unfortunately, DS Evans's prints and DNA have also been found at the scene of last night's murder.'

'Then someone's trying to set her up!' stated Vicky, staring first at Forrester, then at Tanner.

'So it would seem. The question is who?'

'Well, it has to be a girl, doesn't it?'

'Tanner was just suggesting that he thinks it might be Robert Ellison.'

She swivelled around to give Tanner a curious look.

With both Vicky and Forrester frowning at him, he knew that he was going to have to further justify his reasoning. Focussing his attention on Vicky, he said, 'I didn't tell you, but when I met him last night, he told me he'd also seen Jenny a few times, before we met him on Sunday, but couldn't remember when. He then said that she'd been late, when they went out for that drink together; and by late he meant *very* late. And as I'm fairly sure she wasn't, I think there's a strong possibility that he was lying.'

Tanner waited for Vicky to respond, but she didn't. All she did was to continue staring at him.

He could tell what she was thinking, even if she wasn't prepared to say it – that his rather slim theory was based more on jealousy than objective reasoning.

'To be honest, Tanner,' interjected Forrester, 'having had a chance to think about it, I'm more inclined to agree with Gilbert on this one. I mean, the idea of a man going about dressing himself up as Evans, whilst knocking off various members of her old junior sailing squad, leaving behind her prints and DNA in order to frame her for their murders, and for no particular reason – I'm afraid it does all seem to be a little far-fetched.'

'Maybe she *was* late,' proposed Vicky, 'and he was telling the truth. Girls often are, you know. And then there's his motive, of course. By all accounts, he's rather taken by her.'

With his hands clenching together in his lap, Tanner could feel a burning jealous rage surge through his body. It wasn't just jealousy. Deep down he was scared witless. Just the thought of losing Jenny to another man petrified him to his very core.

Doing well to hide his emotions, Tanner turned to Forrester. 'I think there's more, sir. Ellison is an active member of DS Evans's sailing club.'

'So...?'

'So he knows more than most when she's been racing there. He'd also know that she was sailing in a boat on her own, so there'd be nobody to reliably vouch for her. And he'd be in a good position to hide, if not destroy, the missing racing results that would prove she'd been there.'

Forrester stared out of the window. 'I don't know, Tanner.'

'Neither do I, sir, but I'd at least like to look into it.'

Reaching a decision, Forrester returned his attention to the room.

'OK, here's what we're going to do. Tanner, get yourself down to that pub where Ellison met Evans. Find out if they have CCTV, and ask inside, to see if anyone remembers seeing them there on the night in question. Then head over to the sailing club. Try to dig up those missing racing results. If they're not there, find out who's responsible for them.'

'I'd like to run a background check on Ellison as well, sir.'

'That's fine, but I suggest you get Sally to do it. You can ask her to chase forensics for the results from that 999 message as well.

'Gilbert, I want you to focus on the two girls we have as suspects – Kelly Fisher and the other one.'

'Carol Mortimer,' Tanner said.

'Have a chat with Cooper about them. See what he's managed to dig up so far. You can get Sally to help.'

'What about Evans, sir?'

'I think the less she knows about this, the better, don't you think?'

'Agreed,' Tanner nodded.

'And from this point on, I don't want her out of our sight, especially after work. That means no more evening sailing, or going out with anyone even remotely connected to this case. Agreed?' Forrester asked, staring directly at Tanner.

'I'll do the best I can, sir.'

'I'm not only worried about her being further implicated.'

'I know. It's just that she can be a little...how can I say...a little headstrong at times.'

'Then you'll just have to tell her that it's for her own safety, won't you.'

It didn't work last time, mused Tanner, but only to himself.

'OK, that's it, and keep me posted.'

As they got up to leave, returning to his monitor Forrester said, somewhat absently, 'Gilbert, stay behind for a moment. I've got a quick favour to ask.'

Tanner raised an inquisitive eyebrow at her as he nudged his way past, heading back out into the main office.

- CHAPTER FORTY -

ONCE TANNER HAD left, Forrester glanced up at Vicky, standing by the still-open door. Without saying anything, he motioned for her to close it, before pushing himself up from his chair and lumbering towards the window. There he stared out, wrapping his sausage-like arms over his barrel-sized chest.

'I just wanted to ask how you thought Tanner was doing?'

'Oh,' she began, clearly surprised. 'He seems all right, I suppose.'

'And Jenny?'

Noting with interest that he'd used her first name, something she'd never heard him do before, Vicky replied, 'She's OK, as far as I know.'

'I assume you're aware that they've been having some sort of a relationship?'

She blushed slightly. She wasn't used to having such private conversations with her DCI, certainly not about something she knew to be frowned upon by the Force. She also wasn't sure if she was supposed to know that they were, even though she did, along with just about everyone else.

Struggling to find a way to confirm that she knew without admitting as much, she eventually came out with, 'I believe they live on the same boat together, if that's what you mean.'

'And how are they getting on, dare I ask?'

'I really wouldn't know, sir,' she replied, too quickly for it to be true. From various conversations she'd had with each of them, she knew they'd been struggling.

'That's what I thought,' extrapolated Forrester.

Clearly agitated, he returned to his desk to re-take his seat.

'To be honest, Vicky, I'm becoming increasingly concerned about the ability of either one of them to be able to conduct themselves in the dispassionate manner necessary to do their jobs properly. And now I hear Jenny has been going out for drinks with one of the suspects, someone who Tanner is clearly jealous of; so much so that he's taken it upon himself to prove that the man is guilty of murder.'

Surprised to learn that her DCI had reached the same conclusion she had about Tanner's rather improbable suspicions relating to Ellison, she did her best to rise to the defence of both her work colleagues.

'I think Jenny's only been out for one drink with Robert Ellison, sir, and she only did so because he asked her as an old friend; and that was before his name came up relating to the investigation. As for Tanner considering him to be a suspect – in fairness, sir, he is!'

'That's as may be, but Tanner seems to have come to the frankly bizarre conclusion that he's the *only* suspect, and is putting some highly dubious arguments forward in an attempt to prove it.'

Finding herself forced to agree with him, she remained silent.

'Anyway,' he continued, 'I'd like you to do your best to keep an eye on him.'

'In what way, sir?'

'Just don't let him do anything stupid.'

None the wiser, she replied, 'I'll do what I can, sir.'

With Forrester's attention returning to his monitor, Vicky was about to leave when he spoke again. 'There's something else I'd like you to do for me.'

'Yes, sir?'

'I want you to do a background check on Jenny.'

'A background check?' she blurted out.

'You know – have a look through her phone records, social media, that sort of thing.'

'Into Jenny?

Glancing up to see the look of horrified discomfort plastered over Vicky's face, Forrester leaned back in his chair. 'I know what you're thinking, but at this stage, I can't take any chances.'

'But – Jenny's got nothing to do with any of this!'

'I'm sure you're right, but unfortunately just about every piece of evidence is suggesting otherwise.'

'That's because someone's doing their best to make it look like she has, not because she actually did it.'

'Again, I agree with you; but as I've just mentioned, we need to approach each and every investigation with dispassionate, unbiased impartiality. That means being driven by the evidence before us, not by the feelings we have towards each other.'

'I understand that, *sir*, but even so, apart from the fact that Jenny wouldn't hurt a fly, let alone go around killing half her sailing friends, what possible motive could she have for wanting to do so?'

'Yes, well, the same could be said for Robert Ellison, but it doesn't seem to be stopping Tanner from having a go.'

'But this is different, sir.'

'Is it?'

'Of course. Jenny's one of our own.'

'Listen, I understand how you feel, but I'm only asking you to do a background check on her. I'm not ordering you to testify against her in court.'

'I'm delighted to hear it!'

'Look, Vicky, we both know Jenny's got nothing to do with this, but the way things stand at the moment, if this went to court, with Jenny in the dock for the murder of both Craig Jenkins and Christopher Street, a jury would have a hard time believing that she *didn't* do it.'

'But they can't convict someone of murder without them having some sort of a motive, can they?'

'Theoretically they could, which is why I need you to take a look at her phone records, email and social media accounts.'

'And how will that help prove she had nothing to do with it?'

'For a start, by establishing the fact that she's made no effort to get in contact with any of them.'

'Apart from Robert Ellison, of course.'

'From what I understand about that, Ellison made contact with her, after meeting at the sailing club. For Jenny to have followed Ellison and Hall around prior to that, as both suspects have said she had, she'd have needed to have researched their whereabouts beforehand. And as we know it wasn't her, the evidence simply won't be there.'

Vicky still didn't look convinced, forcing Forrester to sit forward to add, 'The very fact that you won't find anything will help to clear her name. I promise!'

'If you say so, sir.'

'Oh, and one more thing. I'd rather you didn't discuss this with Tanner, or anyone else for that matter.'

'So, who should I report to?'

'On this occasion, you can report directly to me. OK, that's it. Make sure to keep me posted.'

- CHAPTER FORTY ONE -

SEEING VICKY FINALLY emerge from Forrester's office, Tanner was exceedingly curious to know what they'd been discussing, especially when he saw how her shoulders slumped as she stomped back to her desk.

'Are you all right?' he asked, watching her pull out her chair.

'Yes, fine,' she replied, forcing a smile at him as she plonked herself down.

Keeping his voice low to prevent Sally from overhearing, he leaned over to ask, 'What was that all about?'

'Nothing,' she replied, with unusual curt dismissal. 'I've been trying to book a holiday, but you know what he's like.'

Wondering what made her think Forrester was going to grant her a holiday in the middle of a double murder investigation, doing his best to sound sympathetic Tanner said, 'It's probably just a question of timing. Anyway, I'm about to head off to the Red Lion.'

'Shall I come with you?' she asked, with an uncharacteristic look of pleading desperation.

'No, you're OK,' Tanner replied, giving her an odd look. 'I think your time is probably best spent here.' Leaning forward again, he whispered, 'And I don't want to take Little Miss Beech, either; so maybe you can find something for her to do in my absence.'

- CHAPTER FORTY TWO -

D RIVING INTO THE Red Lion's car park, Tanner left his XJS between the only two cars there. Stepping out, he immediately began scanning the building's exterior for CCTV cameras. Heartened to see that there was one pointing down towards the pub's rear door, he straightened his tie and made his way inside, wondering who'd be behind the bar and, more to the point, if they'd recognise him. After all, Jenny and he were locals. They may not be regulars, not to the point where everyone knew their names, but they were at least recognised when they did stop by, normally for Sunday lunch.

Knowing that left Tanner feeling awkward. To ask the questions he needed to, he was going to have to formally introduce himself. That meant the whole pub would soon know his profession, something he preferred to keep to himself. He'd discovered a long time before that the moment someone found out what he did for a living, they immediately treated him differently; more often than not with a raft of fake smiles and insincere geniality, which he felt were a front to hide their guarded contempt.

Entering the virtually empty pub, he skirted

around the tables and chairs, heading for the bar. There he found a grey-haired middle-aged lady with a plump pale face plastered with makeup, who he immediately recognised.

She glanced up with a welcoming smile.

'Hello! We don't normally see you in here at this time. What can I get you?'

Reaching into his inside jacket pocket, Tanner cleared his throat. 'I'm afraid it's work related.'

He fished out his ID to open up and hold out for her.

Stooping down to read it, she looked up with a start. 'I'm sorry,' she said, her face and neck instantly flushing. 'I'd no idea!'

'Yes, well, it's not something I go around telling people.'

'We're not in any trouble, I hope?'

'Not at all, no. I'm just trying to find out about someone who told us he was in here recently.'

'When was that?'

'Tuesday evening.'

'OK,' she replied, glancing up at the ceiling. 'I'd have been around then. Who was it in particular?'

Swapping his ID for his phone, Tanner showed her a picture of Robert Ellison.

After studying it for a moment, she looked up, nodding. 'I'm fairly sure he was here then, yes.'

'Any idea what time?'

'It was in the evening, but I can't remember when exactly.'

'I saw you've got a CCTV camera over-looking the car park.'

'We do, yes.'

'I don't suppose there's any chance you'd still

have the footage from that night?'

'Er, I think that's unlikely, I'm afraid.'

'Could you check?'

Glancing furtively around the bar, she leaned over the tall beer pumps in front of her to whisper, 'Don't tell anyone, but it's not real.'

'Shit,' Tanner muttered under his breath. Letting out a heavy sigh, he met her eyes to ask, 'Can you at least tell me if he was with anyone?'

'Not at first, no, but someone did –'

Stopping mid-sentence, she stared over at Tanner.

'I remember now. He was with that pretty girl you're always coming in here with. I was thinking at the time that it was odd, seeing her in here with someone else.' Joining the dots, she suddenly asked, 'Is that why you're here? To find out if she's been cheating on you?'

Tanner shifted uncomfortably from one foot to the other. 'I'm not here about that, no,' he declared. 'They're old friends. I knew she was coming.'

'Oh, I see,' the barmaid replied, sounding unconvinced.

'What I need to know is how long he was here for, before the girl showed up?'

'I can't remember, but it was a while.'

'Approximately...?'

'Maybe an hour?'

Tanner could feel that knot inside his stomach tighten again. His reason for coming over there was to prove Ellison had lied to him; that he hadn't been early, and that Jenny hadn't been late. But what this woman was telling him was only serving to support his story.

Lifting his phone higher, he asked again, 'Are you sure this was the man?'

'Quite sure, yes. He was propping up the bar, just about where you are now, doing a crossword. I remember because he didn't seem to be doing very well and kept reading the clues out to me – not that I was much use. I've never been much good at those sorts of things.'

With a growing sense of unease, Tanner headed out of the pub to find his car, his mind a mess of unanswered questions and disquieting emotions. Amidst the mental turmoil, two main thoughts kept rising to the surface. The first was that if Ellison wasn't behind all this, then who the hell was? The other concerned both Ellison and Jenny. Had she really been late, or was it more that Ellison had been early? Without any way to find out what time either had arrived, it was impossible to know.

Checking his phone for messages – of which there were none – he considered calling the office, to see if Vicky or Sally had been able to come up with anything on either Kelly Fisher or Carol Mortimer. Knowing Vicky would have called if they had, he discarded the idea.

As far as he could work out, there was only one avenue left to prove Jenny's innocence, or at least that she'd not been the one following Marcus Hall around, making it far more likely that someone was deliberately attempting to frame her. He had to find those race results. With that in mind, he brought up Barton Broad Sailing Club's website again, to see if anyone had posted them.

They hadn't.

Checking the time, he wondered if there'd be someone there who'd know where they'd be kept.

Without bothering to try calling the club's phone number again, he fired up the engine to begin speeding his way over.

- CHAPTER FORTY THREE -

TANNER ARRIVED AT the public car park outside Barton Broad Sailing Club about ten minutes later. It was only after he'd stepped out of his car and had walked over to the gated pedestrian entrance that he remembered it would be locked. He'd need the key code to gain entry, and he had no idea what it was. Cursing, he considered phoning Jenny to see if she knew, before dismissing the idea. She'd only end up asking him what he was doing there.

Pressing his face up against the wire mesh, he attempted to peer up towards the club, hoping to catch sight of someone he could call out to. But from what he could make out, the place was deserted.

Standing back, he wondered if he'd be able to climb over, but seeing the barbed wire running along the top, he knew he wouldn't.

After rattling the gate with frustration, he pulled out his phone to try the club's number again.

Standing there, his phone pressed to his ear, listening to it ring without being answered, he was about to give up when he saw a gleaming Volvo Estate turn into the car park and drive down towards him.

Seeing a man of senior years behind the wheel, hoping it was a club member Tanner put his phone away and waited for him to park.

'Are you trying to get in?' asked the driver, heaving himself out.

'Trying to, yes,' Tanner replied. 'I was hoping to speak to someone from the sailing club.'

'Are you interested in membership?'

Tanner paused before answering. He still hoped to join at some point, but it was hardly the time to go into that.

'I was actually looking for the person responsible for your racing results.'

'You're a bit keen, aren't you?' the man grinned.

'I'm sorry?'

'I assume you want to see how you're doing on the leader board?'

'Oh, I see – er, no. It's not for me, it's for a friend, Jenny Evans. She's a member here. You may have heard of her?'

The man thought for a moment. 'The name does ring a bell. How long's she been a member?'

'Only about a month.'

'And you say you're looking for the race results?'

'We are,' Tanner confirmed.

'Then I think you'd best take a look at our website.'

'We've already tried there, but couldn't find them, at least not the most recent ones.'

'Yes, well, they can take a while to get posted up. Paul Lawrence is the man you need to talk to. He's responsible for all that sort of thing.'

'I don't suppose I'd be able to have a quick look inside the clubhouse for them?'

'Well, you could, I suppose,' the man replied, eyeing Tanner with suspicion.

'It's just that Jenny asked if I could pop by,' Tanner said, hoping to avoid having to declare his profession. 'She's trying to persuade me to become a member,' he added, which was true enough, 'so I thought I'd be able to take a look around at the same time.'

'I suppose you'd better follow me then, hadn't you?'

After ushering him in through the pedestrian access gate, the elderly gentleman led Tanner up towards the old wooden clubhouse, in much the same way Jenny had the Sunday before.

'Can you sail?' enquired the man, shuffling along the concrete hardstanding.

'Not really, but it's probably high time I learnt.'

'Oh, yes? And why's that?'

'Well, I live on a boat, so it makes sense for me to learn.'

'A sailing boat?

'It's a forty-two-foot traditional gaff-rigged cruising yacht.'

The man stopped where he was to take Tanner in with renewed interest.

'And yet you can't sail?'

'Not as such, no,' Tanner admitted. 'My friend's been trying to teach me, but without much luck. That's why she's suggesting I learn to sail a dinghy first.'

'I suspect she's right,' the man agreed, continuing their journey up to the clubhouse. 'The Broads are hardly the best place to learn to sail a forty-two foot yacht. Not a huge amount of room for error – at least not when you're navigating the rivers. Besides, dinghies are much more fun.'

'So I've been told.'

'Cheaper as well!'

Climbing the steps up to the veranda, he produced a large bunch of keys from his trouser pocket and rifled through them. By the time they reached the door, he'd found the one he'd been looking for and opened up to lead the way inside.

'We used to pin the results up here,' he continued, stepping over towards a large noticeboard, 'but we don't seem to bother anymore. I can't say I agree, but whenever I bring it up, everyone tells me that it's easier to post them up to our website, which is all well and good, but someone's still got to do it.'

'Didn't you say it was Paul somebody's job?'

'Paul Lawrence, yes, but he hardly comes in anymore. That means someone has to either post them to him or take them home and scan them in before emailing them over. But all that means is that half the time they get lost. I'm told the new system is for someone to take a photograph of them, and email that to him. Anyway, the race officer of the day is supposed to leave them in here,' he added, resting his fingers on the lip of a clear plastic leaflet dispenser attached to the wall, crammed full of crumpled-up pieces of water-stained paper.

Lifting them out, he laid them on a small table below, attempting to flatten them enough to be able to read what they said.

'This one's dated Wednesday, 6th May. When

was that, about a month ago, wasn't it?'

Unable to remember the dates Marcus Hall had said he'd seen Jenny, without having to resort to taking his notebook out, Tanner replied, 'The missing ones are from the last three weeks.'

Leafing through the pile, the old man eventually said, 'I can't find any here that are particularly recent. Maybe they've been kept somewhere else. Either that or someone's taken them home. What was your friend's name again?'

'Jenny Evans.'

'Jenny Evans,' he repeated, looking more closely at each page. 'You know, I can't help but think that I've heard the name somewhere before.'

'She used to be a member of Horning Sailing Club, and was part of the Junior National Squad.'

'Yes, of course!' the man exclaimed, staring up. 'Jenny Evans! She really was rather good. I'd no idea she was a member here.'

Amused to discover Jenny was almost famous, Tanner asked, 'Did you know her back then?'

'I wouldn't say I *knew* her, no; but I remember when she came to our junior open events – her and her friends. They were all extremely good, for children at least. They'd inevitably end up dominating the medal table. I remember because we'd spend months after each event, sitting around discussing ways to improve the standard of our own junior sailing, something which was always sadly lacking. Nothing we tried ever worked, mind. We only had one junior who ever showed any real interest, but we could never get him to race. All he wanted to do was sail off around the world.'

With the description sounding familiar, Tanner

asked, 'That wasn't James Boyd, by any chance?'

'It was. Why? Did you know him?'

'I didn't, no, but I was here on Sunday, when his...when he was found.'

'Yes, of course. Very sad.'

'I was here with Jenny. The intention was for me to have a taster session, before signing up, but it was too windy. It was her who set off in the safety boat, with someone called Robert Ellison.'

'Rob, yes. I was told he went out with a new member. I didn't know it was Jenny Evans, though.'

'She tells me that Robert was in the same Junior National Squad as her, when they were children.'

'He was.'

'I don't suppose you know if he was a member here at the time?'

'Sadly not, no. As I said, we only had one junior sailor who was any good.'

'I heard that he was kicked out of the squad – Robert Ellison that is. Would you know anything about that?'

The man cast a guarded eye up at Tanner.

'You're not some sort of a reporter, are you?'

Realising he'd been bombarding the man with questions, none of which were pertinent to the reasons he'd given for wanting to take a look around, feeling he had no choice, he delved into his inside jacket pocket.

'I'm a Detective Inspector for Norfolk Police,' he replied, pulling out his ID.

'I see,' remarked the man, not looking at all impressed.

'I'm sorry. I should have said earlier. It's just

that I am hoping to become a member here and, well, to be honest, I didn't really want everyone knowing my profession.'

'Well, fair enough, but still – you should have said. But I do know what you mean. My son's a policeman.'

'Oh!' exclaimed Tanner, with genuine surprise. 'What, here, in Norfolk?'

'I'm afraid not, no. He took his family down to London about ten years ago. More career opportunities down there, apparently. Anyway, I assume you're actually here to look into what happened to James Boyd?'

'In part,' Tanner replied, even though he wasn't, at least not officially.

'I'm sure you know the original thinking was that he'd taken his father's boat out to the Isle of Wight, never to return. But I presume you now have a more nefarious theory.'

'We are treating it as suspicious, yes.'

'OK, but I sincerely doubt it was any of his friends. If I were you, I'd look closer to home.'

'How d'you mean?' Tanner asked, his curiosity piqued.

'The police at the time may have reached the conclusion that he was lost at sea, but most of us here thought something different.'

Tanner waited in silence for him to continue.

'His father, Frank.'

Tanner pictured James Boyd's parents, the day he and Jenny had been to their house to ask them to identify the items of clothing which had been found.

'Why do you think he may have had something

to do with it?'

'Well, he had a certain way about him.'

'And what was that?'

'For a start, he was always shouting at James, and when I say shouting, I mean really shouting; and in public as well.'

'OK, but I can't imagine he's the first parent to do so.'

'Someone also said that they'd seen bruising on James's back and arms, when he was getting changed.'

'Anything else?' asked Tanner, clawing out his notebook.

'Then there was the child abuse claim.'

Wondering why they hadn't found anything relating to this in the original Missing Persons report, Tanner asked, 'Did nobody tell the police about this at the time?'

'I doubt it. I mean, it's not the sort of thing you go around telling people; at least, it wasn't back then.'

'That's as may be, but if they'd known, I'm fairly sure they'd have taken the fact that he'd gone missing a lot more seriously.'

'Perhaps, but as I said, it was only a rumour. Nothing was ever substantiated.'

'What about the bruising?'

'James said he got them from playing rugby.'

'And the child abuse claim?'

'It was only alleged.'

'I assume it wasn't James who'd made the accusation?'

'No. It was one of the junior squad members.'

'But...' began Tanner, confusion knitting his

brow, 'I thought you said that you didn't have any squad members at the club?'

'We didn't, no. James's father, Frank Boyd was the Head Coach for the Junior National Squad.'

- CHAPTER FORTY FOUR -

ONCE BACK AT his car, Tanner checked his phone for messages. Finding one left by DS Gilbert, asking him to call, he leaned against the car and did so.

'Vicky, it's Tanner. You called?'

'I did, sir, yes. I just wanted to let you know that Chris Street's wife has formally identified his body.'

'Oh, right. OK. Was that it?'

There was a pause from the other end of the line.

'We've also had news back from forensics, about that voice on that 999 call.'

'Go on,' Tanner replied, somewhat hesitantly.

'Well, sir,' Vicky began, 'they confirmed that it was definitely a woman who'd made the call.'

'Anything else?'

'They're suggesting her age would be between twenty-five and forty. They're also saying it's likely she would have been born and bred in Norfolk.'

Tanner thought for a moment. 'OK, but all that means is that it was someone from around here. It doesn't mean it was Jenny.'

'No, sir, but it doesn't exactly help to exonerate her either.'

She was right. It was just one more piece of

evidence a court prosecutor could use to help persuade a jury of her guilt.

Tanner forced the thought to the back of his mind.

'How've you been getting on with Kelly Fisher and Carol Mortimer?'

There was a pause from the end of the line, before Vicky came back to say, 'It's going to take a little time, sir.'

'Fair enough; but as a priority, I'd like you to get hold of a sample of their voices, so we can compare them to the one left on that 999 call. After all, they're both Norfolk girls, the same age as Jenny.'

'Yes, sir, but, er...any idea how – unless you want me to arrest them, of course?'

'We only need a voice sample. How about taking a look at their social media posts, to see if there's anything there we can use?'

'And if there isn't?'

'Then I suppose we can always ask them if they wouldn't mind volunteering one.'

'And what about Jenny?' Vicky whispered down the phone.

'What about her?'

'Should I try to get a sample of her voice as well?'

'It's not Jenny!' Tanner spat, raising his voice.

'Yes, of course, I know, but wouldn't it help to clear her name if we could prove that the voice definitely wasn't hers?'

Tanner hesitated. It was an obvious idea, but there were two reasons he found himself reluctant to agree. Firstly, what would Jenny think if she found out Tanner had authorised such a thing, and secondly, and of far more concern, what if they came back to say that they thought the voice was hers?

'I'll think about it,' he eventually replied. 'Hopefully, it won't come to that. Besides, I have a new lead.'

'What's that?' asked Vicky, her voice lifting.

'I've just been chatting with this old guy from Barton Broad Sailing Club.' He glanced around the car park, making sure nobody was around to overhear him. 'He told me something about James Boyd's initial disappearance – that there was a rumour going around that his father may have had something to do with it.'

'His father?'

'Frank Boyd. He was known at the time for being openly aggressive towards James – shouting at him in public. There were also reports of bruising on James's arms and back.'

'So he thinks it was Boyd's father who murdered him?'

'That's what was being rumoured at the time. I also found out that he'd been accused of child abuse.'

'Why's none of this in the original Missing Persons report? Surely it must have been flagged?'

'Probably because it was all just hearsay, and the child abuse claim was only alleged. But it's where the accusation came from that's of most interest.'

'Not his son, I presume?'

'No. It was one of the children from the junior sailing squad.'

'But – why would he have been hanging around with *them*?'

'Because, apparently, Frank Boyd, James's father, was the Head Coach for the Junior National Squad!'

Silence followed, as Vicky digested that hitherto unknown piece of information.

'So – he knew them all then,' she eventually said. 'Jenny included.'

'It would appear so.'

'You're thinking he's the one who's behind what happened to Craig Jenkins and Christopher Street?'

'At the moment I am, yes.'

'Any idea as to a motive?'

'Not yet, no, but all this started when his son's body was found, so it has to have something to do with that.'

'You mean – he found out that they knew he'd killed his son?'

'It would certainly explain the timing. As long as James Boyd's body remained hidden, his disappearance was likely to be filed as nothing more sinister than a missing person. That all changed on Sunday.'

'But why go to so much trouble to make it look like Jenny was responsible?'

'To push the blame on to someone else. Or maybe –'

Tanner stopped mid-sentence.

'Maybe what?'

'Maybe it's the other way around.'

'How d'you mean?'

'Maybe he didn't kill his son, but thinks one of his sailing squad friends did.'

'But that doesn't explain why he killed two of

them, whilst going around trying to make it look like it was Jenny.'

'Unless he blames them all, as a collective?'

A moment of silence followed.

'If that is the case,' Vicky concluded, 'it could mean he's not finished.'

Tanner checked his watch. It was getting late.

'Anyway,' he continued, 'I'm going to head over to James Boyd's parents' house, to see if I can have a word with his father. Whilst I do that, if you can have a go at getting hold of those voice samples?'

'Well, I can try.'

Before ending the call, Tanner asked, 'Is Jenny still there?'

'She is.'

'Can you do me a favour? If I'm not back in time to take her home, do you think you'd be able to?'

'Of course!'

'And then stay with her, until I get back?'

'Absolutely. No problem at all.'

- CHAPTER FORTY FIVE -

ABOUT TEN MINUTES later, Tanner turned his XJS into the drive of James Boyd's parents' house and parked where he had before. Climbing out, he marched over to the door, rang the bell and waited.

A few moments later the door was opened by the very man he was so keen to speak to, staring out at him with a quizzical look.

'Good evening, Mr Boyd. Sorry to bother you again. I just had a few more questions.'

'Really? Well, I'm sorry, but I'm afraid it's not a good time,' he replied, glancing over his shoulder. 'We're just about to sit down to eat.'

'It will only take a minute.'

'Who is it?' came his wife's voice from the back of the house.

'Hold on, darling,' he replied, before re-engaging eye contact with Tanner. 'Can't you come back tomorrow? It is rather late.'

'I won't be long, I assure you.'

Boyd let out a heavy sigh of reluctant resignation, standing back to hold the door open. 'Then I suppose you'd better come in, hadn't you?'

'Actually, it's probably better if we talk out here.'

'Why? What's it about?'

'It concerns the relationship you had with your son, Mr Boyd.'

'My *relationship?*'

'With some of the other children as well, one of whom I've been told accused you of child abuse.'

'Christ! Not this crap again!'

'Are you coming or not?' came his wife's voice once more, echoing down the hallway.

'I'll be there in a minute, darling.'

Pulling the door closed behind him, Mr Boyd looked Tanner right in the eye.

'Listen. I've explained all this countless times,' he said, his voice harsh but low, 'to the child's parents *and* the RYA. I was doing nothing more harmful than helping the boy to get his sailing boots on. That was it! End of story!'

'To be honest, Mr Boyd, I'm not here to talk to you about that.'

'Then what *are* you here to talk to me about?'

'Well, first of all, I'm curious to know why you didn't think to mention anything about being the Head Coach for the Junior National Sailing Squad, when we came around to talk to you on Monday?'

'Er, I'm not sure,' he said, with heavy sarcasm, 'but I think it may have something to do with what you've come all the way over here to remind me about – an accusation that cost me my job, and very nearly my marriage as well! On top of that, I'm fairly sure I had other things on my mind at the time, seeing that you were standing there telling me that you'd found my son's body hidden inside an air-tight bag at the bottom of Barton Broad, dragged up from the depths by the upturned mast of a dinghy!'

Tanner took a moment to cast a questioning eye over the man's thin, youthful-looking face. 'I wasn't aware we mentioned anything to you about how the body was found, or indeed, how it had been hidden.'

'What?' Boyd said with a start, his eyes darting between Tanner's. 'Then I must have read about it in the papers.'

'Fair enough,' Tanner mused, pulling out his notebook. 'I assume you heard about what happened to Craig Jenkins and Christopher Street?'

'I'm sorry. Who?'

'The two men found murdered earlier this week.'

'Oh, of course. I didn't know their names.'

Tanner glanced up from his notes.

'But you recognise them, though? They were in your squad.'

He shrugged. 'There were over a hundred children in the squad, selected from all over the country. You don't seriously expect me to remember them all, do you?'

'But you remember Kelly Fisher, right?'

'Obviously, yes, but only because she was dating my son.'

'What about Robert Ellison? Have you heard of him?'

'I haven't, no.'

'Jenny Evans?' Tanner enquired, carefully studying the man's face.

'Again, no.'

Tanner raised an eyebrow at him, before returning to his notes.

A few moments passed in silence, before Boyd tentatively asked, 'May I go back inside now?'

Ignoring the question, Tanner stopped writing to ask, 'What about James?'

'What about him?'

'He wasn't in the squad.'

'No, he wasn't, but only because he didn't want to be.'

'Why was that, do you think?'

'He was never all that interested in racing, I suppose.'

'That's right. "He always had his eyes on the horizon,"' Tanner quoted Boyd's own words back to him.

'Yes, he did,' the man agreed, holding Tanner's gaze.

'I don't suppose you have any idea *why* he spent his time dreaming about sailing off to distant lands, away from you?'

'I don't, no.'

'That's interesting.'

'Is it?'

'I heard something else today.'

'Oh, yes? What was that?'

'That James was seen with his arms and back covered in bruises.'

'He played rugby,' Boyd replied, a little too quickly for Tanner's liking.

'Rugby, yes, of course.'

'Anyway, are we done?'

'One last question. Can you tell me where you were on Tuesday and Wednesday nights?'

'I was at home, with my wife.'

'Are you sure?'

'Quite sure, yes.'

From behind him came the sudden sound of his wife, flinging open the door to say, 'Just what on earth is going on out here?'

With a start, Boyd turned to her. 'Sorry, darling, the police just had a few questions, about James. I didn't want to bother you with them.'

'Is there any news?' she asked, glaring out at Tanner. 'Do you know who -?'

Tanner slowly closed his notebook to rest his eyes on her husband. 'Not yet, no. But I'm becoming increasingly confident that it won't be long before we find out.'

- CHAPTER FORTY SIX -

AFTER ARRANGING FOR a forensics officer to stop by to collect samples of their fingerprints and DNA, and with the sun beginning to set, Tanner made his way home.

Pulling into the car park, downriver from his boat, he was just in time to see Jenny stepping out of her car. Parking up, he leapt out. 'I thought I told Vicky to drive you home?'

'Nice to see you too,' she replied, in a tense, condescending tone.

'Sorry, yes, of course,' he apologised. 'It's just that I asked Vicky if she could bring you back.'

'And I told her that I'm quite capable of driving myself. Where've you been, anyway? I've hardly seen you all day.'

'Chasing leads,' replied Tanner, closing the car door to make his way over towards her. 'Why didn't you tell me that James's father, Frank Boyd, used to coach you?'

Jenny shrugged. 'I didn't think it was relevant.'

'Just like you didn't think it was relevant that you were in the same squad as Robert Ellison.'

'Frank was the head coach for the entire Junior National Squad. I'm not sure he ever said two words to me, at least not directly. So yes, I know who he is, in much the same way that I know who Superintendent Whitaker is; but that doesn't mean I go around telling everyone that I know him personally.'

'Even so, it would have been useful to have known.'

'OK, then I'm sorry. The next time we have to ask someone if they can recognise some dead guy's clothes, I'll make sure to tell you if I've heard of them or not.'

'There's no need to be quite so facetious.'

'I'm not being facetious, I'm being sarcastic.'

'Did you know anything about the rumours being circulated about him at the time?'

'I didn't, no. Why? What were they?'

'That he was the one who'd killed James.'

'I see,' she replied. 'And those rumours were based on what, exactly?'

'That he was known for being openly aggressive towards him at the sailing club – always shouting at him, and that James was covered in bruises. Mr Boyd was also accused of child abuse, apparently by someone in the squad.'

'I must admit, I didn't know anything about that,' she conceded, slipping her handbag off her shoulder to begin rummaging around for her notebook. 'So, you think he may have had something to do with what happened to James?'

'It's possible. It's also possible that he thought someone else knew.'

'Craig Jenkins?' Jenny asked, sending a questioning look into Tanner's eyes.

Tanner didn't answer. 'I assume you heard that we found another body last night?'

'Cooper mentioned something about it, yes.'

'Well, I'm afraid to say that it was another of your junior squad friends, Christopher Street.'

'Are you sure?' she asked, her face draining of colour.

'His wife identified the body this afternoon.' Tanner hesitated. 'So now I'm worried that the killer thinks you may know something as well.'

'But I don't know anything!' Jenny insisted.

'Maybe he's not prepared to take that chance.'

Jenny shook her head from side to side. 'This is ridiculous. There's no way the man who used to head up my old junior training squad is out to kill me.'

'There's another theory which I feel could be just as compelling.'

'What's that?'

'That he thinks one of you is responsible for murdering his son. Maybe he thinks you were all involved, which would explain why two of you are now dead.' Jenny studied the ground in silence. 'I assume you're not going out tonight?'

'Sam asked me round again,' she replied, absently.

'You're not going, are you?'

'I told her I would, yes.'

'But – you can't!'

Jenny glared up at him. 'Please stop telling me what I can and cannot do. It really isn't appreciated.'

'I'm sorry, but with what I found out today, I really do think it would be better if you stayed here, with me.'

'Why, because you think my old sailing coach is

out to murder me because of what happened to his son?'

'To be honest, at this stage I'm more concerned about him successfully framing you for the murders of Craig Jenkins and Christopher Street.'

'I thought we'd been over this?'

'We have, yes, but since then, more evidence has been found to further implicate you.'

'I see, and what's that?' she demanded, taking a defiant stance.

Tanner cast his mind back to the conversation he'd had with Forrester earlier that day. At the time he'd been in full agreement to remain quiet about what they'd learnt since, so as not to cause her any unnecessary anxiety. But from what he could make out, she didn't seem to be nearly worried enough.

Tanner took a deep breath. 'Your DNA and prints were found at the scene of Christopher Street's murder.'

'You mean Craig Jenkins, don't you?'

'I mean Craig Jenkins *and* Christopher Street!'

As Jenny's eyes darted between his, Tanner continued. 'I met Robert Ellison last night.'

Jenny gave Tanner an ominous look.

'I asked him about the night of Craig Jenkins' murder, when you met him at the pub. He said you were late.'

'Wow!' Jenny exclaimed. 'That's a first.'

'He said you were *very* late, a comment later confirmed by a barmaid.'

'You're telling me that you went to the Red Lion, asking questions about me?'

'No. I went to the Red Lion to ask questions

about Robert Ellison. I was expecting to find his statement to be false, but instead the barmaid only seemed to confirm it.'

'What – that I was late?'

'We've also had forensics come back on what they found at the phone box, where the 999 call was made. They basically said your fingerprints were all over it. And the analysis of the recording said that it was the voice of a local woman between the age of twenty-five and forty. I've already told you that there are witnesses saying someone matching your description was using it.'

By this time Jenny was staring open-mouthed at Tanner, her face ashen white. 'You think it was me, don't you?'

'What? No! Of course not!'

'I can't believe it. You actually think it was me.'

'It just means someone is doing their damnedest to make it look like it was you.'

'And they've done such a good job, my boyfriend is all set to read me my rights.'

'Please, Jenny, I'm trying to help you.'

'By going around asking questions about me? Next thing I know you'll be telling me that you've got Sally bloody Beech doing a background check on me.'

'But it's reaching the point where questions are going to be asked.'

'Like what? Did I murder Craig Jenkins and Christopher Street?'

'Like why you were so late for your meeting with Robert Ellison?'

'I wasn't!' Jenny fumed.

'But he said you were, and the barmaid

confirmed it.'

'Then maybe we got the times mixed up, so he ended up thinking I was later than I actually was.'

As it dawned on Tanner that the explanation could very easily be that simple, he brought the conversation back to where it had started. 'Anyway, the bottom line is that I think it's safer for you to stay here tonight.'

'That's nice, but since discovering that my middle-aged boyfriend thinks I'm some sort of a demented serial killer, I'm in dire need of at least one glass of wine, and not with you. So if you'll excuse me,' she said, barging past him to get to her car, 'I'm going to see Sam. Don't wait up.'

- CHAPTER FORTY SEVEN -

Friday, 5th June

TANNER WOKE WITH a start. He was lying sprawled out on one of the bench seats, outside in the cockpit, still wearing his suit and tie, an empty bottle of rum clutched in one hand and a glass tumbler in the other.

Realising it was broad daylight beyond the boat's canopy, he lifted his hand to see the time, so spilling the remnants of his drink over his shirt.

'Shit,' he cursed, lifting himself up, only to feel his stomach turn as a bolt of pain shot through his head.

Forcing himself to sit up, he ditched the bottle and glass onto the table to stare down at his watch. It took a full moment for him to work out what time it said: just gone quarter past eight. He was supposed to be at his desk by nine!

Wondering why his alarm hadn't gone off, he peered down into the cabin for visual confirmation of what he already knew.

Jenny wasn't there. That meant she'd not come home that night.

Finding his phone lying discarded on the floor, he reached down to check for messages. There weren't any. No missed calls, no texts, nothing.

With his head pounding even harder, he stood for a moment, trying to decide what he could get away with *not* doing in order to make it into work on time. He could probably skip having a shower, but he'd need to shave. His stubble was too dense for him not to. He'd also need to change his shirt. There was no question about that. Coffee would have to wait.

Driving as fast as the traffic would allow, he pulled into Wroxham station at two minutes to nine, pushing open the heavy front door less than a minute later.

Pleased with himself for having made it in on time, after a quick nod over at the duty sergeant he stepped through to the main office, staring about for Jenny, but there was no sign of her. He couldn't even see Vicky.

Thinking it was unusual for both of them to be late, he ducked his head into the kitchen.

They weren't there either.

Pouring himself a coffee, he made his way over to his old desk where DI Cooper was sitting.

'I don't suppose you've seen Vicky?' he asked, glancing nonchalantly about.

'She's in with Forrester.'

'Oh, right.'

Continuing to look around, as casually as he knew how he asked, 'And Jenny?'

'She's not in yet,' came Cooper's curt response, his attention focussed on his monitor.

Tanner glanced down at his watch. It had now gone nine, but only just.

'OK, thanks,' he replied, and headed for his desk.

He turned on his computer before peering over to Forrester's office. Through the partition window he could see Vicky standing in front of the DCI's desk, deep in conversation.

Finding himself exceedingly curious to know what they were discussing, Tanner took another sip from his much needed coffee. He was about to sit down to log in when out of the corner of his eye he saw Forrester, waving at him to come over.

Raising one of his eyebrows, he downed his drink, left the cup on the desk and wandered over.

'You wanted to see me, sir?' he asked, poking his head through the door, catching Forrester's eye before noticing Vicky's tense and pale face.

'Come in, Tanner,' Forrester replied. 'And close the door. DS Gilbert has just shared with me some news which, frankly, is of grave concern.'

With the knot inside his stomach tightening, Tanner took up his position beside Vicky, who'd taken to staring down at the carpet.

There followed a moment of silence. Eventually, Forrester sat forward in his chair to rest his elbows on the desk.

'Yesterday afternoon, I asked Vicky to run a background check on DS Evans.'

'You did what?' Tanner demanded, hot blood pumping into his face.

'And it's exactly that reaction, Tanner, which forced me to do so without discussing it with you first!'

'I see! And what did she find, may I ask?' he questioned, as if she wasn't in the room with them.

Vicky lifted her head. 'I found pictures of her on Facebook, back when she was in the Junior National Squad.'

'Well, there's a surprise! On that basis, I can't believe you haven't sent out an armed response unit to have her picked up.'

Forced to ignore his glib sarcasm, Vicky pushed on by saying, 'Some of them show her with Craig Jenkins, whilst in others she's with Marcus Hall and Chris Street. Robert Ellison as well, I'm afraid.'

'So what? She's never denied knowing them.'

'Other posts go on to suggest that she'd been having relations with them all.'

Tanner stood for a moment in stunned silence.

'I'm sorry, I don't believe it,' he said at last. 'She'd have told me if she'd been going out with any of them. You must be reading something into them that just isn't there.'

'There are pictures of her with James Boyd as well,' Vicky continued. 'And I'm afraid those are...intimate.'

Tanner's face burned with indignation. There was just no way he was going to believe that Jenny had lied to him – that she knew James Boyd, let alone that she'd been having sex with him. But what was really making him fume with primal rage was that he knew what was coming next.

Splaying his large fat hands over the desk, Forrester let out a heavy sigh. 'I'm afraid, Tanner, a criminal prosecutor would see this as motive; not only for having killed James Boyd, but also for the deaths of Craig Jenkins and Christopher Street.'

'I've never heard anything so ridiculous in all

my life!' Tanner stated. 'Actually, I'll go further to say that it's bloody insulting to think that you'd even suggest such a thing! This is Jenny we're talking about, not some dysfunctional tart.'

'We're all aware who's under discussion, thank you, Tanner,' Forrester said, his voice remaining calm and controlled, 'but we're duty-bound to follow the evidence, no matter where it may lead.'

'Yes, but – to Jenny?'

'And what we've uncovered so far gives me little choice but to hand this over to Professional Standards.'

'You can't do that!' Tanner yelled. 'You know their reputation. They'll dig up anything they can to make her appear guilty. Even if they come up short, just the fact that she's been investigated will pretty much end her career.'

'I'm sorry, Tanner, but we don't have any choice.'

'Please, sir,' Tanner begged, 'give me a chance to find out who's really behind all this. I mean, everyone knows it's not Jenny.'

Forrester didn't respond; but took to staring down at his hands instead.

With the realisation that he'd already made up his mind, Tanner took in a series of calming breaths.

'Look, sir, it's Friday. Just give me till Monday. I had a really good lead yesterday that I've yet to chase up.'

'What's that?' Forrester enquired, bringing his eyes up to meet Tanner's.

'James Boyd's father. I found out that he used to be the Head Coach for the Junior National Squad, something he'd neglected to mention before. That means he knows every single person involved, just about. On top of that, he lost his job over child abuse allegations, and there were rumours flying around that he'd physically abused James. He verbally abused him, that much is certain. If he murdered his son and thought the other squad members knew about it – or if he suspected one or more of them had done it, then he'd have one hell of a motive for killing them, whilst doing his best to frame Jenny in the process.'

Forrester sat back in his chair to steeple his fingers together, his elbows propped up on the armrests. After a few moments he turned his head to face Vicky.

'What do you think?'

'I think it sounds entirely plausible, sir.'

'I just need time to get hold of his prints and DNA,' Tanner continued, 'and then run them by forensics, to see if they have anything that matches what's been found at the two crime scenes, as well as the phone box. If they do, then I reckon we have our man.'

'But all the evidence is pointing towards this being a woman, Tanner. Even the voice on the 999 call has been confirmed as such.'

'Then maybe it's the man's wife; or maybe it's Kelly Fisher, or Carol Mortimer. Or maybe the person who'd made the call was exactly as it sounds – someone who just happened to find the body and for whatever reason didn't want to be identified. It could be any number of people, but one thing I do know with absolute certainty: it's not Jenny!'

The room fell into an uncertain silence, as Forrester began tapping his fingers against his tightly closed mouth.

'To be honest, sir,' Tanner continued, driving home his advantage, 'I think you should be far more concerned that Jenny could be the next victim. If she is, and she happens to be murdered, a much-liked young police officer, one with a faultless record of service who's nearly lost her life in the line of duty, her blood's going to be on your hands, *sir*. And I'm damned sure Superintendent Whitaker will come to the exact same conclusion, as will just about every newspaper and news media organisation up and down the country.'

As Tanner was talking, Forrester's lips tightened as his face drained of colour, leaving behind patches of purple spider-veins running over his bulbous nose and plump fat cheeks.

'I do hope, Tanner, that you're not trying to manipulate my judgement by making veiled threats?'

'I'm simply endeavouring to state the obvious, sir.'

More silence followed, as Forrester and Tanner continued to glare at each other.

Pushing his chair away from his desk, Forrester heaved himself up to walk towards the window where he stared out at the passing cars, his hands clutched behind his back.

After a few moments, he turned slowly around to face both Tanner and Vicky.

'OK, here's what's going to happen. Tanner, you *have* to come up with something substantial against someone other than Jenny, and you have to do it fast. I'm more than happy to provide you with every resource at my disposal, including all the staff working here. I'm even willing to contact HQ, to ask for their help. At the end of the day, I'm in complete agreement with you about Jenny. The idea of her being some sort of psychotic serial killer *is* ridiculous. However, the crimes she's found herself implicated in are far too serious for me to try and sweep under the carpet. If it were to leak out that I'd endeavoured to do so, even for a minute, it wouldn't just be my job on the line. I'd be facing a charge of gross misconduct, closely followed by a criminal charge of obstruction, as would you.'

Shifting his gaze momentarily towards Vicky, Forrester added, 'In fact, anyone who knew what was going on would be. It's for that reason, and that reason alone, that I have no choice but to contact Professional Standards.'

The room descended into a cold hard silence. He was right, and Tanner knew it.

Glancing down at his watch, Forrester asked, 'Is Jenny in yet?'

'She wasn't when I came in, no, sir,' he replied, his mind becoming numb to what was going on around him.

'OK, now, just to be clear, I'm *not* saying this, but I think it may be a good time for her to take a few days off. Maybe she could go away for the weekend, somewhere which would mean she'd be out of contact for a while. Perhaps she could send me an email, to let me know she's not coming in. Having found no less than two bodies in the last week, she'd certainly have good reason to ask for some time off.'

As it dawned on Tanner what Forrester was proposing, his face visibly brightened.

Without responding directly, Tanner turned to make his way towards the door, saying, 'Excuse me, sir, but I just need to make a call.'

- CHAPTER FORTY EIGHT -

OUTSIDE FORESTER'S OFFICE, Tanner shot a look around to see if Jenny had turned up. After poking his head inside the kitchen, he hurried over to Cooper's desk.

'I don't suppose there's been any sign of Jenny yet?'

Noting the conspiratorial tone of his voice, Cooper glanced down at his watch. 'Not yet, no.'

With no real idea if that was good or bad, Tanner thanked him before hurrying outside.

With no sign of her car, he pulled out his phone to dial her number. 'Please answer,' he prayed, pressing the phone against his ear.

He was just about to hang up to try again, when Jenny's voice broke over the line.

'Hi John – yes, I know, I'm late. I overslept.'

'That's fine,' Tanner replied, momentarily adrift on a wave of relief. 'Where are you?'

'Just passing Beeston Church, about ten minutes out.'

'Are you on speaker phone?'

'I am, yes, why?'

'Is anyone else in the car with you?'

'No. Should there be?'

'I need to talk to you before you come in. Better

still, perhaps we can meet somewhere?'

'You want to meet me before I arrive?'

'Uh-huh.'

'Sorry, but – why?'

Instinctively glancing at the entrance doors behind him, Tanner slunk away, making a beeline for the side of the building.

'Forrester's upped the stakes for us to find out who's responsible for the murders of Craig Jenkins and Christopher Street.'

'But I thought I was working with Cooper, on the James Boyd investigation?'

'He wants me to head that up as well.'

'Oh, OK, but I still don't understand why that means we have to meet up?'

'I think it's better if I explain in person.'

'I think it would be better if you explain now.'

Tanner sucked in a lungful of air.

'He's decided to contact Professional Standards.'

The line fell momentarily silent.

'To investigate who?'

Reaching the end of the building, Tanner stopped to stare blindly about, searching for the words to tell her what Vicky had been ordered to do, and what she'd discovered in the process.

'John? Are you still there?'

'I'm still here.'

'So...? Who's he contacting Professional Standards about?'

'Yesterday afternoon,' he said, 'Forrester told Vicky to start running a background check on you.'

'I'm sorry?'

'In doing so,' he continued, forcing the words out, 'she found photographs of you on Facebook, with various members of your Junior National Squad.'

'And? So what?'

'She says they're suggestive of you having *relations* with them, including two who are now dead – Robert Ellison as well.'

'I assume by "relations" you mean *sexual* relations?'

'I believe that was what she meant, yes.'

There was no response to that from Jenny, forcing Tanner to continue.

'She also said that she found similar pictures of you with James Boyd.'

'*Me*, with *James Boyd?*' she repeated, her voice incredulous.

'That's what she said – bringing Forrester to the conclusion that they provide a motive for you to have done what the physical evidence has been pointing towards.'

'Jesus Christ, John! He must know someone's trying to set me up, surely?'

'Of course he does. We all do.'

'Then why the hell is he reporting me to Professional Standards?'

'I'm not sure he has much choice. It's the evidence. It's just become too compelling for him not to. If he doesn't, and word gets out that he didn't, he'd probably face a formal charge of gross misconduct, along with possible criminal charges for obstruction – not only him, but everyone else who knew about it, Vicky included. But it doesn't mean he's not one hundred percent behind you, which is why everyone at the station is now focussed on finding out who's really doing all this.

He's even offered to ask for HQ's support.'

As she remained silent, he continued. 'He's also given me the chance to give you the heads-up, hence the call. He suggested you send him an email, to let him know that you need a few days off to recuperate from having discovered two bodies over the past week. He's then suggesting you turn your phone off and disappear for a few days – maybe longer.'

In the background, Tanner could hear the hard rhythmic clicking sound of Jenny's indicator, followed a moment later by her voice.

'Where do you suggest I go?'

'Somewhere where nobody will think to look for you.'

'Not my parents, then?'

'Definitely not your parents, no.'

'I suppose I could ask to stay with Sam for a few more days.'

'Maybe you two could go away somewhere together, where you could claim there was a really bad mobile reception, or nowhere to plug your phone in. A campsite, for example?'

'OK, I'll give it some thought. Do you think it would be OK if I pick up some stuff from home?'

The word "home" sent a river of emotion flowing through Tanner's heart. Such a simple word, but one which meant so much.

'Of course. I'm sure that will be fine. I can't imagine anyone out looking for you for a while. If you do decide to stay with Sam, do you think you could ask her to text me every now and again, just to let me know that you're OK?'

'Yes, of course.'

'But make sure she doesn't mention your name, or where you are, just in case they decide to start monitoring my calls.'

Sensing the conversation was coming to an end, knowing they'd likely be out of direct communication for a while, Tanner took in a breath.

'Listen, Jen, I know we've had a rough few days, and I know that I don't say this nearly as often as I should, but – I love you. You do know that, don't you?'

There was a pause before Jenny's voice cracked over the line to say two simple words. 'I know.'

- CHAPTER FORTY NINE -

BACK INSIDE THE building, a station-wide briefing was quickly thrown together, resulting in Forrester and Tanner standing in front of the whiteboard.

'If I could have everyone's attention,' the DCI began, calling the meeting to order.

'As I'm sure you're all aware by now, over the course of this week, we've allowed our attention to be divided between two separate investigations: a cold case centred around the body of James Boyd, and the two recent murders of Craig Jenkins and Christopher Street. From this point forward, those two investigations are now one and the same.

'What most of you are not aware of is that the person who found the body of James Boyd – our own DS Evans – has since been implicated in the murders of Craig Jenkins and Christopher Street.'

A collective gasp rose up from the floor as everyone began staring about, trying to catch a glimpse of the person they all knew so well.

As Tanner shifted uncomfortably from one foot to another, Forrester continued.

'Naturally, it is our firm belief that there is someone out there who is attempting to make it look like she's involved, by planting physical evidence and hacking into her social media accounts in order to create a false narrative as a motive. Unfortunately, they've managed to do such a good job that I've had no choice but to alert Professional Standards.'

A whirlwind of whispered remarks flew around the office, as again people tried to see where she was.

'There's no point looking for her,' Forrester continued. 'What with her having found two bodies in less than a week, she emailed me this morning to let me know that she's decided to take a few days off. And as it's not my position to form any judgement as to her guilt in this matter, but only to forward the collected evidence to the relevant authorities, I'm more than happy for her to take as long as she needs. Hopefully she'll decide to wander off somewhere without telling us where she's going, whilst maybe forgetting to take her phone with her at the same time.'

With it being abundantly clear to everyone in attendance what he was implying, a conspiratorial ripple of laughter circled the room.

'But all that means is that we've managed to buy ourselves some time. We have to find out who's really behind all this, and we have to do so fast. With that in mind, I'm handing you over to DI Tanner.'

Tanner stepped forward. 'Thank you, DCI Forrester. I'm not going to use this time to go into the ins and outs of what's been going on so far. You can find all that in the relevant case files, which you'll be given access to as soon as this meeting has concluded. What I will be doing is updating you with what we discovered yesterday in relation to a new key suspect, before allocating lines of enquiry for you to follow.

'As soon as I'm done here, I'll be inviting James Boyd's father, Mr Frank Boyd, in for formal questioning. For some as yet unknown reason, when we first met with him, he neglected to tell us that he used to be the Head Coach for the Junior National Sailing Squad. Considering the conversation we were having with him at the time, that did seem like a rather odd omission to make.

'We've since learned that just before his son disappeared, there were rumours circulating that he'd physically abused him. There were also reports that he'd verbally abused him as well – in public. At around the same time he was also accused of child abuse, and although the charges were never formalised, they did end up causing him to lose his job. So, first up, I want us to find out what he's been up to since, in particular if he's been in contact with any of our victims, or anyone else in the Junior National Squad. At the same time we need to have a poke around his house. We're looking for the nail gun that was used to kill Christopher Street, along with anything else that may have a bearing on the case. DC Beech, I'm leaving all that with you.'

Hearing her name mentioned, Sally sat bolt upright before meeting Tanner's eyes to give him a single solemn nod.

It had been Tanner's deliberate intention to highlight her name so prominently. He needed everyone in the room to have the same agenda, working towards the exact same goal, and hoped that doing so would give her the perception, at least, of being a key player.

With an expression of professional intent imposing itself over her heavily made-up face, feeling confident he'd succeeded, Tanner added, 'Use whoever you need to help you, and coordinate what you find with me during the interrogation process.

'Cooper, I'd like to ask if you can make a concerted effort to track down Craig Jenkins's missing car. We know he drove it to the car park, so it seems likely that whoever murdered him must have driven it away. And as they'd have struggled to do so without leaving behind some sort of DNA evidence, we need it found. Chase up the council; and get a press release out, asking if anyone's seen it. When you've done that, I want you to join me in the interview room.

'Gilbert, I want you to get in contact with forensics again. Have them analyse those photos we found of DS Evans. I've no doubt they've been doctored. Whilst you're there, ask them how her social media accounts could have been hacked, and if there's any way for them to trace the person who might have done so. Even if they're unable to, if we can at least prove the photos aren't real, and someone planted them there, then there's a good chance Evans will be in the clear.

'When you've done that, I want you to organise a press conference for DCI Forrester and myself. If today's too short notice, set it up for tomorrow, preferably in the morning. Oh, and ask if the murder victims' wives are prepared to take part. Having them there will make a huge difference. We need witnesses to come forward who may have seen anything unusual – anything at all – near to either the industrial estate in Great Yarmouth, or in and around the car park where Craig Jenkins was found – which reminds me. Did you have any luck matching that 999 voice call?'

'I was able to pull samples of both Kelly Fisher's and Carol Mortimer's voices from their public Facebook sites, but neither was anything like our mysterious caller.'

'OK, then we need to make a plea for someone to come forward who either made that call or knows who made it. And as a reminder, anyone who is able to provide us with information will remain strictly anonymous.

'OK, that's it for now. Keep me posted.'

- CHAPTER FIFTY -

'SORRY TO HAVE kept you,' Tanner said, as he and Cooper re-entered the interview room where Frank Boyd was sitting alongside his assigned legal counsel, Mr Clive Percival.

Taking their respective seats, Tanner leaned over the table to re-start the recording device.

'Recommencing the interview of Mr Frank Douglas Boyd of 42, Wisley Gardens. The time is now...' glancing down at his watch, Tanner exclaimed, '16:58! Crikey. I'd no idea it was so late.'

'How long's all this going to take?' moaned Mr Boyd. 'I've been sat here for over four hours already.'

'My client does have a point,' interjected the solicitor. 'You've yet to present a single valid reason as to why he's here, other than he vaguely knew some of the victims.'

'Sorry, I thought one of them was his son?'

'I was referring to those identified as Craig Jenkins and Christopher Street, as you well know.'

'Yes, of course, but we still have the legal right to question your client for another...' he made a point of looking at his watch again, '...nineteen hours, before needing to request an extension, so I suggest he'd better make himself comfortable.'

'But you can only do so with a valid reason, otherwise I'm going to recommend he makes a formal complaint for false arrest.'

Ignoring him, Tanner opened the file he'd brought in with him before presenting the suspect sitting directly opposite him with a thin smile.

'Mr Boyd. How are you?'

'I've been better, thank you.'

'My colleagues have spent the last few hours conducting a search of your house, as well as the garage and shed at the back, and have come up with one or two items of particular interest.'

'As I said when you arrested me, I've got nothing to hide.'

'Perhaps not, but I think somebody did.'

'Am I supposed to understand what that means?' questioned Boyd, glancing over at his solicitor.

'We found something hidden inside what I believe used to be your son's bedroom,' continued Tanner, catching the suspect's eye.

'Don't tell me he had a secret stash of porn mags?'

'It wasn't a collection of magazines, Mr Boyd, but a single book in the form of a diary.'

Boyd's eyes flickered with alarm.

Delighted by the response, Tanner returned his attention to the file.

'Most of it is naturally extremely dull,' he continued, pulling out a couple of A4 sheets of photocopied paper, 'but there are one or two passages which do make for a riveting read. In fact, let me read some of them out to you.'

'What possible right have you to go through my son's personal diary?'

'If it relates to you, then I believe we have every right.'

With no further objections, Tanner selected one of the pages to begin reading in a flat monotone voice.

'*Sunday, 22nd April. My bastard so-called father just beat me up again. This time he used his belt, wrapped around his fist. The guy's a fucking psycho. At least Mum's OK.*

'*Tuesday, 15th May. Dad just kicked me down the stairs, just because I was trying to help Mum. He even put the boot in when I got to the bottom. Mum's locked herself in the bathroom. I can still hear her crying. I can't stay here, not even for Mum's sake.*'

'Shall I go on?'

Boyd stared at his hands, his face pale and drawn. Tanner passed the photocopy taken from his client's deceased son's diary for the solicitor to see. 'We found something else hidden as well, in the shed, at the back of your garden.' Removing a photograph from the file, he spun it around and pushed it over the table for Boyd to see.

'Do you know what this is?'

'It's a nail gun. So what?'

'Surprisingly, we came to the same conclusion, which was of interest to us for three reasons; firstly that we found it hidden in the shed, when all your other tools seemed to be stored in the garage; secondly, that there would appear to be blood on it; and last but by no means least, that something remarkably similar was used to kill Christopher

Street – one of the boys from the junior sailing squad you used to coach, before you were kicked out for child molestation.'

His cheeks reddening, Boyd glared up at Tanner. 'I've already told you about that. I was trying to help some moronic child put his sailing boots on.'

'I remember, yes,' Tanner confirmed. 'I also remember what you said when you first came in, concerning your whereabouts on the various dates and times we ran past you. One was last Tuesday, when you said you were down the Bittern, enjoying a drink with your mates, and the other, the Wednesday before, that you went to the cinema, on your own, which I still think is a rather odd thing to do. Anyway, that aside, I can only assume you didn't know that the Bittern has CCTV cameras, front and back, else you'd have proposed a different pub, and the car park outside the cinema complex you said you went to runs a vehicle number plate recognition system, and yours wasn't recorded.'

'Then I must have my dates muddled up.'

'And the other days I mentioned to you, outside your house the other day, when you said you were at home: I'm afraid your wife is adamant that you weren't.'

'Well, she would say that, wouldn't she?'

'What makes you say that?'

'Because she'd no doubt love to see me locked up for something I didn't do.'

'What – you mean for beating her up on what would appear to be a fairly regular basis, or for losing it completely to end up murdering your son?'

'Now look! Ok, I admit that I used to be a little

rough with the wife.'

'A little rough,' muttered Tanner, taking notes.

'And sometimes I may have given James the occasional clip round the ear.'

'Clip round the ear,' Tanner repeated, still writing.

'But there was no way I would've ever hurt him, not seriously.'

Taking a further few seconds to finish his notes, Tanner looked up to give Boyd a confused look. 'Sorry, but I don't suppose you can describe what you mean by "not seriously", exactly?'

'I meant to the point of killing him.'

'I see, but you are admitting to having beaten him to within an inch of his life, and on a fairly regular basis?'

Before he had a chance to answer, Mr Percival placed a steadying hand on his client's forearm, leaning in towards him to whisper something into his ear.

'For the benefit of the recording,' Tanner said, smiling at Cooper, 'Mr Boyd is being given verbal advice from his legal representative who, if he's got any sense, will be telling his client to keep his mouth shut.'

- CHAPTER FIFTY ONE -

BACK OUT IN the corridor, Cooper closed the door to quietly ask, 'What do you think?'

'I think we have our man, but we're going to have to prove it. Get that nail gun over to forensics and ask them to take a look at that blood. Then have someone go through the local CCTV footage for the nights in question. Hopefully we'll be able to find out where he really was.'

As they walked back into the main office, Constable Higgins leapt out of his chair. 'We've found Craig Jenkins' car, sir!'

'Good work, Higgins. Where was it?'

'Left in a side street, in Irstead.'

'OK, I want forensics over there as a matter of urgency.'

Reaching his desk, he felt his mobile phone buzz. Before sitting down, he fished it out to find a text had appeared from an unknown number, which read, simply, 'Hi. Sam here, How's life?'

Knowing it was Jenny, Tanner smiled before replying, 'Good. By the way, I think we've found that thing we were looking for.'

Pressing send, he only had to wait a moment before it buzzed again.

'I knew you would. Keep me posted.'

'Will do xxx.'

Straightening his face, he caught Sally's attention to ask, 'How's everything going?'

'I've just about finished searching through Frank Boyd's emails,' she replied, with professional solemnity.

'Anything?'

'Nothing obvious.'

'How about you, Vicky? Did you hear back on those photos of Jenny?'

'Not yet, no,' she replied, picking up the phone. 'I'll chase them up. By the way,' she added, directing Tanner's eyes towards their DCI's office, 'Forrester's got visitors.'

Looking over to see two tall thin men, each wearing a suit and tie, Tanner muttered, 'Professional Standards,' as if the words were a personal insult. 'Right,' he continued, tucking his phone away. 'I suppose I'd better see what they're planning to do about Jenny.'

A minute later, Tanner rapped his knuckles on Forrester's door and barged straight in.

'Sorry to bother you, sir,' he began, making a point of eyeballing the two unknown men, 'it's just that we have news on the prime suspect under interrogation.'

Half standing, looking distinctly uncomfortable, Forrester made the introductions. 'Gentlemen, this is my senior DI, John Tanner, who's leading the investigation we've been discussing. Tanner, this is DI Rawlinson and DS Hadfield, Professional Standards.'

Pushing themselves up from their respective

chairs, they took it in turns to shake Tanner's hand, the older one asking, 'Is that the same investigation your colleague, DS Evans, has been involved in?'

'She was, yes, but as DCI Forrester has no doubt told you, we pulled her off the moment we found out she had a personal connection.'

'That she knew both victims, as well as all the primary suspects?'

'At the time it was just the one victim, Craig Jenkins,' Tanner corrected.

'And since then you seem to have amassed what could be considered substantial evidence that she had a direct hand?'

'We found what *could* be considered incriminating evidence,' confirmed Tanner, 'but is far more likely to have been planted, and by the very man we currently have in custody.'

Directing his attention to Forrester, Tanner continued. 'We've unearthed a diary, sir, hidden under the floorboards of his son's bedroom. The contents confirm the rumours at the time; that Frank Boyd *had* been physically abusing his son. We also discovered a nail gun, with signs of blood on it. And Craig Jenkins' car has been found, which forensics are about to take a look at. On top of all that, none of Mr Boyd's alibis have checked out, so we're making good progress.'

As he said that, there was another knock on the still open door, closely followed by Vicky's head.

'News back on the photographs, sir,' she said, catching Tanner's eye. 'They've definitely been doctored.'

'Can they tell if her Facebook account's been

hacked?'

'They haven't come back on that yet.'

'OK, well,' Tanner continued, re-engaging with the others in the room, 'I think that alone proves beyond all reasonable doubt that DS Evans is innocent, and someone is trying to implicate her.'

Clasping his hands together, Forrester beamed a triumphant grin over at the two men. 'Well, chaps. It looks like you've had a wasted journey after all. Sorry about that.'

Ignoring the DCI's comment, the taller of the two plain-clothed officers turned to face Tanner. 'Assuming you're talking about the photographs of DS Evans mentioned in the report, it's also possible that she placed them there herself.'

Fixing the man's eye, Tanner asked, 'And what possible reason would she have for doing that?'

'I'd have thought that was obvious. Once she knew she was under suspicion, she created them herself, to leave for you to find. She'd have known you'd check them, to see if they'd been altered, and that you'd subsequently come to the natural assumption that someone else must have left them there, so deflecting suspicion away from herself.'

'Jesus Christ!' exclaimed Tanner. 'Is this how all you lot think about your fellow officers, or is it just you?

The man returned a thin, devious smile. 'We don't enjoy it, I can assure you of that, but we do have to approach each case on the basis that the officer under investigation has a good understanding of police procedures, and is therefore able to use them to their advantage.'

The man turned his attention to Forrester. 'We

also understand that DS Evans hasn't shown up for work today.'

'She emailed me this morning to request a few days off.'

'I assume you turned her down?'

'Actually, I didn't, no.'

'Despite having only just sent over the report detailing the mounting evidence you have against her?'

'I only did that in accordance with our code of conduct, Detective Inspector,' Forrester replied, taking a defensive stance. 'It's not my place to determine the guilt of one of my officers.'

'Maybe not, but you had only just identified her as being a prime suspect in a double murder investigation.'

'Neither is it for me to decide if one of my officers is even a suspect,' Forrester continued, forcing himself to remain calm. 'All I'm required to do is to inform you of what we've found, which I've done. As far as I'm concerned, DS Evans remains a much-valued member of my staff. She's also overdue some time off. I'd even recommended such, long before all this kicked off.'

'But even so. To allow an officer under suspicion of murder to "take a few days off", as you so eloquently described it, could easily be considered to be misconduct of your sworn duty.'

'Are you levelling that accusation at me?' Forrester demanded, his face filling with blood.

'Not yet, no.'

'Then I suppose it would be worth reminding you that you're talking to a Detective Chief Inspector. And if I thought for a single moment that you *were* accusing me, for no good reason, I'd be the one filing charges of gross misconduct. That much I do know!'

Without looking as if he was the slightest bit perturbed, the plain-clothed officer let out a heavy sigh. 'I assume you're able, at least, to provide us with her address?'

'Of course. She lives on board a boat.'

'A *boat?* repeated the man, with a clear note of incredulity.

'A boat, yes,' Forrester confirmed. 'It's quite normal around here,' he added, despite not thinking it was.

'Then may I ask its name, and where it's moored?'

'Erm – I'm not sure. To be honest, I don't think I've ever asked.'

'But you must have an address for her?'

'Oh, yes, of course. I've even gone to the trouble of writing it down for you.' Plucking a folded piece of paper from the top of his desk, he handed it over. 'I've included her mobile phone number, as well.'

After staring briefly down at what he'd been given, with a confused frown the officer looked up to say, 'But this is the address for a post office?'

'That's the address she's provided us with, yes.'

'It's called Post Restante,' Tanner chipped in with a knowing smile.

'*What's* called Post Restante?' questioned the man.

'The service the post office provides. It's for people with no fixed address, which around here more often than not means people who live on boats.'

'I see. You do know that this won't stop us from finding her?' the officer stated, a comment aimed at both Tanner and Forrester.

'What on earth makes you think we don't want you to find her?' retorted Forrester, his face a mask of befuddled intrigue.

'Right, if that's the way you're going to play it, we'll begin making our own enquiries. I think we'll start with your staff. I'm sure one of them knows where she is, especially once they've been reminded about the consequences of deliberately obstructing an investigation, which, by the way, I think you should all keep in mind. I assume you won't object if we use one of your interview rooms?'

Without waiting for a response, the senior officer marched the more junior one out, leaving Tanner to muse, 'I take it that was a rhetorical question?'

After Gilbert had closed the door, Forrester resumed his seat.

'I doubt it's going to take long for them to find out that you and Jenny live on the same boat together, so even if you have moved it, you'll end up having to tell them where it is.'

'Which is why she's not on board.'

'Do you know where she is? Actually, don't answer that. The fewer of us who know, the better. Anyway, I think they've made it abundantly clear what their intentions are, despite what we've uncovered.'

'I forgot to mention earlier that I've asked for the nail gun to be sent off to forensics,' said Tanner. 'If the blood matches Christopher Street's, then we've got him.'

'It would be a start, I suppose, but I doubt it would be enough; not on its own. A defence attorney would simply argue that Mr Street must have borrowed it one day, which was how his blood came to be on it. Unfortunately, we're going to need a lot more than that, especially when there's so much evidence piled up against Jenny. We have to be able to link him physically to the scenes of the murders. We must just hope that forensics can match either his prints or DNA to what they've already found. Meanwhile, I suggest we find out where he really was on the nights in question, as well as attempt to establish some sort of a motive. Did he kill them because he murdered his son, and thinks the victims found out, or was it because he thinks they were the ones who killed him, and he's out for revenge? We're also going to have to establish that Jenny's Facebook account *was* hacked, and preferably by the person we currently have in custody.'

- CHAPTER FIFTY TWO -

I T WASN'T UNTIL gone eleven that night that Tanner finally got back to his boat. Since the meeting with Forrester, and the flurry of activity immediately afterwards, the station's progress had been painfully slow. Nothing more had been unearthed that could tie Frank Boyd directly to either of the recent crime scenes, let alone the murder of his son, James. Nor had anything been produced that could be considered to be a motive for him having killed either Jenkins or Street, and time was fast running out. They'd already had him in custody for over twelve hours, which meant that by the time everyone arrived back at work the following day, they'd only have a few hours left before either having to charge him, or to seek an extension from the local magistrate; and with the little direct evidence they'd collected so far, he doubted it would be granted. Their only hope now was that forensics would be able to come up with something, preferably more than just a match on the blood found on the nail gun, although even that would help.

Having grabbed some food on the way home, Tanner climbed on board to pour himself a generous glass of rum before immediately draining half the contents.

Tumbler in hand, he lay down on the bench seat, feet up, head resting against one of the colourful cushions Jenny had brought from her flat, when she'd first moved on board. With the tumbler resting on his chest, he spent a few quiet moments allowing his mind to wander as he listened to the rhythmic lap of the water knocking gently against the hull.

A ping from his phone woke him with a start. He'd promised himself that he wouldn't lie there for long enough to fall asleep, as he'd done the previous night, but without realising it, he already had.

Without raising his head, he placed the tumbler on the table to dig out his phone. Seeing it was a text from Sam, assuming it to be Jenny, he lifted his head, just enough to be able to read it.

'All good here, will text again in the morning.'

'OK. Thank you. Sleep well,' he messaged back, before placing the phone down on the table.

Grateful to hear that she was still tucked safely away, Tanner smiled, resting his head back against the cushion as he did. Closing his eyes, he said to himself, 'Just another five minutes,' and drew in a deep, relaxing breath.

- CHAPTER FIFTY THREE -

Saturday, 6th June

TANNER AWOKE IN much the same way as he had the previous morning, sprawled out in the cockpit, in almost the exact same position he'd been in after replying to Jenny's text.

Cursing himself, he checked the time. 'And I've overslept!'

Wondering why his alarm hadn't gone off *again*, he pushed himself up to dig out his phone.

Squinting down at it, it didn't take him long to work out why. It was Saturday. His alarm was only set to cover the weekdays. He'd forgotten to change it before passing out.

'Shit,' he mumbled, massaging his stubble.

Before pushing himself up, he quickly checked to see if Jenny had messaged him. She hadn't, but that was hardly a surprise. There was no reason for her to get up at seven thirty, as he was meant to have done.

Within half an hour, Tanner was driving into work, hoping to make it in for nine, when he noticed the fuel gauge. The needle was deep in the red, threatening the zero mark. Knowing he only had a few more miles before being stranded on the side of the road, he had no choice but to pull into the petrol station just outside Wroxham.

He filled up, and was heading inside to pay when his phone rang.

Wondering if it was Jenny, he ducked down one of the aisles to fish it out.

It was the office.

'Tanner speaking.'

'Hi, John, it's Vicky.'

'Vicky, yes. I'll be in soon. I just had to stop for petrol.'

'Sorry,' she apologised, 'I didn't know what time you'd be coming in today. We've had a report back from forensics.

'Go on.'

'It's not good, I'm afraid. They've found no evidence that Frank Boyd was at either murder scene, and the blood on the nail gun belonged to him, not Christopher Street.'

Tanner cursed out loud, causing an elderly customer to glare at him.

'There's more, I'm afraid,' Vicky continued. 'We found out where he'd been on the nights in question. It was the Snowdon Vale Hotel.'

'Why does that name sound familiar?'

'It's the hotel we've had those reports about – the one being used as a knocking shop for male prostitutes, which would explain why he was so keen to keep quiet about what he was up to.'

'Great. So we're back to square one again.'

'Looks like it, yes. Sorry, sir.'

'What about Jenny's Facebook account? Any news on whether it's been hacked, and by who?'

'Nothing yet, but that was my next call.'

'And Craig Jenkins' car?'

'Again, no, but I'll chase them.'

'OK, well, as I said, I'll be there in a few minutes.'

Ending the call, Tanner's thoughts immediately turned to Jenny. If Frank Boyd wasn't the murderer they were after, that meant two things; firstly, that Jenny was going to have to remain the prime suspect, at least she would in the eyes of Professional Standards. Secondly, and of more concern, was that whoever murdered Jenkins and Street, maybe even James Boyd as well, was still roaming free. If that person knew Jenny hadn't been arrested, despite their best efforts, they could easily change tack, and instead of attempting to frame her, they could decide on a more permanent form of vengeance.

After paying for his fuel, Tanner hurried out to his car. With a sudden urge to speak to Jenny, he was about to dial Sam's number when he caught sight of a bullet grey BMW, parked half-in, half-out of the entrance to the petrol station, causing cars to lean on their horns before steering around to gain entry. With a suspicion that he knew who it was, and what they were doing there, he snuck around the pumps to try and get a look at who was inside, without being seen doing so.

It was the two officers from Professional Standards. They'd obviously found out he and Jenny were an item, and with no other way of locating her, had decided to follow him, no doubt hoping he'd lead them straight to her.

'Sneaky little bastards,' he muttered to himself.

With his finger poised to place the call, he stopped. From where he was standing he had a clear view straight through the BMW's windscreen, where he could see the more junior officer in the passenger seat, staring down at something, his hand pressed against his ear. Having had a few run-ins with Professional Standards before, during his time down in London, he knew their job had more to do with surveillance than anything else, including the use of the latest tech in mobile phone listening devices.

Tucking the one held in his hand back into his suit jacket, he skirted around the pumps to climb back into his car. At this stage he felt he had no choice but to contact Jenny. The last time he'd updated her was when he'd sent her the text the day before, the one which would have given her the impression that they'd found the person responsible, when in fact they'd done nothing of the sort. For a moment he toyed with the idea of sending her another message, via Sam's phone, but rejected it a moment later. If they were monitoring his calls, no doubt they'd be following his texts as well. He had no choice. If he was going to warn Jenny about them, and the fact that the killer was still at large, he was going to have to tell her, face to face. That meant losing the tail he'd managed to pick up.

Shouldn't be too difficult, he mused, firing up his Jag's over-sized V12 engine. Pulling on his seatbelt, he checked the rear-view mirror and began pulling slowly out of the garage forecourt. *As long as they think I don't know they're following me, it should be a piece of cake.* With a mental plan of how he was going to shake them off, he indicated right and pulled out onto the road, heading back the way he'd come, drifting slowly past their car as he did.

Once past, he watched them through his rear-view mirror. The moment they began the awkward process of doing a three-point turn in the middle of the street, with the noise of belligerent horns being sounded, Tanner jammed his car's accelerator pedal into its plush carpeted floor. The XJS hardly had the best handling in the world – far from it – but its massive engine meant it could outpace most modern, more sensible cars: at least it could in a straight line.

As the automatic gearbox dropped down two notches, the entire car hunkered down onto the road before surging forward, forcing Tanner's head back against the headrest as he held on to the steering wheel.

Speeding past the car in front, with Wroxham disappearing fast behind, he rounded a bend in what had quickly become flat open countryside, jamming hard on the brakes to slide the thirty year-old XJS into Beeston Church's car park. Doing a handbrake turn on the gravel, he slid the car behind a hedge, near to the entrance, and waited.

It wasn't long before he saw the bullet grey BMW streak past.

Taking his foot off the brake, he crept out.

Checking the road was clear, he spun the wheels out and sped back the other way, heading for Wroxham once again, and Sam's flat about five miles beyond.

- CHAPTER FIFTY FOUR -

ARRIVING AT THE address Jenny had given him the day before, Tanner found a young woman wearing jeans and a coat, lugging a large suitcase into the back of a nondescript car.

Tanner caught her eye. 'Is it Sam?'

'Who's asking?' she replied, slamming the car's boot closed.

Wondering how much Jenny had told her about him, he introduced himself. 'Sorry, I should have said. I'm John, Jenny's friend from work.'

The woman eyed him with suspicion. 'She wasn't expecting you to turn up here.'

'I know, yes, but someone may be monitoring my phone,' Tanner replied, stepping towards her whilst digging out his ID for her attention.

Leaning in to examine it, she looked up to give him a more relaxed smile. 'Sorry, yes, I'm Sam. Jenny said there might be people coming around looking for her.'

'That's not a problem,' Tanner replied, returning the smile before looking over at the modern two-storey block of flats they were standing outside. 'I don't suppose I could have a quick word with her?'

'She's not here, I'm afraid.'

A prickle of alarm tugged at his heart.

'But – I thought she was staying with you?'

'She was, yes, but I'd planned to see my parents this weekend. I did invite her to join me, but she got a better offer.'

'Who from?'

'Bob – or Rob. Something like that.'

'Robert Ellison?' The knot in his stomach tightened.

'I think so, yes.'

Tanner's face drained of colour. If the murderer was Ellison after all...?

Turning to race back to his car, he called out, 'When did she leave?'

'Oh – it was only about half an hour ago,' Sam replied, somewhat surprised by his reaction.

Reaching the car, Tanner tugged open the door, then turned back to face her. 'If she calls you, tell her that she *has* to contact me. Is that understood?'

'Well, yes, but – is she all right?'

'Just tell her to call me,' Tanner reiterated, before ducking inside to start the engine, spin the car around and race off, leaving Sam standing with her mouth half open, a cloud of burnt rubber hovering in the air in front of her.

- CHAPTER FIFTY FIVE –

URSING THE TRAFFIC, Tanner drove as fast as the narrow country lanes would allow, heading for the mansion he had visited before.

A little over ten minutes later, he was indicating left, looking for the hidden entrance that marked Ellison's residence. Seeing the familiar opening set within a bank of trees, he turned in to see Jenny's car parked beside the same three that were there when he'd been before, just beyond the ornate centrepiece fountain.

Pulling up next to them, Tanner climbed out to take in the immense Edwardian pile, noting how rundown the place looked in the cold light of day. Black paint flaked off the dozens of window frames, a drainpipe had come away up near the gutter beneath the roof, and ivy had been left to crawl freely along the walls. There were even a few broken panes of glass, and the gravel-lined driveway Tanner was standing on was strewn with weeds. What he couldn't see was any sign of Jenny; in fact, the whole estate seemed unnaturally quiet. Even the security cameras were lifeless and still.

Stepping over the drive towards the arched wooded front door, over which age-old varnish rippled and peeled, Tanner searched for a bell. Where he thought there should be one were only a couple of rusty old wires, poking out through the doorframe.

Lifting the lion-headed metal knocker instead, he banged it down twice, then stopped to listen, as the sound echoed around the courtyard. Knocking again, he stood back to look first up at the house, then at the cars behind him.

'Mr Ellison?' he called up to the seemingly empty house. 'Jenny?'

There was no response but the chatter of magpies from somewhere high up in the trees.

Stepping over to the nearest leaded window, Tanner cupped his hands to try and peer through; but years of dust and dirt combined with yellowing net curtains prevented him seeing into the darkened room beyond. He tried the next one along, then the next, but it was the same story.

'Jenny?' he called out again, much louder that time, scaring the magpies who clattered away, leaving nothing but the sound of his own barren voice reverberating around the lifeless courtyard.

Looking for a way in, Tanner skirted around the side of the house, the back of which opened onto a vast overgrown garden. There, a lumpy unkempt lawn was surrounded by a dense tangle of flowers and shrubs, fighting for space against a blackened dilapidated fence.

Stepping onto a wide oval-shaped patio, where weeds flourished between the cracks, and a grimy circular table was surrounded by weather-battered chairs, he turned to gaze up at the house. Directly in front of him was a single door with a large window. Shading his eyes, he peered through the glass. Despite being veiled by another net curtain, there was enough light inside to see that the door led into a kitchen, which, although it may not be clean, at least looked to be in regular use. With still no signs of life, he continued down to what would have once been a pair of elegant steel-framed patio doors. The metal frames had long-since warped, making it impossible for them to close, leaving an ugly uneven gap between each. Realising that there were no curtains of any kind to obstruct his view, he approached the doors with more caution. Peering inside, he stopped in his tracks, not daring to move. Behind the glass was a spacious dining room with dark wood-panelled walls where hung a series of lavish oil paintings, each one depicting an iconic scene of the Norfolk Broads. From the ceiling hung a stately chandelier underneath which sat an elderly couple, tucked in around a dining table laid ready for a feast; their hands resting besides yet to be used cutlery. In the middle of the table sat what was left of a single white candle, its flame flickering just above the table's surface, as it burnt steadily down to the base of its wick.

It took a full second for Tanner to realise that there was something deeply wrong with the scene before him. Arching down from the chandelier were lines of cobwebs, each one thick with dust. What was left of the food was nothing more than putrefying waste, and the elderly couple weren't resting their hands on the table by choice. Their hands were held there, the flat heads of rusty nails jutting up from the backs of each.

Horrified, Tanner took a faltering step away to

begin frantically searching for his phone, when a flash of light caught his eye from inside the room. Glancing back, he saw a purple flame emanate out from the table's centre, rippling over the surface as it raced towards the elderly couple's frail, outstretched hands.

Realising the candle had been used as a fuse to light either petrol or paraffin, unable to think of anything but the lives of the couple inside Tanner leapt over to the patio's dilapidated furniture.

Fetching up a chair, he hurled it at the patio doors, shattering the glass on impact.

Tumbling in after it, he reached out for the man seated with his back to the doors who remained motionless, despite the fact that his clothes were already ablaze. It was only when Tanner grabbed hold of his collar to try and drag him back, that he realised that he was nothing more than a dried-up corpse; a withered skeleton wrapped in paper-thin skin.

As the flames leapt off the table, down to the floor, Tanner's mind returned to the person he'd come in search of.

Abandoning the bodies now consumed by flames, he forged his way through to the back of the room, flinging himself through the open door at the end. Slamming it closed in a bid to stop the fire from spreading, he stumbled into a vast opulent entrance hall where no less than two sets of opposing stairs swept up to the balconied floor above.

'JENNY!' he bellowed, spinning around. 'ARE YOU IN HERE?'

Hearing nothing in response but the sound of

his own voice, echoing its way through the seemingly empty house, he dived towards the first door his eyes fell upon.

Barging into a room shrouded in darkness, he stopped and stared about, giving time for his eyes to adjust to the low level of light. He was in some sort of artist's studio with an empty, paint splattered easel propped up in the corner. Littering the floor were discarded pots and tubes, and covering the walls were dozens of paintings and drawings, some made using harsh bright colours, others sketched with seemingly violent rage. But what made Tanner stop, his heart pounding hard, was that they were all of the exact same person.

Feeling his knees buckle, he turned to wrench open the heavy cloth curtains, drawn over the window. With the room flooding with light, he looked again at the artwork plastered over the walls, desperate to discover that his eyes hadn't been painting pictures of their own. But the influx of light only served to confirm his deepest, darkest fear.

- CHAPTER FIFTY SIX -

PLUNGING HIS HAND down into his suit jacket's inside pocket, he dragged out his phone, woke it up and with trembling hands, and put a call through to DS Gilbert's direct line.

'Vicky, it's Tanner. Jenny's not here,' he began, the words tumbling out. 'Her car is, but she's not – just pictures of her stuck all over the walls. And the dining room's on fire, where his parents are. I need the fire brigade – and backup. I'm going to keep looking, but the place is huge. If the fire spreads before I find her-'

'John, stop!' Vicky demanded. 'You're not making any sense. Where are you?'

Attempting to rein in the fear-stoked thoughts rampaging through his mind, Tanner grabbed hold of the window ledge to take in a series of short shallow breaths.

'I'm at Robert Ellison's place,' he eventually resumed, his voice quieter – more stable. 'It's him. I know it is. He's got paintings and drawings of Jenny stuck up all over the walls, and I think I've just found his parents, what's left of them at any rate. It looks like he's nailed their hands to the dining room table and just left them to rot. They must have been there for years.'

'Jesus Christ!'

'And I think he's deliberately set the place on fire. If Jenny's here, I've got to find her. Can you send backup?'

'Yes, of course.'

'But call the fire department first. I've tried to contain it, but I doubt it will last.'

After making sure she had the address, Tanner ended the call to stare up, once again, at the many images of the girl he was so desperate to find.

Putting the phone away, he ran out of the studio, back into the entrance hall. There, he stared over at the dining room door which he'd closed just a few minutes before, to see tendrils of smoke seeping out from underneath.

With his eyes fixed on the door, he tried to decide what to do. Should he attempt to control the fire, or use the little time he had to begin a search of the house?

As he continued to stare, his feet feeling as if they'd been glued to the floor, he watched as decades of varnish began bubbling up over the door's surface. At least five minutes had passed since he'd closed it. The fire behind must have since become a raging inferno. There was no way he'd be able to control it, and he'd be a fool to try.

Having made up his mind, he sprinted over to the base of the nearest staircase to circle up and around, skipping past the first landing to continue up to the floor above. There he began flinging open the doors, diving inside the rooms beyond to conduct the most basic of searches, all the while calling Jenny's name, hoping she'd be able to respond in some way to let him know where she was. But every room was the same as the last; void and empty, each covered in a dense tangle of spiderwebs, weighed down by a lifetime of dust. None of the rooms looked as if they'd been used in years. They certainly didn't seem to be hiding the girl for whom he was searching so frantically.

By the time he'd finished checking through the uppermost floor, the air was already thick with smoke, catching at the back of his throat. He was halfway down the stairs to begin searching the floor below when he stopped to glance up. He'd forgotten to check the attic. He knew the house had one from the numerous dormer windows built into its sloping tiled roof. Then he remembered seeing a dusty old step ladder, resting behind a door in one of the rooms. Realising it could be used to access the roof, he doubled back up the stairs to come to a halt on the landing. There, he stared about at the doors, all of which he'd closed to help prevent the spread of the fire.

Cursing himself for not having realised what the ladder was for when he'd first seen it, he began flinging open the doors again to stare wildly behind each one. Finding it behind the fourth, he scanned the ceiling to spy a closed hatchway in the far corner. Dragging the ladder over to it, he kicked it open and clambered up, lifting the hatch to peer over the ledge.

'Jenny!' he called, squinting his eyes through wisps of dust and smoke. The space beyond was vast, piled high with decades of junk. It didn't look like anyone had been up there for years.

'Jenny!' he called again, examining the lip of the hatchway. It too was lined with dense grey dust.

The only place it had been disturbed was where his own hands had been.

Confident nobody had been up there recently, he closed the hatch and rattled back down the steps.

Leaving the ladder where it was, he dived back onto the landing, heading for the stairs, only to be met by a wall of thick black smoke, billowing up the stairwell.

Choking, he stumbled back. The fire must had taken hold of the house.

The sound of approaching sirens gave him the courage to continue his search. Holding his breath, he ripped off his suit jacket to cover his mouth and nose before plunging down the stairs, hoping the floor below would offer some respite. But the further down he went, the worse it became. The air had become so thick with smoke that even using his jacket as a filter, attempting to breathe left him choking.

Stumbling onto the landing below, he flung himself at the nearest window to begin clawing at its latch. But although it would turn, the window itself wouldn't budge.

Giving up, he took a half-step away to crack his elbow against its leaded glass, breaking it on impact.

He made a hole, and forced his head through the narrow gap, cutting the sides of his face as he did so, coughing and choking, forcing out the poisonous fumes to suck at the clean fresh air outside.

The moment he regained control of his breathing, he dragged his head back inside to stare about him; first at the landing he was now on, then down at the remaining stairs that would take him to the floor below. He knew he was trapped. The entire lower level was a raging inferno. Even if he was somehow able to make his way down, there was no guarantee he'd be able to find a way out – certainly not the way he'd come in.

His mind returned to Jenny. If she was on the floor he was on, and he could find her, then maybe they could jump to safety. A quick glance out the window made him think it would be possible, just about.

Knowing he'd never be able to forgive himself if he abandoned the search without having done all he could do to find her, he nudged out a larger hole in the glass to stick his head through and refill his lungs. That done, he pulled himself back.

Just as he turned to resume his search, a blast of searing white heat slammed into his chest, knocking the breath from his lungs to leave him suspended in the air, the scream of a drill filling his ears as it burrowed down into the depths of his brain.

- CHAPTER FIFTY SEVEN -

TANNER AWOKE, GASPING for air, but something was being held over his mouth. He fought to wrench it off, only for it to be forcibly put back on, as a stranger's voice began repeating his name.

'Mr Tanner! Mr Tanner! Can you hear me?'

Tanner nodded, before trying to speak, only to begin coughing with painful fury, ripping what he found to be a plastic oxygen mask off his face.

'Just relax, Mr Tanner,' the stranger continued. 'You're going to be fine.'

As memories of where he'd been began flooding his mind, through a rasping voice he asked, 'What happened? Where am I?'

'You're in the back of an ambulance, Mr Tanner. You've just been pulled off a garage roof.'

'Jenny!' he exclaimed, lifting himself up to peer out through the ambulance's open back doors, beyond which he could see what used to be Ellison's stately home, but was now nothing more than a smouldering ruin. 'Did they find Jenny?'

'I'm –' the paramedic began. 'I'm not sure. I think you'd probably best ask the fireman.'

Assuming that to be permission for him to leave, Tanner attempted to sit up.

'I didn't mean now,' stated the paramedic, resting a hand on his shoulder to prevent him from moving. 'You're in no state to be going anywhere.'

'I'm fine!' Tanner insisted, pushing the man's hand away.

'You may feel fine, Mr Tanner,' the paramedic informed him, replacing his hand, 'but I can assure you that you're anything but. You've got at least one fractured rib, a perforated eardrum, lacerations to your face and neck, and significant bruising of your spinal column. I suspect you're also in shock, as well as being concussed. The only reason you're able to move is because I've just given you a heavy dose of oxycodone, which is about the strongest painkiller I have.'

As he scowled down at his arm, where there was a tube leading up to a saline drip, Tanner's eye caught sight of a bald-headed man, peering in through the doors at them. He knew it was Forrester, but he looked nothing like he'd ever seen him before. His rotund face was tired and drawn, his eyes were bloodshot, and his skin was smeared with thick black soot.

'How's he doing?' the DCI asked, directing the question at the paramedic.

'I'm right here!' Tanner stated, with disgruntled resentment. 'And I'm fine, thank you for asking. Actually, better than fine. To be honest, I'm feeling rather good.'

'I suspect that's the painkillers talking,' said the paramedic with a wry look.

Forrester focussed his attention on Tanner. 'Did you know you were pulled off the garage roof?'

'So I heard.'

'Well, bearing that in mind, along with the fact you were only found about ten minutes ago, I'd be very surprised if you *were* fine. The fireman said you must have been blown out through one of the windows, when the building exploded.'

'I was wondering what happened,' mused Tanner, staring down at himself.

'And I was wondering what you were doing inside the building in the first place?'

'I was looking for Jenny, obviously!'

'Inside a mansion, soaked in petrol, with all the gas valves left open?'

'Yes, well – I didn't know about the gas.'

'But you did know about the petrol?'

Ignoring the question, Tanner stared over Forrester's shoulder at the smouldering ruin. There he could see Cooper, Vicky, even Sally Beech, picking their way around the edges of the blackened debris, alongside uniformed police officers, firefighters and forensics. 'What about Jenny?' he forced himself to ask. 'Has anyone found her yet?'

Forrester took a moment to follow his gaze. 'We've discovered the remains of two people, a man and a woman, near the back of the house, but Dr Johnstone thinks they're too old.'

'I think they were Ellison's parents.'

'Well, they're the only two people we've found so far. However, we haven't given up, not yet, but we are beginning to consider the possibility that she's not here.'

'But her car is. Ellison's as well.'

'There are ways of getting about other than by car, Tanner.'

Remembering the vintage ones Tanner had seen in the garage, during his first visit, he motioned to pull the needle out of his arm, only to be stopped by the paramedic.

'I'm sorry, but I really don't think that's a good idea.'

Tanner fixed the man's eye. 'Perhaps, but that's my choice. So either you take it out, or I will.'

The paramedic let out a world-weary sigh. 'Very well, but don't blame me when the oxycodone wears off and you can barely move, let alone breathe.'

With the needle removed, it was only when Tanner began climbing off the bed and out through the back of the ambulance that he had a taste of what the paramedic had warned him about. Placing any weight on his arms left his chest feeling like it was being compressed by a vice, and the second he tried to stand, the lower half of his spine ached under the strain.

Watching him wince with pain, Forrester took a steadying hold of his arm, helping him down.

'Are you really sure you should be doing this?'

'I have to find Jenny,' Tanner muttered, his jaws locked with resolute determination.

'No, Tanner. *We* have to find Jenny.'

'OK, fine; but there's no bloody way I'm going to allow myself to lounge around in bed whilst you do.'

'Fair enough, but – can you even walk?'

'No offence, sir, but of course I can bloody walk!' Tanner fumed, his voice raised in angry frustration.

Pushing himself away from Forrester, he began limping over to the line of stable-like garages.

There, he peered in through the windows, just as he'd done the first night he'd been there. But the view through each hadn't changed. The same two cars were still there, as was the boat.

Finding his phone, he first tried Jenny's number, only to hear what he'd expected; that the line was unavailable. He then placed a call through to Sam.

'Hi, it's John. Jenny's friend.'

'Oh, yes. Hi John. Did you manage to find her?'

'Not yet, no. I assume she hasn't been in contact with you?'

'Not since I saw her this morning, no.'

'I don't suppose she said anything, before she left?'

'Like what?'

'Like if she was planning on doing anything, with the guy she went over to stay with?'

The phone fell silent for a moment, before Sam's voice came back over the line.

'She did mention something about going to the Three Rivers, if that's of any use.'

'Going to, or taking part in?' Tanner questioned, his interest most definitely piqued.

'I'm not sure. I assumed it was a pub.'

Thanking her for her time, Tanner ended the call.

If Jenny had meant the Three Rivers Race, having taken part the year before, with Jenny helming and him doing his best to be a competent crew, he knew exactly what it was: a non-stop weekend-long regatta, the entrants of which had to navigate around a complex fifty-mile course comprising the rivers Bure, Ant and Thurne, making decisions as to which route to take based on tide tables and the ever-changing wind direction. With hundreds of boats taking part, most of which would sail through the night, it would be the perfect place for Ellison to keep her hidden, at least long enough to –

Seeing Forrester deep in conversation with his colleagues, their faces smudged with soot, Tanner began hobbling his way over to them.

'Anything?' he called out, catching their attention.

'I'm sorry, John,' Vicky replied, her face a blackened mask of disappointment.

'Then he must have taken her somewhere else. I don't suppose anyone knows if the Three Rivers Race is on this weekend?'

'It is,' Forrester confirmed. 'We've got patrol boats out to keep an eye on them. Why?'

'I just spoke to Sam, one of Jenny's friends. She said Jenny mentioned something about going to the Three Rivers. She thought it was a pub, but I suspect Jenny meant the race.'

Directing his attention over towards Vicky and Sally, Tanner asked, 'Do either of you know if Ellison owns a sailing boat?'

Sally shook her head. 'I didn't find anything about one.'

'Vicky?'

'Nothing came up, no, but I can't say that we were looking for one.'

'OK. Can you give the Broads Authority a call? See if they have anything registered under his name.'

'Of course.'

Tanner turned to Forrester. 'I'd like to head over to Horning Sailing Club. That's where the race starts and that's where they'd have to sign on, if they're taking part. If they are, then at least we'll know where to find them.'

'OK, but you're not driving. Cooper can take you.'

'I'm quite capable of driving myself, thank you, sir.'

'It's not up for discussion, Tanner. It's either that, or you stay here, and Cooper can go on his own.'

'Fine!' Tanner snapped, and without waiting for his unwanted chauffeur, began making his way over the courtyard, skirting his way around the various emergency vehicles, as Cooper followed behind.

- CHAPTER FIFTY EIGHT -

DRIVING INTO THE heart of Horning, where the village's ancient narrow streets heaved with tourists and cars alike, Cooper soon gave up looking for somewhere legal to park. The moment he managed to squeeze his way past the entrance to the Swan Inn, he turned left onto a pedestrian track, to leave the car on an area of grass littered with picnic tables and people alike.

Ignoring the many disapproving glances from families having their lunch, Tanner heaved himself out to follow Cooper, as fast as his various injuries would allow, heading for a footbridge at the end of the track, above which was a sign for Horning Sailing Club.

Crossing a narrow dyke, they picked their way through a group of wetsuit-clad young sailors, chattering with excitement as they strained at the handles of a line of dinghy trollies.

They soon entered a white wooden building offering open views over the River Bure, to find a table behind which sat two elderly gentlemen, one of whom was squinting at the screen of a laptop, whilst the other collected together what looked to be a pile of entry forms.

Clearing his throat, Tanner pulled out his ID.

'Excuse me, gentlemen. Detective Inspector Tanner and Detective Inspector Cooper. Norfolk Police.'

The elderly men stopped what they were doing to stare up at Tanner, mouths hanging open. Remembering the state he was in, and that they weren't the only ones gawping at him, Tanner lowered his voice. 'We're looking for a couple of people who we believe may be taking part in the Three Rivers Race.'

'Oh yes?' queried the man in charge of the laptop. 'We've just finished entering everyone's names onto the computer. Who are you looking for?'

'It'll be either a Robert Ellison or a Jenny Evans.'

'Ah, well, I know Jenny, of course, but I can't say I remember seeing her here. What was the other person's name again?'

'Robert Ellison.'

'Hold on. I'll have a look, but it might be a while. We've had a record entry this year – over two hundred boats!'

Leaving him to it, Tanner dug out his phone to give DS Gilbert a call.

'Vicky, it's Tanner. We're at Horning Sailing Club. How'd you get on with the Broads Authority?'

'They don't have anything registered under the name of Robert Ellison, but there was one listed under another Ellison. We think it might be his father, but it was a few years ago.'

'Did they say what sort of boat it was?'

'A Broads sailing cruiser – thirty-eight foot. At the time it was moored at a place called Perci's

Island.'

'Where the hell's that?'

'Opposite the Swan Inn.'

'I don't suppose the boat has a name?'

'Providence.'

Thanking her, Tanner ended the call.

Turning back to the table, he caught Cooper's eye. 'Anything?'

'Nothing yet.'

'We have a Robert *Alderson*, if that's of any use?' offered the elderly gentleman, squinting at the screen.

'Nothing for either Ellison or Evans?'

'Nothing, no, sorry.'

'How about boat names? Do you have a record of them?'

'We asked, but not everyone gave one.'

'Can you have a look for a boat called Providence?'

'Providence,' muttered the man, returning his attention to the screen. Repeating the name again, a few moments later he glanced up to say, 'Not that I can see, no. But as I said, not everyone left one.'

Tanner sighed, tapping his fingers against the top of the table.

'He could have signed on under a different name,' Cooper proposed.

Tanner gave him a nod of agreement. 'He could have, but it doesn't help our cause much.'

'What did Vicky say?'

'Only that the Broads Authority don't have a boat registered under Ellison's name, but his father had. It's supposed to be moored just downriver from here. Somewhere called Perci's

311

Island, opposite the Swan Inn.'

'And that's the one called Providence?'

'Uh-huh. But it was a while back. It could easily have been sold since then.'

'Or maybe his son hasn't bothered to keep up its registration fee.'

Staring out through the club's large white-framed windows to the Bure beyond, Tanner reached a decision. 'I think we need to check out that mooring, to see if it's there.'

'And if it isn't?'

'Then either it's been sold, or Ellison's got Jenny holed up in it out there somewhere. Either way, we're going to have to take a look.'

- CHAPTER FIFTY NINE -

HAVING BEEN ABLE to commandeer one of the club's spare safety boats, a bright orange affair with a tiller-controlled outboard engine, Tanner steered the way between various white snub-nosed hire boats to reach Perci's Island, a small private mooring cut into the trees on the opposite side of the river, just down from the Swan Inn.

Tying up to the central pontoon, they took one side each. It didn't take them long to search the berths, half of which were empty, looking for a boat named Providence.

'Anything?' asked Tanner, breathing hard, a hand clamped over his ribs, which ached more with each passing minute.

'Nothing, no,' replied Cooper, who'd hardly broken into a sweat.

'OK, then we need to start searching through the fleet.'

'Not on our own we can't! Not if there are over two hundred boats!'

It was a valid point. Finding one amongst such a large number, spread out over a meandering fifty-mile tidal river system, would take hours; at least it would if they were on their own.

'I'm going to call Forrester,' Tanner decided, digging out his phone. 'We need every police boat out looking for it. Then I'm going to take you back to the sailing club. I want you to find the club's commodore and get a radio call out to all their safety boats. Give them the boat's name and tell them to radio in the moment they see it; but under no circumstances are they to go anywhere near it. Is that understood?'

Cooper nodded.

'I don't want any of them trying to be a hero, especially if Ellison's got a knife pressed against Jenny's throat.'

'What about you?' asked Cooper, watching as Tanner dialled Forrester's number.

Fixing Cooper's eye with a look of dangerous intent, Tanner raised the phone to his ear. 'If Ellison has Jenny out there, then I'm going to find him!'

- CHAPTER SIXTY -

T HE LIGHTEST TOUCH of a breeze flirted with the sail hoisted high above Jenny's head before dropping away to leave nothing but the sound of the water, lapping gently against the Broads sailing cruiser's varnished mahogany hull.

'The wind's dying,' Jenny observed, casting an anxious look over the vast stretch of water that made up Hickling Broad. As she stared out, what few ripples remained of the wind, brushing against the water's surface, seemed to flee before her eyes, leaving nothing but the reflection of the cerulean blue sky above.

Sitting cross-legged on top of the coach roof, a large folding sailing knife in her hand, she returned to her job of prising open a stubborn knot caught in one of the mooring lines. With the knot finally giving way, she closed the knife to throw down for Ellison to catch, before gazing up at the small flag hoisted at the very top of the mainsail.

'I think I may have been wrong about coming this way,' she eventually said. 'In hindsight, we should have gone south, like everyone else.'

'Well, it's too late now,' Ellison remarked, dropping the knife into his shirt's open breast pocket.

'The tide won't be in our favour either, when we sail out,' added Jenny, chiding herself for having made what she now knew to have been a major tactical error. 'That's *if* we can sail out. At this rate, we'll be stuck here for hours!'

Ellison joined Jenny in scanning the water, looking for any sign of the wind. 'It might pick up,' he said, in an optimistic tone. 'Besides, we don't know what's happening with the rest of the fleet. For all we know, they could have been stuck like this half an hour ago.'

'I suppose.'

'Anyway, we may as well make the best of it and have something to eat.'

'Tell you what,' said Jenny, leaping down to the cockpit's floor with agile ease. 'I'll dig out the hamper, if you can do me a favour and send John another text?'

'No problem,' Ellison replied, happily fishing out his phone. 'What shall I say this time?'

'Just tell him that I screwed up on tactics, and we're stuck in the middle of Hickling Broad without so much as a shred of breeze. Something like that.'

Seeing Ellison take his hand off the boat's curved steel tiller to begin tapping his thumbs over the screen, Jenny ducked down the companionway steps, into the gloomy wood-enclosed cabin below. There she began rummaging around for the picnic hamper they'd brought with them in the taxi, a few hours before.

Discovering it under the table, she reached down to prise it out, just as Ellison made his way down the steps to join her.

'It was on the floor,' she said, placing it gently down on the table to begin wrestling with one of two brass buckles holding the lid's leather straps in place.

'My fault,' Ellison apologised. 'I should have made it more secure.'

'Did you manage to get a text out to John?' she asked, undoing the first buckle and moving on to the second.

'I did,' he said, phone still in hand.

'Any reply?'

He glanced down at the screen. 'Nothing yet.'

Jenny raised a concerned eyebrow. That was the third text she'd asked him to send that morning, but John still hadn't responded.

'Is the reception OK?'

Ellison held the phone up in the air. 'Seems to be.'

As Jenny lifted the hamper's lid to peer inside, craning his neck he asked, 'Everything still in one piece?'

'Well, the sandwiches look a little past their sell-by date, but at least the wine glasses haven't broken.'

'As there isn't much going on up top, we may as well eat down here,' Ellison commented, turning around to bring the doors closed, plunging the cabin into a gloomy semi-darkness.

A sense of unease swept over Jenny. She didn't like being enclosed in such a confined dimly lit space, especially with a man she was only just getting to know again.

She turned her head to glance out of one of only

six small oval-shaped portholes. 'Wouldn't it be better if we ate outside? To keep an eye out?'

'I don't think there's much point. There's not an ounce of wind. We may as well make ourselves comfortable down here for a while. Besides, there's something I'm rather keen to have a little chat to you about.'

- CHAPTER SIXTY ONE -

HAVING DROPPED COOPER back at Horning Sailing Club, with scant regard for the four miles per hour speed limit Tanner roared down the River Bure, the safety boat skipping over its calm smooth surface as the outboard engine's propeller drove it through the water, leaving passing motor cruisers wallowing in its wake.

Knowing that the boats taking part in the race would have to sign themselves off at various checkpoints, Tanner decided that the fastest way to find Providence would be to visit each one in turn. It was unlikely to be the way entrants would approach the course, but with little need for him to worry about either wind or tide, it would certainly be the most logical.

With a plan in place, assuming the checkpoints would be the same as the previous year, he banked left at the mouth of the River Ant to plough north. Finding only a handful of small sailing dinghies, he sped back around, blasting back to the Bure before taking a sharp right towards the checkpoint at the entrance to South Walsham Broad. With no sign of Providence there either, he spun round again to fly over the water, back up to the Bure to turn right, heading for the mouth of the River Thurne.

Nearing what was effectively a T-junction in the river, the Bure turning sharply to continue meandering south with the Thurne flowing in from the north, Tanner eased back on the throttle to look first one way, then the other. This was where the fleet would have to make a critical decision, the same dilemma Tanner was now faced with. North would take sailors under the bridge at Potter Heigham, up to the checkpoint at the far end of Hickling Broad, whilst following the Bure south would take them under Acle Bridge, down to the checkpoint at the Stracey Arms drainage mill.

Tanner was about to head south, when he remembered what Jenny had told him, when they found themselves looking for new moorings the autumn before – about how the Broads were far quieter north of Potter Heigham, thanks to its medieval bridge, which was so low, only the most intrepid tourist would risk taking their boat under. If Ellison had lured Jenny out on his long-dead parents' boat, with the intention of doing her harm, either Hickling Broad or maybe even Horsey Mere would be the perfect place.

Easing the steering column towards him, Tanner drove the boat forward to once again begin roaring over the surface, leaving a streak of churned up water fanning out towards the dense yellow reeds that flanked him on either side.

- CHAPTER SIXTY TWO -

INTRIGUED TO KNOW what Ellison had to talk to her about, Jenny raised a curious eyebrow as she began lifting the somewhat bedraggled sandwiches out of the hamper to place them carefully down on the table.

Reaching for the nearest one, Ellison made himself comfortable on the companionway steps that led out into the cockpit.

Peeling back the clingfilm, as if opening the leaves of a delicate rare flower, Ellison eventually asked, 'How've you been coping since we found that body last weekend?'

'Oh, of course,' Jenny replied, relieved to hear what was on his mind. Having had so much going on, she'd almost forgotten about what had happened back then, and that it had been Ellison she'd been in the boat with when they'd hauled it up. 'To be honest, it's been such a busy week, I've hardly had the chance to think about it.'

Ellison took to staring down at the cabin's wooden floor, a haunted expression clouding his face. 'I must admit,' he said, his voice barely more than a whisper, 'I've found myself unable to think about much else.'

Jenny took a moment before answering. It was

clear that the event had upset him far more than she'd realised.

Having weighed up a suitable response, speaking with empathetic delicacy, she eventually said, 'I'm very sorry to hear that.'

'It brought back memories, you see,' Ellison continued, his voice so quiet, Jenny could barely hear him. 'Seeing him rise up from the grave like that. And you there with me, at the same time. It was obvious what it meant.'

'How d'you mean?' Jenny enquired, surprised by his choice of words.

'It was a sign.'

'A sign?' she repeated, staring over at him.

'Actually, no; not so much a sign. More as if I was being given permission.'

Lines of concern rippled over her forehead.

'I'm sorry, Rob, I'm not with you.'

'To finish what I started,' Ellison continued, glancing up to give her a disturbing look of fateful intent.

A bolt of alarm slammed hard into her chest. As a mass of thoughts flooded through her mind, refusing to accept what every sinew of her body was screaming at her, she blurted out, 'But – you haven't started anything!'

'Oh, I'm afraid I have,' Ellison continued, his eyes trailing away. 'And a long time ago now. For many years I laid the blame squarely at my parents' feet.' With a shrug, he added, 'I suppose we all do, to some extent. Mine in particular really weren't very nice to me, but I was eventually able to forgive them. I must admit, it did take me a while. I had to drug them first, at Christmas dinner. I then had to spend the next five days watching their lives ebb slowly away, the hands they used to abuse me nailed to the table they were about to feast from.'

As he spoke, with the jarring sound of her heart pounding behind her ears, Jenny's mind raced uncontrollably as her body remained fixed to her seat. There was no question about what his intentions were. He was going to kill her, or at least he was going to try.

'What about James Boyd? I assume it was you who...?'

'He wasn't very nice to me either. None of you were, leading me on like you did, only to brush me off, as if I didn't exist. You've no possible idea how difficult that was for me; but how could you – a pretty girl like you? You must have had men twisted around your dirty little fingers ever since you were old enough to blow them a kiss, just like you did me.'

'I was never anything but completely honest with you!'

'LIAR!' screamed Ellison with such violent rage that Jenny's heart stopped for a full moment before pounding even harder.

'You led me around in little circles; winking – smiling – all your slutty remarks. And when I finally found the courage to make a move, what did you do?'

Jenny's mind dragged her back to the party she knew he was referring to.

'I-I can't remember,' she lied, lowering her head in shame.

'You laughed at me! You fucking laughed at me!'

Jenny could see Ellison's eyes filling with tears, as his face began trembling with emotion.

'You just sat there, in the middle of the bloody room, surrounded by everyone we knew, and you laughed at me!'

'I'm sorry, Rob. Really I am. I didn't mean to. I was drunk, and –'

'Oh, I think you knew *exactly* what you were doing, just like Craig and Chris did. They both seemed happy enough to tell me that they loved me, daring me to kiss them, only to dissolve into fits of hysterics when I tried. I spent *years* asking God for the strength to forgive you, all of you, but He never did. So I did my best to forget. And for years I did, until guess who came waltzing into my sailing club, all grown up?'

Ellison turned to offer Jenny a thin, lurid smile.

'Now that *was* a sign. No doubt about it. Of course, I didn't let on that I'd seen you, not until God stepped in again, arranging for us to walk straight into each other, when you came over with your so-called boyfriend. I'd made my plans long before then, though. I was just waiting to be told that my idea was…acceptable. At the time, I didn't know how, but I knew He would find a way. Then it happened. He raised James from his watery grave, where I'd left him all those years before, for both of us to see. I couldn't have asked for a more obvious sign than that.'

Jenny watched with growing horror as Ellison placed his uneaten sandwich down on the table to fish out the sailing knife she'd returned to him earlier.

Fixing his eyes on hers, he flipped open the

blade. 'So, anyway, I think the time has come, don't you?'

Desperate to delay the moment for as long as possible, forcing saliva down into her paper-dry throat, she gulped enough air into her lungs to splutter, 'If your plan was nothing more imaginative than luring me out here to kill me, what was the point of making it look like I was the one who killed Craig and Chris? I assume that was your intention?'

'I must admit, it was, yes. Tell me, did you rush to help poor little Craig, when you found him? I did my best to keep him alive for you. Did you leap to his aid?'

Jenny didn't answer. Her mind was busy, frantically trying to think of a way out.

'Anyway, it didn't matter. I'd already covered the scene with your prints and DNA.'

'And just how did you get your hands on those?'

'Oh, that was easy. I lifted your fingerprints from a mug you used at the sailing club, and then I plucked some hair and skin samples from off the clothes you left hanging in the girls' changing room.'

'I assume it was also you who hacked into my Facebook account?'

'Of course. I must admit, I did take more pleasure than perhaps I should have done in creating those images, as I did dressing up as you.'

'You've still not told me why, if your only intention has been to kill me.'

'You really don't get it, do you?'

'Get what?'

'No, well; to be honest, I'm not sure I ever

thought you would. But don't worry, I've left a full confession with a reliable firm of solicitors, along with a detailed explanation as to the hows and whys. It's just a shame it will be such a long time before anyone can read it. You see, I've given them strict instructions to only make it available after a period of thirty years has passed.'

Without taking his eyes off Jenny's, Ellison lifted himself up until he was standing, one foot on the floor, the other perched on the steps behind him.

Sensing the moment had come, Jenny eased herself half off the bench she'd been sitting on to reach inside the hamper.

'You'd better know that I'm not going down without a fight,' she sneered, pulling out the bottle of wine that was in there, clutched in her hand like a club.

Ellison smiled at her. 'Good for you, Jen. Good for you. But I'm afraid to say that your life here, on Earth, is very far from over. Mine, on the other hand, is about to come to a glorious end.'

'But – wait – what?'

Ellison spread out his arms, the blade of the knife glinting in his hand. Gazing up towards the roof, through a joyful grin he began to speak. 'Out of the depths I cry to you, oh Lord. With shouts of grateful praise, I sacrifice myself.'

'Stop! Wait! What are you doing?'

'What I have vowed, I will now make good.'

Closing his eyes, Ellison plunged the knife deep into his chest, letting go to leave the handle jutting out, as a dark stain of crimson blood spread out over his shirt.

Jenny could do nothing but stare, her eyes wide, her skin the colour of stone.

His stance faltering, Ellison staggered forward, a hand taking his weight against the table's edge. Spitting out blood that bubbled up through his open mouth, taking short rasping breaths he leered down at Jenny. 'The chasms of Hell await you, my dear; but not before Earth's cold bars of steel.'

As he bared his blood-stained teeth in a wide demonic grin, his supporting arm gave way, sending his body crashing down onto hers, his final words puncturing Jenny's very soul, as her fractured mind began to scream.

- CHAPTER SIXTY THREE -

DUCKING HIS HEAD as he steered the safety boat under the low central arch of Potter Heigham's ancient medieval bridge, Tanner continued to tear his way up the Thurne, his eyes peeled for any large wooden yachts as he did. When he made a sharp left-hand turn into the cut which led up to Hickling Broad, the water opened up before him, and he eased back on the throttle's twist grip to stand up in the boat and peer around.

Up ahead he saw a traditional Broads sailing cruiser, its giant canvas sails hanging listless in the stagnant summer air.

Screwing up his eyes, he tried to read the ornate gold lettering emblazoned across its stern. Unable to see, he returned to his seat to twist the throttle the other way. As the boat surged forward once again, the slender figure of a girl emerged from its cabin, her hands guiding strands of hair from out of her eyes.

It was Jenny.

'Thank God,' Tanner muttered, raising a hand to wave at her.

Seeing her wave back, he slowed the boat down to call out, 'I was worried about you. Are you OK?'

It was only then that he saw the blood. Her clothes were covered in it. And she hadn't been brushing hair away from her eyes, but torrents of mascara-filled tears, leaving blackened smudged streaks down either side of her desperately pale face.

Fighting against a tidal wave of panic, Tanner slammed the safety boat into the side of the yacht, wrenching out the kill cord, leaving the engine choking to a halt.

'Are you hurt?' he cried, leaping up to tie the boat up.

Her reply came through short juddering breaths.

'It's Rob – Robert Ellison. He's – he's –' she spluttered, an unsteady hand pointing into the cabin below.

'He's what?' Tanner demanded, leaping on board.

'He's stabbed himself – down there, in the cabin.'

Taking her shoulders in his hands, Tanner sent a questioning look down into her tear-filled blue eyes.

'He *stabbed* himself?'

Jenny nodded, her body trembling under his touch.

'Is he still alive?'

'I-I think so.'

She turned her head to stare back down. With sudden clarity of thought, she stared back into Tanner's face. 'You've got to help him, John! You can't let him die!'

'If he had the good sense to try and kill himself,

I fail to see why I should help him.'

'B-because his blood,' she stammered, staring down at her clothes, 'I'm covered in it. And the knife he used,' she continued. 'He'd given it to me, just before. My fingerprints will be all over it.'

'OK, listen – try not to worry. Everyone at Wroxham is fully behind you, Forrester included. And I'm going to give Commander Bardsley a call. He's bound to know a good lawyer.'

'I don't want a lawyer!' Jenny declared, fixing Tanner's eyes. 'I need Robert Ellison alive!'

'But Jen – if he's psychotic enough to stab himself, just to get you locked up for his murder, were we to help him, he's just going to tell everyone that you tried to kill him. That's attempted murder right there, and it will only add to the evidence that you killed the others. I really think we're better off with him dead.'

'You've got no idea just how demented the man is. He told me he's left his confession with some lawyers, but they're not allowed to make it public for another thirty years. He wants me put away for life, John, only for everyone to find out that I was innocent after all. If we can make him tell us who the solicitors are –'

Tanner didn't need to hear anymore, pushing past her to plunge down into the cabin. There, lying face-up on the table, a knife sticking out of a blood-soaked shirt, lay the body of Robert Ellison, his eyes closed, his face deathly pale.

Lifting the man's arm, Tanner felt his wrist for signs of life as he leaned over his head to pull back his eyelids.

'I can't feel a pulse,' he said to Jenny, who'd

followed him down.

Dropping the arm, Tanner pulled out his phone, turned on the torch app and shone the light down into the man's eyes.

'OK, he's alive; but only just. We need to get him to a hospital, but I doubt he'll survive if we move him; not if we have to drag him up into the cockpit, over the stanchion lines and then down into the safety boat.'

With Jenny staring at him with imploring desperation, Tanner had an idea.

He handed Jenny his phone. 'Call an ambulance. Get them to meet us at that pub at the end of the broad. What's it called again?'

'The Pleasure Boat Inn,' Jenny replied, taking the phone to stare at it with absent eyes. 'But how are we going to get there? There's no wind, and the boat doesn't have an engine.'

'Yes, but I do,' Tanner replied, brushing past Jenny to launch himself back up the companionway steps.

- CHAPTER SIXTY FOUR -

SECURING A ROPE from the yacht's bow to the back of the safety boat, Tanner eased on the power, bringing the line taut before twisting the grip around to full throttle, but the thirty-eight-foot mahogany-built cruiser remained stubbornly where it was, as if being held in place by an anchor.

'Nothing's happening!' shouted Jenny, from the back of the yacht, her hand held fast around the tiller. 'We're not moving!'

With the safety boat's engine reaching full power, the water around the propeller boiled as smoke billowed out from the exhaust. When the boat's plastic orange snub-nosed bow began lifting spasmodically into the air, Tanner was about to give up when he felt the Broads cruiser behind him finally begin to slip forward.

Gaining momentum, with the sound of sirens fast approaching, they were soon passing Hickling Broad Sailing Club to turn into the narrow dyke beyond. Up ahead was the Pleasure Boat Inn: a picturesque British pub with magnolia-painted walls and a line of picnic tables running parallel to the dyke, where a number of small motorboats were moored.

As Tanner and Jenny guided the two boats into the moorings, an ambulance came careering its way into the pub's gravel-lined car park, lights flashing, siren blazing.

Leaving Jenny to tie up the boats, Tanner leapt onto the hardstanding, clutching at his fractured ribs. Running as fast as his injuries would allow, seeing two paramedics jump down from the ambulance he stopped where he was to pull out his ID. With a hand on his knee, through short painful breaths, he pointed back at the dyke. 'We've got a man with a single stab wound to the chest.'

'Whereabouts?'

'Inside the wooden yacht's cabin.'

'OK, got it.'

Left alone, Tanner glanced about, searching for a seat to help take the pressure off his spine, when the sight of DCI Forrester's portly frame came into view. Flanking him on either side were the two officers from Professional Standards: DI Rawlinson and DS Hadfield.

'What the hell are *they* doing here?' Tanner demanded, forcing himself to stand up straight.

'Jenny left her name, when she made the call,' Forrester replied, his eyes filled with regret.

'Well, they can just turn around and sod off back to wherever it was that they came from.'

'We're here to bring DS Evans in for questioning,' the taller, more senior of the two men stated.

'Over my dead body you are,' Tanner replied, blocking the man's way.

'What's going on?' called out Jenny, jogging up to join them.

'You'd better tell your boyfriend here to stand down,' sneered Rawlinson, his face now inches from Tanner's.

Keen to prevent his senior DI from doing something he'd later regret, Forrester drove himself between the two men, forcing them apart.

'Is anyone going to tell me what's going on?' Jenny demanded, coming to a halt beside them.

'I'm sorry, Tanner,' Forrester began, 'but we're going to have to let them do their job.'

'I appreciate that, sir, really I do,' said Tanner, his words thick with sarcasm, 'but Jenny didn't do it. It's Ellison. He even admitted as much.'

'He admitted as much to who?'

'To Jenny, sir, before he went and stabbed himself. He was hoping to pin his death on her as well. The guy's a complete psycho!'

'Is that true, Jenny?'

'He did, sir, yes. He openly admitted to having killed Boyd, Jenkins and Hall, all because they spurned his affections when he was young. Then he went and stabbed himself, knowing I'd be blamed for the deaths of all four of them.'

Rawlinson locked his arms over his chest, leering over at both Tanner and Jenny. 'You're honestly expecting us to believe that he murdered *himself?*

'Personally, I don't give a rat's arse what you believe,' Tanner growled. 'Anyone with half a brain would understand that DS Evans couldn't have done it.'

'As they say, it takes all sorts. For all we know, you two came up with the idea together, whilst banging each other inside that floating bathtub of yours.'

Tanner lunged violently at the man.

'ENOUGH!' shouted Forrester, forcing him back.

'I suggest you let your boy go,' taunted Rawlinson, with a wide antagonistic grin. 'I'll then be able to add assault to the charge of obstruction I'm already considering.'

Keeping Tanner at arm's length, Forrester fixed one of his beady eyes on the Professional Standards officer. 'And if *you're* not careful, I'll be filing a complaint of misconduct against *you!*'

'Misconduct?' Rawlinson laughed. 'I think you've been getting too much sun on that shiny bald head of yours. On what possible grounds could you file a complaint for misconduct?'

'For attempting to provoke one of my officers, for a start,' Forrester began, his face darkening with blood. 'You seem to be forgetting, young man, that you're bound by the same Code of Ethics as the rest of us. You're also forgetting that you're addressing a senior officer, and I will *NOT* be spoken to with such blatant disrespect!'

The volcanic power of Forrester's voice left Rawlinson humbled into silence, his mouth left opening and closing like a dying fish.

'Now, before I *really* lose my temper and have you and your colleague thrown in the river, I suggest you'd better carry on with your *so-called* duty.'

With Rawlinson's grin creeping back over his face, he returned his attention to Jenny. 'Detective Sergeant Evans, I'm arresting you on suspicion of murder. You do not have to say anything...'

'John?' Jenny cried, taking hold of Tanner's arm to send him a look of panicked desperation.

'...but it may harm your defence if you do not mention when questioned something which you later rely on...'

'You can't let them do this, sir,' interrupted Tanner, placing himself squarely between Rawlinson and Jenny. 'Not with what's just happened. We need more time!'

'Tanner – Jenny, I'm sorry, really I am, but my hands are tied. There's simply nothing I can do.'

- CHAPTER SIXTY FIVE -

PROMISING NOT TO leave her, Tanner followed Jenny and the two Professional Standards officers over to Norfolk's Police Headquarters in Norwich, tucked into the back of a squad car. On arrival, he watched in helpless agony as Jenny was led away for processing before being taken to a secure interview room.

Meanwhile, Tanner was offered a desk to work from, up on the second floor. There he spent the next several hours staring vacantly at a computer screen, drifting in and out of sleep, jumping in his seat every time the door behind him was opened, hoping for news. But none was forthcoming.

Come the evening, with his ribs hurting so much he could hardly breathe, he asked around for some painkillers before taking the lift down to the canteen. With some food inside him, and the painkillers doing their job, he returned to his temporary desk on to which he lifted his feet, reclined the back of his chair, and leaned back to fall into a dreamless sleep.

Sunday, 7th June

A familiar distinctly British voice woke him with a start.

'Morning, John. I was told I'd find you here.'

Forcing his eyelids open, just enough to confirm what his ears had told him, Tanner found himself peering into the stern but affable face of Commander Matthew Bardsley, the senior ranking policeman who'd been a friend to his late father, going on to act as a guardian to Tanner and his family since the time of his passing.

Whisking his feet off the table, Tanner sat up to wince with pain, grabbing at his ribs.

'Are you all right?'

'Just about,' he groaned.

'Here, I brought you a coffee,' Bardsley responded, placing one of two sealed Styrofoam cups down on the desk in front of him.

Tanner eyed it with due caution.

'Don't worry. It's premium grade filtered.'

'Thanks for this,' Tanner replied, lifting himself up to peel off its lid. 'I owe you one.'

'Only one?' Bardsley smirked, watching as Tanner wrestled a couple of painkillers out from their foil-encased dispensers.

'Nobody told me you were coming,' commented Tanner, swallowing them down.

'Your DCI was kind enough to give me a call,' Bardsley replied. 'He told me what happened, so I thought it would probably be best if I came up. I did try to call, to let you know, but you weren't answering.'

'The battery on my phone must have died,' Tanner replied, tugging it out to discover that it had. 'What time is it, anyway?'

'Just gone half-ten.'

'What? In the morning?' Tanner queried, his head whipping around to stare over at the line of windows surrounding the large open-planned office.

'I'm afraid so. You must have been out cold.'

'Yes, well. I've had a busy few days.'

'It looks like it. To be honest, you look like you've just driven over a landmine.'

'Funny you should say that,' Tanner muttered, grimacing up at him.

'Anyway, whilst you've been lounging around up here with your feet up, your team's been keeping itself busy.'

'They have?'

'I've been chatting with your colleagues, Cooper and Gilbert. They sent me over the case files you've been working on. You'll be pleased to hear that they've had some positive news concerning the abandoned car they found, as well as Jenny's social media accounts. Forensics were able to find traces of Robert Ellison's DNA inside the car, and their digital counterparts have been able to establish that Jenny's Facebook account had been hacked. They've also been able to source the IP address of the person responsible.'

'Ellison again?' questioned Tanner, with a look of hopeful expectation.

Bardsley smiled his confirmation.

'Furthermore, they managed to find out that he spent a number of years seeing a psychiatrist and have put in a court order to access his medical notes. I suspect they'll reveal him to be somewhat disturbed. Added together, it should be enough for a conviction.'

'Am I to assume he's still alive?'

'He's on life support, but yes, for now he is.'

'And Jenny?'

'Ah, Jenny. I was wondering when you were going to ask about her.'

With Bardsley falling silent, Tanner was forced to ask, 'Well?'

'I'm afraid Professional Standards can be a little, how can I say, over-enthusiastic at times.'

'I hope that means they're not going to charge her?'

'With what your team's been able to unearth on Ellison, I think it's fairly obvious that he'd been doing his best to frame her; at least that's what I've been endeavouring to make them understand.'

'So, they're going to release her?'

'They've yet to say,' Bardsley replied, digging out his phone. 'But I've told their director that if I don't hear something to that effect by eleven o'clock this morning, I'll be putting a call through to the Home Secretary.'

- EPILOGUE -

Saturday, 20th June

A LUMINOUS BAND of sunlight shone down on Hunsett Mill, lighting it up against a dense black cloud that stretched out over the wide flat horizon.

With the second glass of their evening's wine poured, Tanner set the bottle down to retrieve his book from the table. Reclining against a cushion in the open cockpit, he took a moment to stare out over the yacht's transom.

'Didn't you say that it wasn't going to rain?' he asked, in a conversational tone.

'Not until later,' Jenny muttered, from the bench seat opposite, her head buried inside a book of her own.

'And tomorrow?'

'All day, I'm afraid.'

'So you won't be dragging me back to the sailing club, then?'

Jenny turned her head to face him. 'Why wouldn't we be going sailing?'

'You just said it was going to rain all day.'

'Yes – and?'

'But we'll get wet!'

'Don't be such a wimp,' she snorted, returning to her book. 'Besides, you're probably going to get wet anyway, so I don't see what difference it makes.'

'I thought you said it wasn't going to be windy?'

'That doesn't mean you won't capsize, not on your first day. Dinghy sailing is a water sport, after all.'

'Great,' Tanner groaned, his tone thick with sarcasm. 'Can't wait.'

'Anyway, if it's going to rain all day, I can't think what else we can do.'

'I can,' Tanner said, sitting slowly up, his ribs and back still aching from two weeks before.

Leaving his book on the seat, he placed his elbows on the table, his hands clasped around something held in front of his mouth.

Eyeing him with suspicion from over the top of her book, Jenny eventually asked, 'What are you up to, John Tanner?'

Without speaking, he placed an object down on the table.

Pushing it over towards her, he returned his hands to hide the smile that had begun playing over his lips.

Without moving her head, Jenny stared down at the object. It was a small black velvet-covered box.

'I didn't know it was my birthday,' she said, an anxious frown creasing her forehead.

'It's not.'

'It's not *your* birthday, is it?'

Tanner shook his head.

'Then what's this for?'

'You'll have to open it to find out.'

Sitting up, Jenny set her book down to spend a

few moments studying the object. About to pick it up, she stopped to cast a wary eye over at him. 'Aren't you supposed to get down on one knee for this sort of thing?'

'The doctor's given me strict instructions not to over-exert myself.'

'I see,' she replied, returning her attention to the box. 'So, you are asking me then?'

'I believe so, yes.'

'I don't suppose you could actually say the words, just in case I think you're asking for my hand in marriage, when in fact you're only looking to borrow a tenner?'

'To be honest, I was hoping for a little more than just your hand.'

'What – you want my arm as well?'

With an amused smile, Tanner glanced down at the box. 'So, what do you say?'

'You haven't asked me yet.'

'You haven't opened the box.'

After eyeing it for another moment, she picked it up, her fingers poised to pull back the lid. 'What if I don't like it?'

'Then I'll buy you another one.'

'I meant the question.'

'Oh, well – then I suppose you can always say no – if you really don't want to.'

'Will I be able to keep what's inside if I do?'

'If you say no?'

'Uh-huh.'

'Er –' thought Tanner. 'I think, traditionally, the two are mutually inclusive.'

'Does that mean I can't?'

'I'd rather you just said yes.'

'OK, let me have a look.'

With that, she opened the box.

After taking a moment to peer at the simple but elegant diamond ring inside, sparkling gently in the evening sun, she closed it again to set back down on the table.

'You don't like it?' Tanner asked, with a growing sense of nervous unease.

'No, I do.'

'What about the question?'

'I'm still waiting for you to ask.'

'You mean, you want me to actually say the words?'

'Yes, please.'

'OK,' he replied. Swallowing, he took Jenny's hands into his to look deep into her eyes. 'Jenny Summer Evans, you mean the absolute world to me. I couldn't imagine my life without you. I'd be truly honoured if you'd accept me as your husband, for better or worse, for richer or poorer, till death us do part.'

There was a momentary pause, before Jenny piped up with, 'Are you saying you want to marry me?'

'What did you think I was asking?'

'Sorry, I wasn't sure. You seemed to go a little off subject at the end. I take it that's a yes?'

'To my question, or to whether or not I was asking you?'

'The latter.'

'I was, yes.'

'Oh, OK,' Jenny replied, returning her attention to the box.

'So?' Tanner asked. Had he known it was going

to be this difficult, he'd have asked someone else to do it for him.

'So what?' Jenny queried, glancing up with a curious expression.

Tanner let out an exasperated sigh. 'Will you marry me?'

'What, now?' she replied, glancing down at her watch. 'Don't we have to book a church first?'

'I think you're supposed to say yes before we send the invitations out.'

'I do hope you're not doing this just to get out of going sailing tomorrow?'

'Well, if you say yes, and we can find a vicar in time.'

Jenny narrowed her eyes at him. 'And I doubt we'd be able to work together anymore.'

'We'll have to cross that bridge when we come to it,' Tanner replied. 'So anyway, was that a yes or a no?'

'Sorry – what was the question again?'

It was Tanner's turn to narrow his eyes.

'Oh yes, the marriage thing. Right.'

Raising her eyes to the sky above, she tapped a thoughtful finger against her chin.

Tanner turned to gaze out over the River Ant, sliding silently past.

'It will be getting dark soon.'

'Oh, go on then,' Jenny finally replied, her eyes sparkling with tears as a broad grin spread out over her face.

*DI John Tanner and
DS Jenny Evans
will return in
Horsey Mere.*

- A LETTER FROM DAVID -

Dear Reader,

I just wanted to say a huge thank you for deciding to read *Three Rivers*. If you enjoyed it, I'd be really grateful if you could leave a review on Amazon, or mention it to your friends and family. Word-of-mouth recommendations are just so important to an author's success, and doing so will help new readers discover my work.

It would be great to hear from you as well, either on Facebook, Twitter, Goodreads or via my website. There are plenty more books to come, so I sincerely hope you'll be able to join me for what I promise will be an exciting adventure!

All the very best,

David

- ABOUT THE AUTHOR -

David Blake is an international best-selling author who lives in North London. At time of going to print he has written seventeen books, along with a collection of short stories. He's currently working on his eighteenth, *Horsey Mere*, which is the follow-up to *Broadland, St. Benet's, Moorings, and Three Rivers*. When not writing, David likes to spend his time mucking about in boats, often in the Norfolk Broads, where his crime fiction books are based.

Printed in Great Britain
by Amazon

51012388R00200